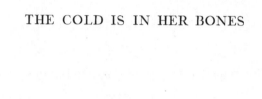

THE COLD IS IN HER BONES

Also by Peternelle van Arsdale

The Beast Is an Animal

the Cold is in Her Bones

Peternelle van Arsdale

MARGARET K. McELDERRY BOOKS
New York London Toronto Sydney New Delhi

MARGARET K. McELDERRY BOOKS
An imprint of Simon & Schuster Children's Publishing Division
1230 Avenue of the Americas, New York, New York 10020

MARGARET K. McELDERRY BOOKS is a trademark of Simon & Schuster, Inc.
For information about special discounts for bulk purchases, please contact Simon & Schuster Special Sales at 1-866-506-1949 or business@simonandschuster.com.
The Simon & Schuster Speakers Bureau can bring authors to your live event. For more information or to book an event, contact the Simon & Schuster Speakers Bureau at 1-866-248-3049 or visit our website at www.simonspeakers.com.
Book design by Sonia Chaghatzbanian and Irene Metaxatos
The text for this book was set in Adobe Caslon Pro.
Manufactured in the United States of America
First Edition
10 9 8 7 6 5 4 3 2 1
Library of Congress Cataloging-in-Publication Data
Names: van Arsdale, Peternelle, author.
Title: The cold is in her bones / Peternelle van Arsdale.
Description: First edition. | New York : Margaret K. McElderry Books, [2019] | Summary: When Milla, sixteen, who has lived a sheltered life on a farm near a cursed village, finally makes a friend, she learns of her connection to the curse's originator.
Identifiers: LCCN 2018015760 (print) | ISBN 9781481488440 (hardcover) | ISBN 9781481488464 (eBook)
Subjects: | CYAC: Blessing and cursing—Fiction. | Demonology—Fiction. | Snakes—Fiction. | Secrets—Fiction. | Farm life—Fiction. | Fantasy.
Classification: LCC PZ7.1.V3583 Col 2019 (print) | DDC [Fic]—dc23
LC record available at https://lccn.loc.gov/2018015760

For Jan

THE COLD IS IN HER BONES

PROLOGUE

THERE ONCE WAS A GIRL WITH TANGLES IN HER HAIR. She liked the tangles. She dug her fingers into them, twirled and spun them with curious, searching fingers. Her name was Hulda.

Hulda had a sister whose hair was as smooth as river water. The mother brushed the sister's hair like it was something precious. "Like spun gold," the mother said. Hulda had never seen spun gold. But if it was anything like the sister's hair, she thought it must be very beautiful.

Maybe, Hulda thought, spun gold was like snakeskin. Snakeskin shimmered like the sister's hair. Hulda wondered if the sister's hair felt like a snake's skin, too. Cool and alive. But the sister didn't let Hulda touch her hair. "Dirty hands," the sister would say, and wrinkle her pretty nose. Hulda's hands were often dirty, it was true. It was only when the sister was sleeping in the bed next to hers that Hulda could creep over and pick up a coil of the sister's hair, spread it across her arm. The hair lay there, lifeless. Not like a snake at all. Hulda let it drop to the pillow. Wrinkled her own less pretty nose.

Every evening after that, she watched with altered eyes while the mother brushed the sister's hair, the firelight turning each strand a different shade of sunshine-yellow. Hulda felt caught in a place between envy and disdain. It was a silly thing to fuss over something so dead. And yet she saw the pleasure the mother took in each stroke, the way the sister's eyes half closed like a drowsy cat's.

The mother used to brush Hulda's hair that way. That was a long time ago. Hulda was little then, years before her first bleed. She could hardly recall the feel of the mother's hands in her hair. The last time, the mother had threatened to cut it all off. "Child, if you can't keep the tangles out yourself and you cry so when I brush it, what choice do I have?" But the father had insisted no. "A woman's hair is her glory," he said. Hulda hadn't known what that meant at the time. Now she did. On her wedding night a woman was supposed to unwrap her hair and offer it to her husband like a gift, something only he was allowed to see and touch. This was why the sister, on her eighteenth birthday, had taken to braiding her hair and winding it around her head, a secret to be revealed to none other than the man she married.

Hulda was sixteen, and such things only played at the periphery of her vision, like a bird fluttering off before she could catch sight of what it was. But birds didn't interest Hulda so much anymore.

When they were little, Hulda and the sister had been always together. When the mother woke them in the morning, she'd find them curled up in the same narrow bed, legs and arms and hair intertwined. After breakfast the girls fussed over the baby animals on their parents' farm. The puffy white lambs and yellow chicks. They'd even taken to naming them. But the parents had admonished them that there was no sense naming something that they or one of their neighbors would someday be eating. The sister lost interest in the game after that, but Hulda had concluded that in the natural order of things, one didn't eat what one named. So she took to naming the creatures that weren't likely to be eaten by anyone in the village. The parents made this difficult, though. It seemed there were few living things in Hulda's world that weren't ultimately headed for someone's dinner table. Deer. Doves. Rabbits. So she turned her attention to smaller things. Ants. Beetles. Butterflies and moths. Fireflies on summer evenings. She'd catch one in her hands, whisper a name into her palms, and then let it go. "Fly, Asmund! Enjoy a nice long life!"

Years passed that way, and while the sister pinned her hair to her head and grew into a woman, Hulda christened salamanders and snacked on wild berries until her lips turned purple. She liked to think each time she named a creature was a sort of blessing, like the pastor's upraised hands at the end of Sunday service. An invocation of some magical, protective gift. She loved to lie in the field near home, the one that gently sank into marsh, and let the wind blow the long grasses softly over her in tickles and strokes. She'd lay perfectly still, her fingernails dug into the earth as if she too were dug in, while bees buzzed around her, flies landed but never bit. She named each one.

The first time a snake slithered over her, she held her breath. It wasn't fright that made her still. It was delight. The feel of snake scale on skin was so delicious it sent a tremor up her spine.

The snake was slender and green and its tiny black eyes regarded her with a calm that made her calm as well. She named it Grön, which seemed only fitting.

After that, the snakes became her special friends. They spoke to her. Not in a way that she could hear, but in a place that she could feel. They told her their secret names, the names they held within themselves. It was a presumption, Hulda realized, to have given a name to the snake she called Grön. When she found him again, she apologized. He flicked her earlobe with his gentle forked tongue and she knew she was forgiven. His name, he told her, wasn't Grön at all.

While the sister stayed at home collecting eggs and learning to churn butter, Hulda escaped immediately after breakfast and rarely returned before supper. This way she mostly avoided the mother's despairing gaze. Still, she felt the mother's eyes following her hands as she reached for bread at the table. When the mother's lips thinned with disgust, Hulda knew what would happen. Once the dishes had been cleared, the mother would take Hulda's hands in her own and scrape the dirt from under her fingernails. Hulda quietly endured the digging of the mother's file in those tender places. While the mother labored, she didn't marvel over Hulda's hands the way she did over the sister's hair. Instead the mother said, "Life is difficult enough without your daughter making it more so."

One day Hulda sat at the roots of a large tree. She was still learning all the snakes' names, concentrating hard on the task, and that was why she didn't notice the approach of the farmer boy the sister's age. He was more man than boy, really—broad in the shoulders and sprouting a new beard.

The snakes were gathered around Hulda, patiently whispering

to her, nestled among the tree roots, and maybe that was why the boy didn't see them until they were almost underfoot.

Hulda's favorite snake had woven itself into her hair like a green ribbon. She and it looked up when they sensed the boy's presence. The boy's eyes widened. He lifted his finger and started to say something. But then he saw the snakes. All the snakes. And the snakes saw him, and they all raised their heads and turned to him. If the boy had known anything about snakes he might have been calmer, but he wasn't that kind of boy. He was the kind of boy who stomped, and that was what he did then. He stomped those snakes, stomped them hard. Hulda screamed. She got to her feet and the sounds coming out of her weren't girl sounds at all, the boy would swear later. The eyes that looked back at him from her face weren't girl eyes, either. He fled.

Hulda ran her fingers over the snakes the boy had bruised with his awful boy feet. They coiled around her wrists, sought solace in the crooks of her arms. The green snake slithered more deeply into her hair.

Hours later, in the cool of dusk, she went home to the sound of crickets. She'd forgotten all about the clumsy boy. She'd learned so many names since then.

They were all there when Hulda got home. The mother and father. The sister. The boy and his mother and father. The memory of the boy's stomping feet came back to Hulda in a rush, and she nearly opened her mouth to tell them how horrible he'd been, but the words dissolved on her tongue. They were looking at Hulda with accusing eyes. The boy's mother said to Hulda's mother, "You'll do as we agreed?" Hulda's mother nodded.

Hulda was sent to bed hungry, and downstairs she heard her family talking.

"We'll keep her locked up. No more running wild," the father said.

"You can't make me sleep in the same room with her," the sister said.

"In the barn with her then," the father said.

"No, not that," the mother said. "Besides, what would the neighbors think?"

"What do the neighbors think already?" the sister said. "I wish I had no sister. She'll ruin us all. Who will want to marry me with a creature like that for a relation?"

Hulda lay in her bed listening to all of this while hot tears stung the corners of her eyes. She remembered when the sister and she had been as woven together as a single braid. She mourned the loss in a rush that emptied her heart and left nothing in its place. She'd never felt so alone.

Just then, a delicate stroke above her left ear reminded her that she wasn't alone, and never would be. The slender green snake slid down her cheek and throat, grazed her earlobe with its tongue, and then wove himself into her hair once again. Hulda fell asleep that way.

Hours later, Hulda woke to a dark room and the sister's screams. "It's crawling on me! It's crawling on me!"

Hulda's hands flew to her hair, searched her scalp. The slender green snake was gone.

The darkness was broken by lamplight and the mother and father in the doorway. "What's happened, child? What's crawling on you?"

Hulda held her breath, but the mother and father found nothing. The sister was untouched, despite her wailing to the contrary. She pointed at Hulda. "It was a snake crawling on me. She did it." The parents looked at Hulda.

"I was asleep," Hulda said. "I woke up to her screaming, same as you. I did nothing."

The sister's eyes narrowed at Hulda and then at the parents. "You believe her and not me?"

"No, child, it's not like that," the mother said.

"What's it like, then? You heard what happened. She's a monster. You'll know it when she's killed me in my bed."

"All right, child. There, there." The mother placed soothing hands on the sister's brow. Stroked her rivers of golden hair. "Nothing evil can befall you here. It was a dream, that's all."

The father said nothing, but looked at Hulda with cold eyes. Hulda lay her head down on her pillow.

The door closed and the room darkened to black again.

Minutes passed and Hulda felt the cool stroke of scales on her cheek, and the green snake nestled himself in her hair once again. Hulda let go of the breath she'd been holding in her chest since the sister first screamed.

Then the sister spoke to her soft and low from across the room. "I hate you, Hulda."

"I hate you, too," Hulda said.

It didn't happen every night. Days might go by when Hulda woke to the dawn and the snake was nestled in her hair, right where he belonged. But just often enough, the sister woke up in the night screaming, and the slender green snake was nowhere to be found. The mother always insisted these were nothing but nightmares. The trouble would pass, she said. Dreams always did. And the father always looked at Hulda with cold eyes.

In the meantime the mother kept Hulda locked inside. When Hulda wasn't helping the mother in the kitchen, or mending socks with uneven stitches, she stared longingly through the window, craving the dirt under her fingernails, the snakes whispering their names in her ears. The slender green snake was a comfort, but Hulda sensed he was ailing. Hulda felt herself sickening as well. As fall sank into winter, leaves browning and drifting, Hulda also withered and drifted. She wasn't really the girl sitting in the chair by the window, the green snake coiled in her hair. Her body was there. But the other part of her, the better part, was gone.

She longed for the voices of the snakes in her ears. They'd been silent to her for so long. The green snake spoke to her still, but his whisper was so faint she had to strain to hear it. *Call to them*, the green snake said, *tell them we're dying*.

In her bones, Hulda knew this to be true. If she didn't get out, she would die here in this chair by the window. She and the green snake.

She begged the mother to let her out for even an hour. "I could help you," Hulda said. "I could fetch father for dinner. I could sell eggs in the village for you."

But the mother always said, "You stay here."

Then one Sunday morning, Hulda woke up and the snake voices were loud and there were so many of them, all talking at once. The words hissed over each other, but Hulda felt their meaning.

Get out, they said. *Get out. He's coming.*

It was the boy the snakes were warning her about. The boy who'd stomped them.

The mother and father had invited him to dinner after church. The sister had made cake.

Sunday mornings were the only time the mother and father let Hulda place a foot on the ground outside their farmhouse, and to breathe air that wasn't still and stale. This wasn't a mercy, Hulda knew. It was because they feared what she might do if they left her alone.

Hulda carried herself like any other girl attending service with her family. Mostly. She sat with folded hands. She bowed her head. And when all the rest of the congregation whispered their prayers, Hulda whispered to the snakes, ever so quietly and under her breath. She felt them far beneath her, in their deep winter dens where they burrowed and warmed each other in the cold. The soles of her feet tickled.

In the back of the wagon on the way home from church, the sister pinched Hulda hard in the fleshy part of her arm. "Behave," she said. "They'll send you away if you don't."

"Good," Hulda said, and smiled in a way that caused the sister to shrink from her.

"There's something very wrong with you," the sister said.

Hulda didn't talk to the snakes while the boy was there that afternoon, but the snakes talked to her. *Get out*, they said. *Get out. He's here.*

Hulda was quiet while the father talked to the boy, asking him polite questions about his family's farm, their yield and horses. The sister smiled and served the boy her cake. The mother smiled and cleared the table while the boy and the sister pulled chairs up to the fire.

Hulda darned socks and rocked with the voices in her head.

She felt the boy's eyes on her, and she wondered why he

was looking at her. She touched her hand to her hair, making sure the green snake was where he belonged. He moved against her index finger. She stroked him and then pulled her hand away.

The sister's eyes were bright, lit by the fire and her desire for the boy's attention. "Why, I daresay Hulda's fixing her hair for you," she said to the boy.

The boy laughed and Hulda felt her cheeks burn. "I wasn't," she said.

The father laughed now, too. "There are worse things than fixing your hair for a boy, Hulda. You're old enough for braiding now." He looked over at the mother where she sat with her own mending.

The mother caught Hulda's eye and what Hulda saw when she looked back was fear. Not fear of Hulda, but rather fear for Hulda. "There's time for that," the mother said. "But not yet."

Hulda's heart filled and opened toward the mother, suddenly and painfully. It had been so long since she'd felt cared for. Her eyes widened and she almost smiled. Maybe this was why Hulda didn't notice how the sister's excitement had grown, and how the sister's hand reached for her, picking up a tangled hank of Hulda's hair.

Hulda's gasp of surprise was drowned by the sister's shriek. The green snake had reared its head and hissed at the moment the sister's hand invaded his home.

The sister fell backward. The father shot to his feet, sending his cup of tea spilling and rolling across the floor. The mother whitened and froze, her needle held midair.

The boy was more decisive. He leapt toward Hulda, grasped the green snake with his fist, and threw him into the fire.

Hulda heard the green snake screaming in her head, and

she matched his screams with her own. Then the green snake screamed no more, but Hulda couldn't stop.

Hulda felt herself being held and she couldn't have said who it was that held her. She thrashed and bucked. The scent of burnt flesh was in her nostrils, and she felt burnt herself, heated up outside and in. Too hot. Too hot. When she could scream words they were words of burning. "I'm on fire," she howled. "On fire."

The snakes in her head were all screaming at once and she could no longer make out what they were saying. Were they burning, too? Were they all burning?

Hulda felt something cold and wet on her forehead and she looked up at the mother leaning over her, resting a cloth there. Hulda was in her bed; she and the mother were alone. "Child," the mother said. "You must calm yourself. This screaming and carrying on, it'll do you no good. Nor any of us."

Hulda looked up at the mother's face, written with concern. This time the mother's concern was for herself, not for Hulda.

"Mother," she said. "If I could. If only I could." And then the snakes in her head screamed and so did Hulda. "I'm on fire," she howled. "On fire."

For three days and nights Hulda writhed, twisted, and sweat through her bed linens.

On the fourth day, a woman appeared in the doorway to Hulda's bedroom. Hulda recognized her: the midwife.

The midwife said, "She looks well enough."

"Well enough?" the mother said. "She's burning up! You can feel it yourself. She'll burn away to ash before long."

"You mistake me," the midwife said. "She looks well, but she isn't well. I believe her . . . suffering . . . is spiritual in nature."

The mother narrowed her eyes at the midwife. "How so?"

"If it were a fever she'd be weak and pliable. But look at her strength! Look how she twists and screams. And that heat. That's not fever heat. No. This is something . . . else."

The midwife stepped gingerly toward Hulda. The nearer she came, the more Hulda thrashed. She felt the midwife closing in, sensed her looming body. She tried to shrink from the midwife; she pressed down into the pillow and bed linens. In her head the snakes were still talking over each other, a jumble of voices that sounded like pain felt. Her skin burned hotter. She couldn't bear it, the heat, the fire, the terrible heat.

She leapt up from the bed and hurled herself toward the open window. She would throw herself through it, she thought. Into the cold and snow. Put out the fire. Then there would be no more burning, no voices screaming in her head. No more frightened faces staring at her from across rooms. No more sitting in chairs looking through windows at places she couldn't go. She could dig her fingers into earth once again, if only to die there.

But before she could leap through the window the father's hands were on her, and the midwife's hands were on her, and where they touched her she felt scorched, as if her flesh might pull away in their grips. She screamed in agony. To make them stop was all she wanted. But they forced her down to the floor, the father holding her arms, the midwife straddling her legs.

So she used the only weapon they'd left her with. She sank her teeth into the father's fleshy earlobe and didn't let go until she tasted blood.

Finally, she wasn't the only one screaming.

✦ ✦ ✦

Later, after Hulda's hands and feet had been tied to the bedposts, the midwife said, "I told you. It's the demon heat."

"Yes, the demon heat," the father said, cradling his ear.

The sister fled to her aunt and uncle's farm and promised she never would return so long as that monster was in the house.

The mother wept. "Why us? We've done nothing to deserve this."

"We cannot know why some are stricken," the midwife said.

"What's to be done about it?" the father said. "How can we purge ourselves of . . . " He gestured at Hulda.

The midwife said that the best way to battle a demon so fiery was to douse its flame. She would freeze the demon out of Hulda. Take her away from the farm, into the woods, and leave her there for three days, long enough for the demon to pass out of her. The third day would be a Sunday, which they all agreed was fitting. After church and praying for the Lord's mercy on her soul, they would return for the child that remained once the demon was gone.

The mother asked if she might clothe Hulda, but the midwife refused. "No, that will only give shelter to the demon."

Hulda was left alone again. When the light through the window had dimmed to afternoon, Hulda felt herself surrounded. She was untied from the bed, and though she thrashed, there were too many hands and arms upon her. They wrapped ropes around her and she could no longer move, only scream.

Her eyes cleared for a moment and she saw the mother there, hands twisted together, face drawn tight. Hulda said, "Mother?"

The mother's hands went to her mouth. Then to her eyes.

Then there was no mother anymore. No father. Only the fire inside Hulda and the screaming of the snakes.

Hulda felt the bite of the cold as she was carried out of the house and into the woods. Her wet nightshift froze to her skin.

They laid her down. Hulda looked up at the branches of an evergreen white with snow. She shook. There was no fire inside her anymore. There were no voices in her head. There was only terror. Cold like the ground she lay upon. Colder even than the snow they piled over her.

"Cover her head, too?" someone asked.

The midwife bent over Hulda, considering. Hulda looked up at her, shivered, felt the meager heat of her own breath as it curled over her lips. "I hate you," she said.

The midwife shook her head at Hulda. "Yes. The head, too." As the first scoop of snow dropped over Hulda's face she heard the midwife add, "Vile creature."

Hulda couldn't say how long it took for the cold to overtake her. Minutes or hours. Time had lost meaning for her, ever since the screaming started.

At first the cold was painful to her, but then that passed, and for a brief while, she felt almost warm. Or maybe it was a memory of warmth. Of a time when she hadn't been made of ice. When there had been warm blood in her veins, warm breath in her chest, heat in the places where her limbs met her body.

But then the cold reached her bones. The cold was in her bones. And that was when she allowed herself one last cry for help.

She didn't cry for her mother or her father.

She didn't cry for her sister.

She cried for no one who had abandoned her.

She cried for the snakes.

She called them by name.

She called to them where they huddled in their dens, warming each other. She asked them to come stroke her cheeks, to curl around her wrists, to remind her of what it had been like when she too felt warm and free to move through the grass, to feel soil on her skin.

And the snakes came. They rose from their near-slumber and worked their way up to her. They wrapped themselves around her limbs and belly. They wove themselves through her fingers. They threaded themselves into her hair. They didn't scream in her head anymore. They whispered to her, soft and sweet. *We're here,* they said. *And we will never leave you.*

The snakes didn't come to her alone, however. They brought another with them.

The morning of the third day dawned bright, clear, and cold. So cold. The mother and father met their oldest daughter at church, and the family sat together and prayed.

After the service, the congregation spilled from the church. The children turned gleeful, the adults murmured and chatted, their eyes drifting to the family with the demon child.

Stories of what happened next would be told many times and in many ways. The people saw what they saw and felt what they felt. And who's to say what they did or didn't?

This is what really happened:

Hulda came to church.

She broke through the trees, a girl made of snakes. A girl with snakes for hair, and arms, and fingers. A girl with snakes for legs. A girl with fangs.

And the people backed away from her; they fled into the church, they tried to bar the doors.

But there was no more backing away from Hulda. With her body made more of muscle than of bone, she pushed through the church doors and blocked their retreat.

Then she spoke.

Or rather, she hissed. It was hundreds of hisses together, thousands. The people felt her hisses in their own heads, and they clapped their hands to their ears, but they couldn't drown out the sound. The hissing only grew louder.

She cursed them. She cursed them all. From the oldest to the youngest. She cursed their mothers and fathers, their sisters and brothers. She cursed the babies they had yet to dream of having.

They would know this curse when it woke up in their homes. They would know this curse when it sat at their kitchen tables. They would know this curse when it reached out for the milk and bread.

The curse would grow among them, and it would spread. And they would never feel peace or contentment again.

The coldness of Hulda's curse sank into them. Babies whimpered. Adults clutched their chests. Children shivered.

And then Hulda left them. She went away where they couldn't find her, even if they'd tried. But her curse remained, and it settled in. It sat on stools in warm corners of kitchens. It fed chickens and milked cows. It cuddled in laps and braided hair. It went to church on Sunday.

The people tried to forget the curse. But the curse wouldn't be forgotten. The curse reached up to them with soft, chubby fingers. The curse held their hands.

PART ONE

I

To protect your home from demons:

I. If you see a snake, kill it. Then burn it.

2. Pour salt where the air comes in—sills, thresholds, hearths.

3. Stay inside after dark. Lock tight doors and windows.

4. Pray.

2

MILLA POURED THE SALT IN A STRAIGHT LINE, LEFT
to right. It was daytime, so the window was open and the breeze
scattered a few grains that caught in the grooves of the wooden
sill. When she was little, Milla would make drifts of the salt, like
snow, then walk her fingers through. She'd furtively lick the tips
when she was done.

But she wasn't little anymore. She was sixteen, and it had
been a long time since she'd done anything as rebellious as wasting salt.

"Don't dawdle so." Milla's mother looked over her shoulder at
Milla, a pinched expression on her face. Gitta's face was a lock,
and Milla had yet to find the key to opening it.

Gitta was already turning away, headed out to fetch some
eggs for breakfast, when Milla said, "Yes, Mamma. I'm sorry."
Milla knew that she had nothing to be sorry for. She hadn't been

dawdling. But this was the way of things, and if Milla wanted to smooth even one line from her mother's forehead, the only thing was to give in. To say: *Yes, I know, I was wrong, and I'll do better next time.* Anything less than agreement would seem like disobedience—or worse, wildness. And that was what the demons wanted; that was how they got you. Run off the path, skip your chores, carelessly leave an opening in the white line of salt around the hearth, and *whoosh* down the chimney a demon would come and make you its own. Next thing you knew, you were waking up in the morning far less you and a lot more *it.*

Milla went to the next window and poured another fresh line of salt. She'd never received a good answer for why salt kept demons away. She'd learned not to ask questions about such things. It was another sign of disobedience to ask a question that shouldn't be asked, had no answer, or that had an answer you should already know. "A question that shouldn't be asked doesn't deserve an answer." That was what her father, Jakob, said whenever she asked why they'd always done things a certain way, why they couldn't do things a different way. Milla had long ago learned that for Pappa there was simply one right way of doing things, and no argument to be made for the wrong way.

Her brother, Niklas, seemed less bothered by the rules than she was. Maybe that was because it wasn't such an effort for him to follow them. He was naturally so pleasant, so good-natured. He was the one person who had the key to their mother's face. When Niklas walked in the room, the lines on her forehead relaxed and she looked years younger, and so pretty. Pretty in a way that Milla could never hope to be. "Pretty is as pretty does," Gitta had always said to Milla. But Milla knew that couldn't be right. Milla had never done anything but behave, and still she wasn't pretty the way her mother was. If she were, she'd know it. She'd see proof of her prettiness in her mother's eyes, or her father's. Instead what she saw there was disappointment. Perhaps it wasn't true that pretty is as pretty *does*. Maybe, Milla worried, it was pretty is as pretty *thinks*. And if that was the case, then Milla was doomed. Because she could control her behavior, but she couldn't control her mind. Her mind would have its way.

It wasn't quite true that Milla had always behaved. There was one time Milla had disobeyed so horribly that it made her never want to misbehave again. This was back when she and Niklas were very young. All one summer afternoon, they'd fought together in the woods, with knobby sticks as their swords. They screamed battle cries that shook the earth and the leaves and sent the birds circling up and up, and terrified their imaginary troll enemies. Just as the sky turned a deeper blue, they walked toward home with dirt under their nails and leaves in their hair and mud smeared across their cheeks.

From the corner of her eye, Milla regarded Niklas—happy Niklas whom their mother loved. He looked so jolly. So confident that he'd be embraced upon his return, no matter how dirty he was, or how torn his clothing. Something came over Milla then, and she wanted to frighten him. Niklas was two years older then Milla, but never as brave. He was fine when the enemy was something big and oafish like a troll, but Milla's imagination traveled to darker places than his. "Oh, Niklas," Milla whispered, "I smell blood. Fresh boy blood. It must be a forest witch. There she is, see her? The blood from her last kill is dripping from her teeth. But she's still hungry. And now she's coming for you. You'd better run."

Niklas paled. "That's not funny, Milla. You shouldn't say such things. I'll tell Mamma."

Now it was Milla's turn to pale. "I'm sorry." Niklas's face was hard and scared at the same time. Then she made the mistake of trying to tease him out of his upset. "Silly. You know I was making it up."

Niklas turned on her, hands on hips. "I'm not silly, and you're a bad girl."

Milla felt his words like a slap. "I'm not. I'm a good girl."

"No. You're not. Mamma and Pappa both say so." His eyes traveled to her hair. "You're a mess. You'll never brush out all those tangles before Mamma sees you. Remember what happened the last time you went home like that."

Milla did remember. She'd cried and cried as her mother ripped the tangles from her hair with her comb, all the while berating Milla for being so rough and wild. Now Milla forgot all about forest witches, and she wanted only to be good and smooth for Mamma. "Oh, Niklas," she said. Her eyes welled with tears and some spilled over.

Niklas seemed to soften. "There, there, Milla," he said, patting her shoulder. "You can cut them out before we get home. Mamma will never know." Niklas pulled his sharp knife from his pack, the one their father had given him when he turned eight. "Here, you can use this."

"Oh no," Milla said. "I don't think I can." Milla was only six, and while she had the heart of a bear about most things, she knew her limits. "You do it, Niklas. Please?"

So, one by one, Niklas sawed the tangled clumps from her hair. He stood back now and then to survey his work. Then he sawed off some more, and some more. Milla looked down at her feet, and it seemed like an awful lot of hair was collecting there. Finally he stopped. She looked at him. "How is it now? Better?"

Niklas smiled. "Much."

As they walked home, Milla gingerly touched her head. It felt so much lighter. And there was so much air on her neck. That didn't seem like a good thing at all, but it felt kind of nice. She told herself that it must be all right, because Niklas had said so.

When they got home, Milla expected to see her mother's usual locked face, the one that opened the moment she turned to Niklas. Perhaps a part of Milla expected a little worse than that. But she wasn't expecting her mother to drop a bowl and shriek at the sight of her.

"What have you done, Milla? What in all of creation have you done?"

Milla looked at her brother, and for an instant, one corner of his mouth turned up with satisfaction. Milla knew in that moment that he'd gotten her back for having frightened him and then laughed at him. At the sight of their mother's shattered bowl, though, his half smile vanished as quickly as it had appeared.

Milla's mouth opened and closed, and her hands went to her head, searching, hoping to find more hair than she now knew there was. For the first time she allowed herself to realize that it was all gone. Her hair was back there in the woods, in a pile. Where she'd once had bark-brown ringlets that grazed the middle of her back, she was left with uneven clumps no longer than her little finger.

Gitta gripped her by the shoulders. "Why did you do that? You stupid, stupid girl."

"Mamma," Niklas said. "It's not her fault. We were playing and her hair got all tangled, and I suggested she cut it. And she wouldn't use my knife to do it, even though I said she should. I did it, Mamma, I'm the one who did it."

"Oh, Niklas," Gitta said. She shook her head at him the way she did when he spilled milk at the breakfast table. Then she looked back at Milla, her face closed again. "Why must you always be so wild? If you hadn't made such a mess of yourself, your brother wouldn't have had to try to fix you." Gitta released Milla's shoulders and turned toward the kitchen. "Pappa won't like this. Not one bit. Now go and get clean and then I'll see what sense I can make of your hair. I suppose the way you look is punishment enough, but your father may think different."

In the kitchen yard, Niklas pumped water into two pitchers and handed one to Milla. "Is my hair so very bad?" she asked him.

Niklas laughed. "Oh, Milla. It's horrible."

Milla burst into tears.

"There, there." He patted her shoulder the way he had back in the woods, only this time she sensed he meant it. "It's all right. I'll handle Mamma and Pappa." Then he took the pitcher back from her, and he had Milla hold out her hands while he helped her wash with a fresh bar of soap. When he finished rinsing her hair he said, "Well, that was quick. Maybe you should keep it this way, right?"

Then she finally stopped crying, because it was impossible to keep feeling awful with Niklas standing there smiling at her.

That was a long time ago.

Once she had laid the salt down in perfect lines along every window and doorway and arching in a perfect semicircle around the hearth, Milla went out to help Niklas finish loading the wagon. She should have stayed behind to help Mamma with breakfast. But she'd go back inside in a moment—after she'd spoken to Niklas.

In the end, she didn't say anything to him at all. He'd finished loading the wagon with strong, confident arms just as she arrived to help him. Then he looked at her and said, "I'm hungry." So they went back inside.

Don't leave me, she had wanted to say to him. But if she'd said it, her brother would only have laughed at her, the way he always did. It would be a laugh that wasn't meant to make her feel stupid, and yet it would have that effect all the same. His face would break into a smile like sunshine, if sunshine were made of teeth.

She'd said it to him many times before when he and father would go off to the market in the village, leaving her and Mamma behind. And each time he'd respond the same way. "Silly Milla." She was silly Milla, just a girl. Silly Milla, just a lonely girl. Silly Milla, just a lonely girl who must stay at home on the farm while her brother went off and had adventures.

"I'm not having adventures," Niklas always said. "I'm working with Pappa. Standing ankle-deep in manure while he haggles with the other farmers. You're lucky you don't have to go. You get to stay here where it's clean, and Mamma takes care of you, and all you have to do is sew and feed the chickens."

"But you get to see things," she'd argue. "I don't understand why I can't go. It's not fair."

Then he'd smile and laugh like always. "Silly Milla."

Milla knew better than to make such arguments to her father and mother. Pappa would ignore her. Mamma would look frightened. Of what, Milla could never figure out. But her mother's fear was always there, always hanging between Milla and Gitta like an impenetrable fog. It lifted when Niklas was at home. Gitta's face lit up then, and she laughed at Niklas's jokes and she swept his hair from his forehead and kissed him there. Niklas wrapped his arms around Gitta's waist, even when she was cooking, and she let him. If Milla had done that, Gitta would have shooed her off and told her not to hang on her so. When Gitta spoke to Milla at all, it was a word of caution. *Don't do that. Be careful there. Watch you don't get dirty. Lower your voice. Brush your hair. Put on a clean apron.* Milla couldn't remember a time when it wasn't that way, and so it didn't occur to her any longer to try to soften her mother toward her. Nor did it occur to Milla to blame Niklas. After all, she loved Niklas best, too. It was impossible not to.

That loving was from a distance these days—ever since Niklas had turned thirteen, five years ago, and Pappa had said he was man enough to learn how to run things. Running things meant packing the wagon, and saddling a horse and driving cows and goats to the village—the village where Milla wasn't allowed to go.

When she entered the kitchen, Milla felt Gitta's eyes on her, scanning her, making sure her hair was smooth, her apron tied, and her fingernails clean of grime before she set the bread in front of Pappa and took her place at the breakfast table. Milla thought it hardly mattered what she looked like, because she couldn't remember the last time her father had really noticed her. Jakob would have noticed if the bread wasn't fresh, or if the meal wasn't hot. But if all was in order, if the meal was served at the right time and his fork was to the left of his plate, Jakob would see nothing else. Milla might have traded places with a goat, she thought to herself. As long as the goat was well-behaved, Pappa would be none the wiser. Milla imagined herself as a goat, placing the big wooden bread board in front of her father with her teeth instead of her hands, and she laughed.

Gitta wrinkled her brow at Milla then. "What's funny," she said. She said it like a statement, not a question. As if she were really saying, *There's nothing funny. And we don't laugh for no reason.*

Niklas came to the rescue, as he often did. "Did you hear Trude's rooster chased Wolf right out of the kitchen yard?" Trude and Stig were their family's only neighbors, and Wolf was their elkhound. Stig worked for her father, and since Niklas was so often away now, either in the fields or traveling to the village, Milla spent as much time sitting and sewing with Trude as she did with Gitta. "That old rooster is more of a guard dog than Wolf is."

At that, Gitta laughed, and that meant that Milla could, too. Because now something was funny. "That rooster is so mean," Milla said. "Poor Wolf."

"That dog's no use if a rooster can run him off," Jakob said. "I told Stig he should put Wolf down."

"Oh, Pappa," Milla said. "No. That's awful."

Jakob stopped chewing and looked at Milla with surprise, as if he'd just that moment seen she was there. "What would you know about it? And wouldn't it be awful if a fox came and ate up all of Trude's chicks, meanwhile Wolf's asleep by the fire? You're old enough to be thinking sense about these things, Milla."

Milla felt blood rush to her cheeks. She couldn't remember the last time her father had spoken so many words to her. The ignoring she'd grown used to, but this was far worse. She looked down at her plate. She wondered if all girls were treated this way, like something to be frightened for, or ridiculed and thought ignorant if they ever did speak, or found useless if they weren't perfectly behaved all the time. How was she any better than Stig's dog? She looked up at her father's square, sun- and wind-hardened face topped by thick, sandy hair mixed with gray. She realized how rarely she looked into his opaque blue eyes. "Perhaps you should put me down, too, Pappa."

The words were out of her mouth before she could stop them, before she even knew where they were coming from.

Her father's cheeks purpled.

"Milla." The expression on Gitta's face was one of horror. Like a goat really had replaced her daughter at the table. A talking goat with horns on its head and clattering teeth. Gitta's disgust was so great she couldn't even utter a *don't* or a *no* or a *take care*. Milla watched while Gitta turned her attention from Milla's disobedience to Jakob's disapproval. Her mother's most immediate job was to soothe the latter. A storm on her father's side of the table would ruin the meal. And a ruined meal was a grave failure. "Jakob," her mother said. "The child is softhearted. That's all it is. You know how she is about the animals." Gitta reached out her hand and barely grazed Jakob's cuff with her fingertips.

Niklas was struck silent. He looked from Milla to their father, then back again. Jakob stared straight at Milla, his cheeks slowly fading to red. It was Milla's turn now to make things right. She spoke softly. "I'm sorry, Pappa." That word. *Sorry.*

Her father said nothing, but stared at her one beat longer as if he wanted her to wonder what might happen next if he had a mind for something to happen next.

After breakfast, Jakob climbed into the wagon and Gitta spoke to him softly while she handed him the food she'd packed for him and Niklas. Milla walked Niklas to his horse. Once he'd mounted it, he said, "Milla, why must you worry them so?"

Milla had to restrain herself from shouting, but instead she kept her voice low enough so only he could hear. "Worry them so? What do I do all day but try not to cause them worry? Try to be sweet and clean the way Mamma wants, and obedient and . . . and invisible the way Pappa wants. I swear to you, Niklas, I thought just this morning that Pappa wouldn't notice if I were a goat. If I were a goat with horns and fur who sat at his table. So long as I set his plate down in front of him at the right time and the right way, it wouldn't matter." Milla laughed then. "Can you imagine, Niklas! I should do it. Dress up one of the goats in my apron and set it loose in the kitchen."

Niklas looked at her in a funny way then. A way that he didn't normally look at her. It was the way her mother always did. Like he was frightened for her—or of her. "You mustn't talk that way, Milla."

Milla took a step back then. "What way, Niklas? Like a bad girl?"

He shook his head. "Don't be silly, Milla." Then he smiled. "I'll bring you back something from the market. Promise not to upset Mamma while I'm away."

Then he rode off, and Milla wondered how she could avoid doing something that she had never tried to do in the first place.

Milla ate a quiet supper with her mother that evening. If it weren't always so awkward between them, Milla might have enjoyed these nights without Pappa and Niklas. There were no men to feed or clean up after. There was so much less food to make. No clumps of soil shaken from heavy boots and trailed across the floor. There was a fire to warm their toes and the pleasing shimmer of their needles in and out of their sewing. And silence. Dreadful silence.

They might have chatted amiably about which chickens were laying and which would end up in a stew. That's what Trude would have prattled on about if she were here. Trude had a way of using a lot of words to talk about very little, and it would have at least filled the air between them. Instead, the dark fog of Gitta's fear hung there, thicker than ever.

Gitta paused her needle in her sewing and looked at Milla. Milla kept her eyes on her sewing, but she felt her mother's examination like fingers on her scalp. "Milla," Gitta said. "We'll say our prayers together tonight."

Milla felt a chill inside, despite the fire. She knew what was coming next. Milla set aside her sewing, and her mother reached across and took Milla's hands in her own, then pulled her down to kneel across from her on the floor.

Gitta squeezed her eyes shut so tightly that it looked more like wincing than praying.

> *Lord, help us to stay on the path.*
> *Lord, help us to do as we should.*
> *Lord, help us to obey.*

It was a prayer that Milla knew well, but tonight it felt different. Tonight it felt like every word her mother spoke was meant for her, either to protect her or to punish her. It was blasphemous to think so, but Milla doubted there was much of a difference between the two.

> *Lord, we have spread the salt.*
> *Lord, we have locked the doors.*
> *Lord, let us not answer the knock of the stranger.*

The knock of the stranger. For as long as Milla could remember, this line in the prayer had given her a secret thrill. There'd never been a knock of a stranger on their door. There had only ever been her mother and father and Niklas, and Stig and Trude just a shout away. Faces she knew so well she would have noticed if a freckle were misplaced.

Milla wanted a stranger to knock on the door. She begged for one. Anything to break the lonely sameness of her days.

Lord, protect us from demons.
Lord, protect us from demons.
Lord, protect us from demons.

Three times. Three times always. Three times was supposed to be the charm. Milla had often wondered what would happen if she said it only twice.

"Amen," Gitta said. Then she opened her eyes and looked hard at Milla, so hard that Milla feared she'd said aloud what she thought she'd only been thinking.

The heat from the fire licked Milla's right cheek, and a cold draft from under the door kissed her left. "Amen," she said.

Gitta held her grip on Milla's hands, and stared into Milla's eyes as if looking for something. Milla resisted the impulse to break her gaze and instead held steady, steady, steady. Soon, Milla thought to herself, soon she'd be free to go to her bed, and then what happened in the space between her ears was her own business and no one else's.

Finally her mother released her, and Milla rose to her feet.

Gitta stayed where she was, kneeling on the floor. As she turned to the stairs to go up to bed, Milla noticed a break in the stream of salt in front of the door. A small gap—but there. If Gitta noticed it, she'd want Milla to do something about it. Milla looked back at her mother and made a decision.

"Goodnight, Mamma," she said.

Milla went to bed then, and in the moments before sleep took her, she thought about a stranger knocking on their door. And then she thought about opening it.

3

SOMETHING WAS HAPPENING. THAT WAS WHAT MILLA said to herself over and over that day. *Something is happening.*

Something was happening. Soon.

Soon her days wouldn't be the same. Soon there would be a new face at the table—at least sometimes. A new face to discover, and a new voice to say new things. Things that might surprise her.

Milla was so excited she spilled the salt. Gitta was too distracted to admonish her for it.

Someone was coming. A girl. A girl just a year older than Milla. Her name was Iris.

Gitta told Milla the news right after Niklas and Jakob had returned from their last trip to the village. The girl was Stig and Trude's granddaughter, the only child of their daughter and son-in-law who lived in the village. And she was coming to live with Stig and Trude now.

When Milla asked Gitta why Iris was coming, Gitta hesitated at first. Then she sighed. Her face became soft, and Milla couldn't tell if it was a happy or a sad softness. Then she thought it was both. "It will soon be time for our Niklas to think about marrying. And Iris is a good girl. Or so Stig and Trude say. So for the next few years she and Niklas will get to know each other, and if they like each other, well, they'll marry. And we'll build them a house here. And things will go on."

Niklas . . . marry? Milla turned the words over in her head. It wasn't that the thought had never occurred to her, but it had seemed so impossibly far away that either of them would have to think about it. And Niklas was her brother, a boy. A boy with a man's shoulders, but still—a boy. "Does Niklas know?"

"That Iris is coming? Of course."

"No, does he know that he's to marry her?"

Gitta looked away from Milla, through the window and at the green of the fields that rolled away from their home, and the darker green of the forest that bordered it. That view through the window was all Milla had ever known. She wondered how her mother could be content with it. With everything always going on and on, the same. She wondered what a girl like Iris—a girl raised in the village!—would think of so much quiet. So much sameness. Then she went back to thinking about her brother marrying. Marrying!

"He knows it's how we're thinking of it," Gitta said. "And he knows he can say no if he doesn't like her. But they've met, and he seems happy enough about it."

"They've met?" Milla couldn't keep the surprise from her voice.

Or the hurt. How long had Niklas known, and he hadn't told her? Once again she felt filled with resentment that his life was so much bigger than her own. His life occupied a whole other world that she hadn't even been allowed to see. And then there was the hurt that her brother, to whom she'd once been so close, now felt so far away. That he hadn't told her something so important about himself. Not to mention, he knew how lonely she was. How much she craved companionship. How could he not have told her that her wish was being granted?

Instead of ringing the bell for dinner, Milla decided to go find Niklas in the field. It was spring, and the sun was warm on her head, but the air was still chilly on her skin, so she wrapped a wool shawl around her shoulders and walked at a clip through the fields to where she knew her brother would be. She called to him the moment she saw him. He looked up, waved, and walked toward her.

When he was not less than thirty feet away, Milla said, "Just when were you planning to tell me that you're to marry?"

He walked closer before he answered her. "Mamma told you?"

"No, Wolf did. That dog talks to me more than you do."

Niklas laughed. Kept smiling. "Don't tell Pappa you're talking to that dog. He considers him a bad influence."

Milla kept her mouth in a straight line. Her eyebrows, too. Niklas would not get her to smile. He would not. "Niklas."

He sighed. "I didn't know what to say."

"How about, 'Milla, a girl named Iris is coming to live with Stig and Trude, and Mamma and Pappa think I should marry her in a few years.'"

"Well, right. I suppose I could have said that. But honestly, Milla, it's all so strange. Imagine how I feel. I've seen the girl at the market with her mother and father, but I haven't spoken to her more than twice. She seems nice enough, and I suppose I'm happy about it. You're not the only one who gets lonely, you know."

Milla looked at her tall, handsome brother. For the last five years she'd imagined him having friends in the village, charming everyone with his smile the way he charmed their mother. It hadn't occurred to her that he got lonely. She only thought about how lonely she was, and how much more exciting his life seemed.

But still. Something was wrong. There was something her brother wasn't telling her. She could see it in his eyes, that there was a closed door in there, and he was trying to distract her away from it.

"I'm mad at you," Milla said. "You should have told me."

"You're always mad, Milla. And you have less to be mad about than you think."

Milla raised an eyebrow. That closed door had just opened a crack. "What do you mean," she said.

The tiniest ripple of consternation crossed Niklas's forehead, then dissolved into a smile. "Nothing, Milla. I just mean you don't know how easy you've got it." He took one of her hands in his own and turned it over. Then he took her other hand, held one of her fingers between two of his own and ran it over the pads of her open palm. "So soft," he said.

"My hands aren't soft," she said, pulling her hands away from him. "I work plenty. Who do you think helped Mamma make the dinner you're about to eat? Who do you think is going to wash the shirt you're wearing?" She rubbed lard into her hands at night, just to soothe the painful, bloody cracks that burned every time she dipped them into soapy water.

Niklas held up his own hands, palms facing her. She touched

them. The calluses were as thick and hard as wood chips.

"Fine," she said. She turned away from him and walked toward home. He chased after her and threw an arm over her shoulder.

"Silly Milla. Let's not fight."

She crossed her arms over her chest so her elbows stuck out hard and sharp.

"Don't you want to know what Iris is like?"

"No," Milla said.

"Oh really?" Niklas said. "You're not curious? You'd cover your ears and run away if I tried to tell you?" He smiled at her, triumphant.

"I hate you," Milla said. But her own smile gave her away.

"No you don't," Niklas said. "And you never could."

Milla sighed. It was true. She couldn't. She couldn't ever.

Milla knelt to sweep up the salt she'd spilled. Stig and Trude had gone to fetch Iris two days before, and the plan was that they'd stay one day visiting with their daughter and son-in-law, and then they would come back here. Milla did calculations in her head, guessing how long it might take them to make the trip. It must be very far, Milla thought. After all, she never saw anyone from the village, so it must be hard to get from there to here. The way Mamma and Pappa talked about it, it seemed like the village was a world away.

Milla stood up, and that's when she heard wagon wheels. Stig and Trude. And Iris. They were back. Milla's hands flew to her hair to tuck away any stray strands. Iris was the first girl she was meeting in her life, and Milla had been worried for days how she might appear to her. If she might look . . . off . . . to Iris. If she dressed the same as the girls in the village. Talked the same.

Wore her hair the same way. Gitta was always so despairing of Milla that she thought she must be very clumsy and awkward. She imagined Iris must be more like Gitta. Pleasing to look at, and graceful. Always knowing what to say and how to act, even without her mother's rules to guide her.

Milla said to her mother, "Mamma, please. May I go meet them?"

"We'll go together," Gitta said. She untied her apron and hung it from a hook, then smoothed her own hair. Milla waited, even though she wanted to take off at a run and not miss even a moment of Iris's arrival.

Milla thought her mother walked slower than usual on purpose, just to teach her daughter a lesson about patience. Everything in Milla's life, it seemed, was a lesson. Milla had asked Niklas that morning if he'd stay home that day so as to be there when Iris arrived. Pappa had answered for him. "Work doesn't wait just because we have a visitor," he said. *A visitor.* That was an odd way of putting it, Milla thought. As if Iris's stay were temporary. As if, maybe, it wouldn't work out. Then it occurred to her that maybe Iris's life would also be full of lessons now, and if Milla wanted her to stay, she'd have to help her learn them very well.

When they reached Stig and Trude's small, neat cottage, Stig was unloading baskets from the wagon, but there was no sight of Trude or Iris.

"Hallo," Stig said, when he caught sight of them. "Trude's showing our granddaughter about the cottage. You wouldn't think that would take very long, but our Trude's a bit excited. I think she's presently giving her a tour of the kitchen table." He walked toward the house. "Trude. Gitta and Milla are here to meet Iris. Hurry along."

Iris emerged from the cottage, and the girl-shaped creature in front of Milla was at once strange and beautiful and familiar and ordinary. She was about the same height and width as Milla. Her hair was long about her shoulders the way Milla's was. Those were all the ordinary parts. Everything else was extraordinary.

Her face was heart shaped, starting with a V at the center of her forehead and ending at the soft point of her chin. Her cheekbones were high, and she had wide, sweeping eyebrows the color of rust, matching her hair the color of rust—if rust were also shiny and liquid. The color of her skin wasn't like Gitta's, which was milky with touches of rose on her cheeks and the tip of her nose. Nor was it like Milla's, which was more yellow, like butter. Iris's skin was more brown, like harvest wheat. And her eyes were at once bright and dark, like syrup. Milla hadn't known that eyes came in that color. She took in all this newness with thirsty eyes.

Then the most unusual thing happened. Iris rushed toward Milla and threw her arms around her. "Milla! I've heard so much about you. We're going to be better than friends. We're going to be sisters."

Milla startled and shook and then something broke inside her. Or opened. Or collapsed. Some structure that had existed inside Milla, which had given form to her world and defined what was possible, shattered and scattered and blew away. And in its place was Iris.

Milla felt Iris's arms across her back and Iris's hair in her face and it was as real and unreal as a dream. Real because it felt so natural, and unreal because it shouldn't feel so.

Stig continued unloading the wagon, completely unaware of the world-shifting event that was presently occurring inside Milla.

Gitta, for her part, seemed less interested in Iris, and more interested in being alone with Trude.

"Milla, walk Iris over to our place so she knows how to find us. And show her the chickens while you're at it. And the garden. Show her everything."

Her mother never gave Milla such freedom, and the idea that she should be the one to show a stranger around their home was as odd as suggesting that Wolf should do it. Milla saw how Gitta had already tilted herself toward Trude's kitchen, urging Trude along with her. She felt that tickle of suspicion again, the same one she'd felt with Niklas. The sense that she was being distracted away from some truth she wasn't allowed to know.

Iris linked arms with Milla and said, "Lead on." Then she smiled.

Of all the things that were most extraordinary about Iris, from her syrup eyes to her liquid-rust hair, what mesmerized Milla most about her was the way that Iris made her feel. Iris didn't make Milla feel upside down—rather she made Milla feel as if she'd finally turned the world right side up. And oh, *this* was how it was supposed to be. And no wonder Milla had felt so off-kilter before.

Another thing: Iris smiled even more than Niklas, which Milla hadn't thought possible. This opened up a world of other possibilities for Milla, who just yesterday had known only five people. Now that she knew six, and this sixth person was so very different from the other five . . . well, it stood to reason that the seventh—if ever she should meet a seventh—would be as well.

She couldn't imagine that the seventh, or eighth, or one hundredth person that she met would ever be as interesting to her as Iris was, though. Milla found herself arrested by the way Iris used her hands when she spoke, tracing lines in the air that seemed to make what she said all the more interesting and original. Iris looked at the same tree that had stood outside Milla's window her whole life, and she said, "What a funny tree! It looks like an old man scratching his head." And Milla looked at it and realized that why, yes, it did look very much like an old man scratching his head and why had she never noticed that before? Maybe it was because she'd seen so little—she had nothing to compare it to. Iris seemed full of memories, and everything reminded her of something else. Buckets and buckets of recollections spilled out of her when she noticed something. Milla showed her Gitta's jars of preserves, and that led Iris to a story about berry picking, and that led her to a story about her favorite berry, and why it was her favorite, and then she asked Milla if she could only ever eat one berry for the rest of her life, what would it be?

Milla paused to ponder while Iris waited expectantly for her answer, her syrup-eyes bright with interest. "Well," Milla said. "I haven't ever thought about that." Iris looked disappointed for a moment, and Milla felt dull and stupid. So she rushed to say more. "What I mean is that I haven't thought about it that *way*. Because I haven't been anywhere or done anything the way you have, so I'm always thinking about what more I could see or do. I don't want to think about doing even less."

It was an unusually long rush of words for Milla, not because she didn't like to talk, but because there was no one to talk to. Even Niklas only half listened when she talked to him these days, so she lost interest in making the effort, and kept her thoughts to herself. She worried Iris would find her very odd.

"Oh, Milla, of course!" Iris said. "That makes complete sense. It was a silly question anyway. Who would want to only eat one berry? Especially when you have so many berries here. We don't have nearly so many in the village." She ran a finger over one of Gitta's jars.

"Really?" Milla said. She hadn't ever thought of there being less of anything in the village. "Will you miss it there?" Milla wondered if she would miss the farm if she were sent away to live somewhere else. But she could only imagine excitement at the prospect.

Iris's face had turned thoughtful. "I'll miss Mamma and Pappa. But maybe I'll visit." She brightened then. "And you can come with me!"

For a moment Milla thought she might rise off the floor with happiness, but then she remembered. "I'm not allowed."

"Oh, Milla. Of course not. I knew that. I'm so sorry. I keep saying all the wrong things." Iris went blank again.

Milla didn't think anyone had ever said sorry to her before. She was always the one saying it. And she felt such a rush of wanting to reassure Iris the way she'd always wanted to be reassured herself, that she reached for Iris's hand. "Oh no, not at all! You're so kind to offer. And . . . maybe things will change? Maybe someday they'll let me."

Iris smiled. "We'll *make* them."

Milla laughed. "You haven't met my father."

Iris said, "Oh, but I have! He's not so bad. And anyway, we'll just leave when their backs are turned. And maybe we won't go to the village at all. Maybe we'll go somewhere else."

Milla's mind took a leap. She'd been so desperate, and for so long, to go to the village that she hadn't thought about there being other places to go. "Where?"

Iris tugged gently on one of Milla's long, dark curls. "Anywhere."

4

THAT FIRST EVENING, THEY ATE DINNER TOGETHER, ALL
seven of them. This only ever happened on holidays, and it felt
festive, like a party. Even Jakob smiled at one point, and warmed
up to tell a story about how he got the best price for a cow. It
wasn't a very good story—there was barely a beginning, not much
of a middle, and no real end. But Iris listened to it attentively
and nodded at all the right places. Milla remembered her father's
word—*visitor*—and she was glad for how well Iris seemed to be
doing at pleasing him. Gitta was harder to read, but Iris's manners
were so pretty that Milla couldn't imagine Gitta not liking what
she saw. And Iris was just right with Niklas, too. Friendly, but
not too friendly. She knew exactly how much attention to pay to
him—just enough that a beloved boy like him would feel was his
due, but not so much that he'd weary of it. Milla didn't think she
could ever grow tired of watching Iris.

After dinner, Jakob and Stig pulled out their pipes and smoked by the fire, and Niklas carved a new wooden spoon for Mamma. "Such a good boy," Trude said, and smiled at Iris. Milla held her breath for a moment. Mamma might not like this special attention paid to Niklas on Iris's behalf—Gitta had always had Niklas for her own, and maybe she would feel . . . jealous. The thought of that made Milla feel odd inside, and she wondered where this suspicion had even come from. What a strange thing to think— that her mother would be jealous of a girl. But there it was. Milla watched her mother and saw a flicker of annoyance in Gitta's otherwise still, locked face.

"It is a very beautiful spoon," Iris said. "And I noticed your others, ma'am. They're so much nicer than my mother's. And I saw that there's only one that's stained purple. Is that the spoon you use when you make preserves? That's so clever. All of my mamma's spoons are stained purple. It didn't even occur to us to keep just one aside for making preserves."

Milla watched her mother's face, and the wariness that Milla always saw there when Gitta looked at her didn't give way for Iris. It was still there. But nonetheless Mamma said, "In the summer, Iris, you'll help us with the preserving."

In the summer. That was months away. That was a kind of promise, wasn't it? Gitta was saying that Iris would still be there in the summer. Milla looked at Iris then.

Iris winked at her.

The next day, Iris was at their door directly after breakfast and just as Jakob and Niklas were headed to the fields. Milla was to teach Iris the rules.

Gitta observed closely while Milla showed Iris the right way to pour salt in a line—no breaks, but no waste, either. Once Gitta was certain Milla hadn't been careless, she left the girls to themselves and went off to see Trude again. Gitta rarely had so much to say to Trude, so this aroused another flicker of curiosity in Milla, but she was too relieved to see her go, and too happy to be alone with Iris, to wonder about it for long.

Once Gitta was out of earshot, Milla said, "I'm sorry. This must be so boring for you. I don't know why Mamma is having me teach you rules you must already know. We'll just do the hearth now, and then we're done. Do you want to do it?"

Iris shrugged. "That's all right. You can do it. I don't see much point."

"Oh," Milla said. She felt ashamed, and she wasn't sure why.

"It's just that if a demon wants you, a demon will get you. I don't think a little line of salt is going to keep it away."

"No?"

Iris shook her head. "No."

Iris seemed so certain, which made Milla think once again how much more Iris must know about the world than she did. "How do you know?"

Iris's face went blank for a moment. This had happened before with Iris, and it was the kind of blank that Milla was used to in other faces—in Pappa's and Mamma's especially. And more recently in Niklas's, too. But she could tell that Iris's face didn't want to be blank. It wasn't a normal state for Iris's face to be so empty of emotion. So shut up tight.

Once again, Milla had that feeling. That feeling that something was being held back from her. "You're not telling me something."

Iris looked at Milla, and now her face wasn't blank, it was

pleading. "I can't, Milla. Please don't make me. If you make me, they'll send me back. And I want to stay here." Then she took one of Milla's hands in her own. "I would tell you if I could."

"But I wouldn't tell anyone," Milla said. "And it's not fair. Why is everyone keeping secrets from me? Why do you get to know, but I don't? Is it something about the village? Is that why I'm not allowed to go there?"

They both heard the clatter of the chicken coop opening and closing. Gitta was back.

"Milla, listen to me," Iris said. "If I ever told you, they'd know. They'd find out and they wouldn't let me stay here anymore."

Milla wanted to protest, but Gitta came inside, and she told Iris that Trude was asking for her.

Then Milla was alone.

Every day since Iris arrived, Milla had rushed through her chores so she could spend as much time as possible with her. Milla couldn't remember ever being so happy in all her life—at least not since she was eleven, before Niklas was taken away from her.

Milla was so happy that she hadn't pestered Iris with any more questions. She decided not to worry about such things for a while. Maybe, she told herself, in this one area she could be a truly good girl. To simply do as she was told and not to ask for more than she should. Maybe in time she could learn to be as in command of herself as Iris was. Iris seemed to know how to be right with everyone. She knew how to be sweet with Stig and Trude, amiable with Niklas, and well-behaved with Mamma and Pappa.

With Milla, Iris seemed to let all that go. For Milla's part, being with Iris reminded her of those days in the forest with Niklas when they were children, fighting off trolls. Milla felt wild

again during her afternoons with Iris—but without the conse-
quences. She knew how to return home with a clean apron and an
innocent face and her hair still long down her back.

When she was little, and Milla and Niklas went off for their
walks in the forest, Milla had been the one making up stories. But
Iris was far better at stories than Milla had ever been. Milla could
conjure a witch with teeth dripping blood, but Iris would make
that witch do and say such horrible things that Milla marveled
at how Iris could ever have thought of them. Milla was used to
Trude's simple stories about trolls and princesses and princes that
turned into frogs and back again, but Iris's stories were different.
Milla's favorite was the one about the snake tree.

One day, a pretty girl named Anna was walking through the
woods picking berries. This girl was so pretty and so good that
her parents let her walk in the woods all by herself without fear
that she would ever do anything wrong, or that anything wrong
would ever befall her.

As Anna reached for a particularly juicy strawberry, a gnarled
hand closed over her own and Anna gasped in surprise. The
gnarled hand belonged to a gnarled and ugly old woman with a
wart on her nose. The wart had its own wart growing on top of it,
and from that wart grew one long black hair.

The ugly old woman was dressed in rags and bent over like a
question mark. She leaned on a walking stick and seemed very
frail, so Anna's fear flew away and she asked the ugly old woman
if she needed help reaching home, and if Anna might carry her
basket for her.

The ugly old woman said, well, aren't you a dear, and you are
such a dear that you deserve a reward for being so good.

Anna liked being told how good she was, and it made sense

to her that she deserved a reward. Because she *was* terribly good, wasn't she?

So Anna thanked the ugly old woman, and asked her what the reward was.

The ugly old woman said that Anna's reward was buried in a clearing in the forest that was too far to reach for such an old woman. It was a treasure, you see, an enormous treasure. And all the ugly old woman required was that Anna go and dig it up. And then Anna could keep half, and the other half she would return to the ugly old woman. Did they have a deal?

Why certainly, Anna said. Most certainly they had a deal.

Anna made her way back to the clearing in the forest. A pretty place. A very pretty place, and just as the ugly old woman had described. Anna used the little trowel her mamma had given her for foraging, and she dug up that treasure. And the moment Anna caught sight of it, her heart embraced that treasure as if it were all her own. After all, shouldn't it be? Wasn't she a pretty, good young girl? And how very old the ugly old woman was. And how very ugly the ugly old woman was, too. Too old and too ugly to need a treasure. What would she do with it, anyway?

So Anna took all the treasure. She packed it up in her basket and she went home and hid it under her bed. She didn't tell her mamma and pappa, because she wasn't sure how to explain to them how she'd dug up and stolen a treasure from an ugly old woman in the forest. That was the second time when Anna felt a little bit afraid.

Anna shook off that fear and she continued on with her life, and for a while she didn't go back to the forest. Eventually, though, her fear was so long gone that she forgot about it entirely and she went back. And just as she was reaching for the blackest, ripest blackberry she had ever seen, a gnarled hand closed over her own.

And Anna gasped.

It was the ugly old woman, and the ugly old woman asked where her half of the treasure was.

That was the third and last time Anna felt afraid.

Anna said there was no treasure. She had dug where the ugly old woman had told her to dig, but there was nothing there. Anna said that the ugly old woman was very mean for scaring her so, and really Anna should be heading for home because her mamma and pappa would be waiting for her.

Then the ugly old woman looked much less like a question mark. She stood as straight as the walking stick that she no longer seemed to need. Black smoke rose from her feet, enveloping her rags and transforming them into a cloak so black that it was blacker than the blackest blackberry. Her hair swirled around her head.

Anna knew then that the ugly old woman was a witch, and this was all a terrible trick.

The witch told Anna that she had one more chance to save her life. She held out her gnarled hand and waggled her fingers over the earth beneath their feet, and from that spot sprouted a low tree with long, skinny leaves. And from one of its branches grew a single green apple. An apple so green it glowed. It made Anna's mouth water.

The witch said that Anna had only to eat that apple, and then all would be forgiven.

Anna reached out and plucked the apple. Then she sank her teeth into it, and for just a moment, Anna thought she had never tasted anything so delicious in all her life.

But after that first bite, Anna wasn't Anna anymore. Or at least she wasn't an Anna-shaped Anna. Anna was a snake. A small, slender, perfect snake. She shimmered as she curled around the green apple where it had fallen to the ground. She wondered at her new station in life.

The witch bent over and plucked up Anna by the tail. She held Anna in the air, and looked into her snake eyes. And she said to Anna: The prettiest snake is eaten first.

Then she dropped Anna into her mouth. And as the witch chewed, enjoying the sensation of Anna fighting back a bit, only just a bit, she also enjoyed the sweetness of the apple she could taste on Anna's snake lips.

When the witch had swallowed Anna down, she waggled her fingers once again and the snake tree disappeared. Then, as the witch continued on down the path, looking for other pretty, good girls and boys, she laughed. These good children, she said. They do love their rewards. . . .

When Iris told Milla that story, she knew exactly when to pause and lower her voice, and she made Milla shiver in places and laugh in others.

One afternoon when the sky was blue and the sun was warm and the shade from the trees was the perfect degree of cool, Iris and Milla sat in a clearing that looked very much like where the witch's treasure was buried. When Iris finished telling Milla her story, she reached over and tugged on one of Milla's long brown curls. "You have beautiful hair, Milla."

"I do?"

"Of course you do. Don't you know it?"

Milla felt such hopelessness in her chest at that moment, such an awareness of the vast, uncrossable distance between what she knew and what she didn't know. "Iris, I don't know anything. And if you don't tell me, I never will."

"Your mother must tell you things."

"All Mamma tells me is how to cook what Pappa likes to eat and how to get things clean."

"Well, I suppose that's useful. And lots of mothers are like that."

"Is yours?" Milla knew Iris missed her mother.

"There's always so much work to be done. And life is . . . hard. But in the evenings, Mamma brushes my hair and we talk. And that's nice. Was nice. I thought it might be that way with Grand-mamma. But she's old and she falls asleep by the fire. So mostly I sit and sew while she and Grandpappa snore. You're lucky you have Niklas."

Milla thought about that for a moment. She supposed she was lucky. She couldn't imagine life without him, with just her and Mamma and Pappa. It would be so dreary. "You don't have brothers or sisters, do you? I just realized that I never asked."

"No. It's only me."

"Your mother and father must miss you so much. I'm surprised they let you leave them." Milla knew she was treading dangerously close to asking Iris more questions, but she couldn't help herself.

"Milla," Iris said. She looked at Milla with her bright syrup eyes that seemed to take in everything so quickly.

"I know, no questions." Milla sighed. "All right. Tell me about your friends. You're the only girl I've ever met. You can at least tell me about other girls."

"Oh," Iris said. "All right. Well, I had a friend, yes."

"What is she like?" Milla had a thought. "Maybe she could come visit you?" Then Milla would get to meet someone else. A seventh person.

Iris went blank. So blank. So blank it was as if Iris weren't there anymore and only an Iris-shaped shell were left in her place.

"What's wrong?" Milla said. "What did I say?"

Iris stood up suddenly and walked away from Milla. "We should get back."

"Iris." Milla caught up with Iris, only to have Iris walk away even faster. "I'm sorry. I didn't mean to upset you. But if you'd only tell me how I upset you, then I'd know not to do it again. As it is I'm so confused that I feel like I'm wrong and I don't even know why. And I'm so very tired of feeling this way." Milla's voice cracked and she realized she was crying.

Iris stopped walking, but she didn't turn around. "My friend's name was Beata."

Was. Milla stopped crying. Wiped her eyes with the back of her hand.

"Beata and I were friends since we were babies. Always together. She taught me all the stories I tell you. You think I'm so smart, but Beata was the smart one. So quick and sharp. But then she got sick."

Iris paused. Then she turned around and looked at Milla. "And now Beata's not Beata anymore."

Beata's not Beata anymore. The line from the prayer came to Milla now. *Lord, let us not answer the knock of the stranger.* Had Beata answered the knock of the stranger? Is that why she wasn't herself anymore?

"You're my only friend, Milla. Be my friend." Iris wasn't crying, and she wasn't pleading. She was telling Milla something, and Milla knew she needed to listen. To collect all that she was being told so she could do something with it later.

"Yes, Iris," Milla said. "I'm your friend. Always."

SPRING WARMED TOWARD SUMMER, AND MILLA NO
longer worried that Iris might be snatched away from her at
any moment. She and Iris had taken to doing all of their chores
together, making short work of them. Sometimes they chatted,
other times they were happy to be quietly in each other's company
while they peeled potatoes or hung the laundry to dry.

On Sundays, when Niklas, Pappa, and Stig rested from
their work in the fields and there was no market in the village,
Niklas joined Milla and Iris on their walks in the forest. Iris
was easy and friendly with Niklas, but she never made Milla
feel as if she really wished she were alone with him. Milla had
been worried about this the first time he had walked out with
them. She wondered if she might feel stupid and awkward and
childish if Niklas teased her in front of Iris. But when Niklas
called her "silly Milla," Iris always came to her rescue, teasing

Niklas back and saying that he was the silly one.

The first time they walked out together, Milla had been so eager to show Niklas how well she knew Iris, and to display Iris to Niklas in all her wonderfulness, that she begged Iris to tell him the story about the snake tree. While Iris told the story, Milla watched Niklas's face and saw that it troubled him. At the end he said, "Why would the good child get eaten? That's not the way stories are supposed to go." So Iris didn't tell any more stories when Niklas was around.

Something else Milla noticed was that whenever conversation took a turn toward the village, Niklas steered it away again. Sometimes she said something about the village just to watch him do it.

"Iris," she said once, "how would you be spending your day if you were back in the village?"

Before Iris could answer, Niklas pointed out a fox to them, a fox that magically disappeared when she and Iris tried to spot it. And then he changed the subject to hunting foxes, knowing that Milla would argue with him and tell him that he should leave the foxes alone. Milla allowed herself to be distracted, because she already had her answer: Niklas knew something she didn't. He was in on the secret, and he was trying to keep it from her.

Milla might have wished Iris could tell her whatever the secret was, but she forgave her for this; she understood Iris's reasons. Iris feared she'd be sent away. Milla felt betrayed by Niklas, though, and it closed a tiny part of her heart to him. She found herself wishing he wouldn't walk with them on Sundays—which shocked her. Not so long ago, she'd wanted so desperately for Niklas to stay with her always. But everything had changed since Iris arrived, and for the first time Milla allowed herself to think that maybe, in this one way, her life hadn't changed for the better. She didn't want to feel this way about Niklas. It made her unhappy. But there it was. The truth was out. And she couldn't put it back in.

On the first hot afternoon of the summer, when Milla and Iris had finished their chores and cleaned up after dinner, Milla told Iris that she'd take her to a spring where they hadn't been before. Without Niklas, they could take off their boots and stockings and hitch up their dresses and wade in up to their knees. It would be heaven.

Milla hadn't known Iris very long, but she'd studied her so closely that soon after they set off for the spring, Milla knew something was wrong. Iris's harvest-wheat skin looked pale on the surface, like a thin veil had been pulled tight across her.

"Are you feeling well, Iris? Are you sure you want to walk so far today?"

"Oh yes, quite well, Milla. Quite well."

Iris sounded odd to Milla, too, as if she were slightly off the beat of the world around her. After Iris spoke, she shadowed her own words, silently reforming them with her lips as if she were making sure of them, or not quite ready to let them go.

"I have a new story for you," Iris said, and she didn't wait for Milla to respond. She spilled it out in a rush of words. "Once there was a prince, who fell in love with a beautiful princess. So he asked her to marry him and she said yes. On her wedding day, white doves flew down and dressed her in a beautiful blue gown. Then they perched on her shoulders and cooed to her while bluebirds flew down and braided her hair. When the prince saw her, he said, my darling, what's that all over your shoulders? And pray tell, what is that in your hair? And the princess looked and saw that the white doves had shat all over her shoulders. And she reached up to her hair and discovered that indeed the bluebirds had shat all over her hair. So the prince beat her and then he ordered her burned as a witch because only a witch would let birds dress her and braid her hair."

"Oh," Milla said. "Oh."

Iris laughed. Then she put her hands to her face and cried. "There's something wrong with me, Milla. Something terribly wrong."

"No, no, dearest. Not at all," Milla said. "I loved that story. It was wonderful. All of your stories are wonderful." They'd reached the spring, and Milla led Iris to a flat rock where they could sit and talk.

"You don't understand," Iris said. "It's happening to me. Just like it happened to Beata."

Milla felt frightened then, because she knew she was about to hear something terrible, and for the first time she realized that perhaps she didn't want to know. Perhaps it might be better not to.

"I'm hearing it in my head, Milla."

"You're hearing what in your head?"

"The demon." Iris tapped her forehead. "It's in here."

"Oh no. No, no, no. That's not possible." Milla felt herself going blank now. She wanted to clap her hands over her ears and squeeze her eyes shut and pretend she hadn't heard any of that. "We spread the salt. We locked the doors and windows."

Iris smiled strangely, in a way that showed teeth but no happiness. "That doesn't work. I told you that. Nothing ever works. The demon gets us anyway."

Milla had a choice to make, she realized. She could tell Iris to be quiet, the way her mother would have told Milla to be quiet if she'd said something troubling. Or she could be the friend that Iris had asked her to be. "Tell me, Iris. Tell me everything."

And Iris did.

It wasn't the oldest girls who were taken by the demon. Or the youngest. Or the ones in the middle. Or rather, it was the oldest *and* the youngest *and* the ones in the middle. It was any of them, sometimes all of them. Very few families were spared entirely. Maybe they had only sons, or they had daughters who managed to escape the demon. Those families considered themselves blessed. But most families could list off sisters or aunts or cousins or daughters who were taken by the demon. And the cruelty of the demon was its randomness. There was no pattern to its grasping, so there was no way to protect against it. The most devout weren't spared, nor were the least. They were all at risk. If you were born a girl, you were fair game.

The youngest girl who'd ever been taken was twelve, and no one could recall a girl over the age of eighteen being taken. This was why Jakob and Gitta had at first insisted that Iris's mother and father wait until she was eighteen before they sent her to live with Stig and Trude to be Niklas's intended. This way Jakob and Gitta could be assured that Iris was out of danger—or rather, that Jakob and Gitta were out of danger of bringing a demon-possessed girl into their home. Trude told Iris that it was Niklas who'd convinced Jakob and Gitta that Iris should come now. After all, she was almost eighteen, and such a good girl. And Niklas said she'd be a calming influence on Milla—because they all had their worries about Milla. She was too much alone. It wasn't healthy. A girl could start hearing things under those circumstances.

That was how it started with the girls who were taken by the demon—hearing things. It was the demon talking to the girls, telling them nasty lies about their mothers and fathers, sisters and brothers. Then the girls began whispering to themselves. Then one morning they woke up seeing monsters in the faces of their families. They screamed at the sight of their own mothers.

When the first girls were taken—long before Iris was born— the village was caught unawares. But as it happened to more and more girls, the demon-possessions became a sad way of life. Fear and grief and suspicion fell over the village like a fog that the villagers continued to walk through in the hopes that one day it might lift. And what choice did they have? Leave their homes and farms and shops? And go where? And eat what?

Then it happened to Beata. Iris's dear Beata. One day Beata confided in Iris that there was a whispering in her head, a whisper-ing that wasn't her own. She asked Iris if she thought the demon was taking her, and Iris had said, *no, no, of course not.* Iris wouldn't let herself believe it, because she couldn't bear for it to be true. Then the whispering grew louder and clearer in Beata's head. It was a voice, strong and certain. And Beata found it increasingly hard to doubt what the voice said to her. *Beata,* the voice said, *your family doesn't love you. They think you're a monster. But they're the monsters. Look at their faces. See the monsters all around you.*

Beata begged Iris to help her leave the village, and for Iris to leave with her. But Iris was afraid. Then Beata woke up one day screaming. She looked at her mother's face at the breakfast table and insisted she was trying to poison her. She looked at her father's face and said he was the devil. And by then it was too late; there was no escape for Beata. Consumed by guilt, Iris pleaded with Beata's mother and father not to let the midwife take Beata away. Iris told Beata's mother and father she could look after Beata herself. But that wasn't allowed. Possession, the midwife said, was contagious. This was why all the stricken girls were taken to The Place, where the midwife looked after them. Families were allowed to visit, and some did. But many found it too upsetting to be reminded of their loss—to look into the eyes of a daughter who sometimes knew them and at other times said terrible things. Hateful things.

Iris didn't know what The Place was, or even where it was. But she knew she didn't want to be sent there. She'd rather die. The Place had become something that mothers and fathers used to scare their misbehaving children. *If you carry on so, the midwife will come and take you to The Place.* So she made Milla promise her that no matter what happened, Milla wouldn't let them take her.

And Milla promised.

"Be my friend," Iris said to Milla.

"Yes, Iris," Milla said. "I'm your friend. Always."

Then Milla and Iris took off their boots, and they walked into the icy water together. As they went deeper, letting the cold sink into them—toes, then ankles, then knees—Iris gripped Milla's hand so tightly that it hurt.

6

M ILLA SEWED WHILE WAITING FOR PAPPA TO YAWN.
When Pappa yawned, Mamma would say it was time for bed.
Then Milla could find a moment alone with Niklas.

All through dinner, Milla had looked at her family with new
eyes. Her mother's fear for her made sense now—and her father's
insistence on obedience. Of course. They were terrified that one
day they'd wake up and Milla would have become someone else in
the night. Or some*thing* else. A monster wearing their daughter's
dress.

Maybe, though, such things only happened in the village.
Maybe that was why they lived so far away, and why Milla was
forbidden to go to the village—because it truly was contagious.
She supposed that was reasonable, but why couldn't they have
told her? Why was Niklas brought in on the secret, trusted in
that way, when her life was the one most at risk? It was infuriat-

ing. She had watched her brother eating his supper, making inane small talk with Pappa, and she wanted to slap their bowls away from them. She twitched.

She pressed a hand to one of her cheeks. Was this how it started? With such violent anger? No. Iris had said it was a voice in your head that was the first sign. But what was a voice in your head? How did you know it wasn't your own voice? What did the voice sound like? Milla had spent so much time alone before Iris came that she had gotten quite used to talking to herself. Sometimes the voice in Milla's head didn't seem quite like her—it seemed sharper. Meaner.

But no, Milla sensed this wasn't what Iris was talking about. Milla remembered how Iris had looked that afternoon, like her usual self-command had been stripped from her. She seemed afraid that she was being rearranged piece by piece and all twisted. This was something different from the odd thoughts that Milla often had. Milla sometimes wondered why she thought the way she did—certainly she felt strange at times. But she felt sure, almost sure, that her thoughts were her own. They weren't anyone else's. She didn't think.

Maybe that's what the other girls thought, too.

And how would Milla ever know if no one told her? Perhaps her family thought they were protecting her by keeping her so ignorant, but they were wrong. She accepted her mother and father's disregard for her as simply the way things were. But Niklas. Her whole life she had loved him best of all. And Mamma and Pappa had loved him best of all, too, and Milla didn't even mind. All she hoped for in return was that Niklas might love her best of all. Or at least think of her sometimes. But now she knew he never had. He wanted to keep her as small and helpless as Mamma and Pappa did. He thought she was too fragile—too strange—to be trusted with the truth about the village and the workings of the demon. He didn't know her at all.

She stared at Niklas where he sat working on a wooden bowl for Mamma. She willed him to look at her, to notice how angry she was. But he blandly ignored her.

She watched Pappa. He smoked his pipe facing the fire—not so much looking at it as pointed toward it. Blank as always. Then she watched Mamma at her sewing. Occasionally Mamma looked up from her work and straight at Niklas. It was as if a thread connected Mamma to Niklas, and the only direction her attention could go was toward him.

Milla turned her gaze back toward her father. *Yawn, Pappa. Yawn.*

Then, finally, he did—a face-cracking yawn that Mamma couldn't help but notice. Mamma folded up her sewing and Pappa tipped the remains of his pipe into the fire. "Bedtime," Gitta said. She followed Jakob upstairs. Milla heard their door close.

"Niklas." Milla hissed his name, and he looked up at her, seeming surprised at what he saw in her face. "I know about the village. I know about the girls, and the demon, and The Place. And I know you've been keeping it all from me."

Niklas closed his eyes and pressed his lips together. He only ever did that when he was very upset. Then he opened his eyes again. Niklas had the kind of green, brown, and amber eyes that changed color with his surroundings. Right now they were black, full of pupil. "Iris told you."

The mention of Iris's name opened up a crack in her chest that filled with cold air. Iris had told her, yes, and the reason Iris had told her was that she was afraid she was hearing the voice of the demon in her head. And if Niklas knew that, he would tell their mother and father, and then Iris would be taken away from her and sent to The Place.

She looked at her brother, registered the fury in his eyes, and thoughts streamed through her head like wheat berries through her fingers. If she tried to catch one, she not only lost it, but ten others slipped past as well.

Milla had made a terrible mistake. She knew it even before Niklas said, "You have no idea what you've done. And what Iris has done in telling you."

"I begged her to tell me. I knew you were keeping something from me. You don't know what it's like to live this way, Niklas. Feeling like there's a world out there that's so different from this one and I'm not even allowed to know how. Or why. It's maddening. Sometimes I think I can't bear it another day."

"Don't you think I know that? You don't even know what I do for you. How lucky you are. Do you think I like going to the village without you? Believe me, I don't. But Pappa made me swear I wouldn't tell you anything about it. He said it was the only way to keep you safe." He stared at Milla, blinking too hard and too fast. "This is all my fault."

Milla struggled with how differently their conversation was unfolding than she'd thought it would. She'd known only her anger a few minutes before, and that was so simple, but this was complicated. Her brother sat in front of her, and instead of hating him, she regretted causing him such anguish. That little part of her heart that she'd closed to him opened back up again, and she felt deep guilt for having closed it in the first place. She was the wrong one. She was always the wrong one. And then she felt angry again. Why was she always the wrong one? It wasn't fair. And so her thoughts went, around and around.

"It's not your fault," Milla said to Niklas. And she meant it. "It's theirs, Mamma's and Pappa's. They've done this to us. They took you away from me, and they keep me here, trapped. And they convinced you it's for my own good. But it's not." Even as Milla said all this, though, another thought streamed through her brain, and this one she caught and held onto tightly. Iris. What would Milla tell Niklas about Iris, and what Iris was afraid was happening to her? Then he answered Milla's question for her.

"I have to tell Pappa and Mamma that you know, and that Iris told you. I can't lie to them."

"Oh no, Niklas. No, you can't." The cold crack in Milla widened. "If you do they'll send her back. You don't want her to go back, do you?"

"Of course not, Milla. I'm the one who convinced Pappa to let her come here now."

"Because you think I'm strange. And you think Iris will make me less strange." Milla's anger was coming back.

Niklas put a hand to his forehead. "Everything I do for you, you turn it all around. I knew Pappa and Mamma wanted her to come eventually, and I know how lonely you've been. I know you, Milla. You may not think I do, but I do."

"If you know me, then you know I love you more than anyone else. And you know I wouldn't lie to you. If you tell Mamma and Pappa that Iris told me, and if they send her back, then I'll run away."

"I'll tell Mamma and Pappa you said that, and Mamma will never let you out of her sight. She'll lock you up. You won't be able to run away."

"If they ever did that to me I'd turn into one of those demon girls." She almost laughed when she said it, but the words horrified her the moment they left her lips.

"You *mustn't* say such things, Milla." He grabbed her hand and squeezed his eyes shut. "Lord protect us from demons Lord protect us from demons Lord protect us from demons. Amen." He looked at her. "Say it, Milla."

"Amen," she said.

He tried to pull his hand away then, but she held on. "Niklas. I promise to be good. I promise not to ask any more questions or ever to speak of the village again. Just please don't tell Mamma and Pappa that Iris told me." She squeezed his hand and looked into his face, so tight and worried. "Please."

Niklas sighed. "As long as you keep your promise, I won't tell them. But I'm going to have to talk to Iris. She needs to know how wrong she was to tell you."

"*No.*" Milla's voice was louder and sharper than it should have been, and Niklas jerked his head back. "Don't talk to Iris, Niklas. Let me do it. It will be better."

Niklas looked at her through lowered eyebrows, and Milla saw an expression there that she hadn't ever seen on his face before. Suspicion.

"I feel guilty, Niklas. That's all. She's still so new here and eager to please, and I made her tell me. And she was so upset about it. She'd be terribly embarrassed if you knew. She thinks so highly of you."

The shadow that had fallen over him lightened, but Milla knew she would have to be more careful now. Something had changed between her and Niklas, because something had changed in her. She had become a liar.

♦ ♦ ♦

The next morning dawned bright and even hotter, and by the time Jakob and Niklas left for the fields, Milla was already sweating under her dress. She'd lain awake a long time the night before, worrying over Iris and the terrible mistake she'd almost made with Niklas. She had come too close to betraying Iris, much too close. She thought through all the things that might have happened if Niklas had told Jakob and Gitta. She thought about what her life would be like if they took Iris away. Then she felt terrible shame that she was worried more for herself than for Iris. Iris had trusted Milla. *Be my friend.* Milla hadn't been her friend last night.

But today that would change. Today, Milla told herself, Iris would feel better, and Milla would be a good girl, and she'd do her chores well, and she'd smile brightly at dinner, and soon the shadow of suspicion would entirely lift from Niklas and everything would be fine.

Doubt tickled her spine when Iris didn't appear at the kitchen door after breakfast. But maybe Trude had given Iris something to do that delayed her. Trude could be baking, and would want Iris's help for that. There were any number of reasons that Iris wasn't there. So Milla continued doing her chores, carefully, ever so carefully.

She poured the lines of salt especially straight that morning, with not a single break.

When every chore was done, and she had been told by Gitta that there wasn't a single other thing that needed doing, Milla walked to Stig and Trude's. She walked no faster or slower than she should have, and she thought that the very normalcy of her stride was proof that this was a fine day, a typical day.

She walked up to Stig and Trude's whitewashed door and she knocked in a way that wasn't too soft or too hard. It was a just-right knock, and then she waited for someone to open the door in a just-right way.

Instead there was no answer. So she knocked again, this time a little harder and louder than just-right. And again. And again. And then she called through the door. "Iris? Trude?"

Milla heard movement and then the door opened. Trude faced her, and Milla knew then what she hadn't allowed herself to know since Iris hadn't come after breakfast. What she'd felt in her gut even last night as she tried to convince herself to sleep. What she hadn't wanted to believe the moment Iris had tapped her forehead and said the demon was in there.

Nothing would ever be just-right again.

7

Trude reached across the threshold and pulled Iris inside. The kitchen was oppressively hot, the windows shut tight.

Iris wasn't there; Milla could feel the emptiness of the house. There were two cups on the table and a pool of spilled tea that hadn't been wiped up. Trude herself looked unwell. Her gray hair, always neatly braided around her head, trailed down her back, undone. Her apron was dirty. Stranger than all of this was the expression on Trude's face, which was usually so plump and pleasant. It was terror. "Where is Iris?" Milla said.

"It's happening, Milla. Here. Where we thought we were safe."

"Where is Iris?" Milla felt that if Trude didn't answer her question this time that she might reach out and shake the old woman by the shoulders.

"She's run off! Stig's gone after her. And if your mother and father find out they'll take her and they'll put her in The Place. And then they'll send us away, too. Because we brought the demon here when we brought Iris here."

"What do you mean she's run off? She's run away?"

"She was so strange last night. So peculiar. And she didn't look well. And Stig and I, we looked at each other, and I think we both knew then, but we didn't want to know. So we all went to bed, and this morning I went in to wake Iris and she took one look at me and she screamed. She said I was a monster and what was I trying to do to her, and then she ran out in her nightdress. Stig went after her, but she ran so fast he said it wasn't even human. It was like something else was in her body making it go. Then he lost sight of her." Trude sobbed into her apron.

Milla had to think. She had to think what to do. She should comfort Trude, she knew, but instead she took a step away from her, wanting only to get away from her wet weeping.

"After that," Trude said, "Stig came back for his rope. He said that if he finds her and she's not herself, he'll tie her up and take her to The Place. Then he'll tell your mother and father that Iris got homesick and went back to the village. He said that was the only way your mother and father would let us stay here."

Milla had to get to Iris before Stig did. She couldn't let him take Iris to The Place. She turned away from Trude, desperate to leave.

"Oh, please, Milla. Don't tell your mother."

Milla held the door handle, her back to Trude. "That's what you care about." She turned around and looked at the woman whom she'd always thought of as a sweet old grandmother. "You don't care about Iris. You only care that Mamma and Pappa don't make you leave."

Trude's face changed, and Milla thought of the ugly old woman in the story of the snake tree, and how she transformed into a witch when angered. "Don't you judge me," Trude said. "Don't you dare judge me. You've never had a worry in your life. You don't know what that village is like. You don't know what it is to be afraid of your own child. You're a foolish little girl."

Milla's chin dropped a fraction lower with each word, each word that hurt even more for being true. She turned her back on Trude and left the door wide open.

Milla ran into the woods, thinking of all the places she and Iris had been together—the clearing that was so like where the witch in the story had buried her treasure. The spring where they'd sat the day before. But Iris wasn't anywhere Milla thought she'd be, and the longer she looked the more frantic she became, and the less certain she was that she would ever find Iris before Stig did.

She needed Niklas. He would calm her, and he would know what to do. She hoped he was alone and not with their father, because she couldn't possibly pretend in front of Pappa that something wasn't terribly wrong. In just over an hour Mamma would ring the bell for dinner, and she had to find Niklas before then.

Milla ran to the edge of the forest. There was a slight rise above a fallow field where she knew Niklas had gone that morning to chop a fallen tree into kindling. She heard his axe first, and then she saw him. He'd paused his work to wipe his brow. His light brown hair was dark with sweat. She waited to call to him until she was closer for fear that Pappa might be nearby and hear her. When she couldn't wait any longer she called to him while running. "Niklas!"

She could tell his first impulse was to smile at her—because that was always Niklas's first impulse when he looked at her. That made her heart break just a little. Then he took in her desperation and ran toward her, swatting aside tall, fluff-topped grass. "What is it?" he called to her. "What's happened?"

"Iris," she said. "She's run off." When they reached each other, she told him everything—how Iris hadn't seemed well yesterday, and what she'd just learned from Trude. "We have to find her before Stig does or they'll take her to The Place. We can't let them take her, Niklas. You love her, don't you? She begged me not to let them take her there, and I promised I wouldn't. Please, Niklas."

All the while she pleaded with him, Niklas moaned and ran his hands through his sweat-damp hair. "Oh, Milla," he said, pressing the heels of both hands to his eyes. "You should have told me last night that Iris wasn't well. And what will we do if we find her? What if she's as Trude says? If she's like the other girls, and the demon's really gotten into her?"

Milla didn't believe it. It couldn't be. "Well, then at least we'll know. But I have to see her, Niklas. I have to talk to her. I can't just let them take her." Then she said something that she knew would get him to come with her. "And neither can you. You said it yourself. You're the reason she's here. You owe it to her." Milla was almost sorry when she saw how her words landed on him. But not sorry enough to say that she was.

"All right, Milla. Let's go. But if we haven't found her by the time the dinner bell rings, and you and I aren't back soon after, Mamma and Pappa will know something's wrong anyway. And then neither of us will be able to protect her."

So *this* was how it felt when it happened. Just last night Milla had wondered if she'd ever heard another voice in her head—a voice that wasn't her own. Now she knew she hadn't ever heard one before, because she was hearing one now.

It wasn't the voice of a demon, though. It was Iris, and she was talking to Milla right inside her head. It wasn't wishful-thinking talking, the way Milla used to imagine that Niklas was with her and what they'd talk about if he were. This wasn't Milla making up the sound of Iris's voice in her head. This was Iris herself, telling Milla things that she didn't know.

Don't tell Niklas. He won't understand. Lie to him. Lose him. Then I'll tell you where I am.

"Have you looked everywhere you went together, Milla?" Niklas looked so concerned as they ran through the woods, choosing paths that Milla hadn't yet searched. She wanted to believe he cared for Iris, that he would help Iris once they found her. That he would keep her secret.

We can't trust him, Milla. He's not my friend. Only you are my friend, Milla. Be my friend.

Milla was sick with uncertainty.

He lied to you, Milla. He kept things from you. Everyone loves him more than they love you. Everyone except for me. Be my friend, Milla.

Milla ran along behind Niklas. Sweat dripped under her arms, and she felt hot and cold at the same time. She slowed. "Niklas," she said. "I have to stop."

He turned around.

"I have to pee," Milla said.

"Now?"

"I'm sorry. It's just that I'm so frightened."

Niklas shook his head. "Well go on, be quick."

"Walk ahead of me," she said. "I'll catch up with you."

Run left. Run fast.

Milla waited, heart beating painfully, as Niklas walked on. When the path took a gentle turn and she could no longer see him, she ran left, and she ran fast.

Keep running.

Branches snagged Milla's sleeves and skirt. Leaves slapped her face and twigs scratched her cheeks. She ran on, wondering if she was still going in the right direction.

You are.

She came to a clearing, and on the far side of it she saw Iris crouched beneath a tree. Her white nightdress spread limply around her. Her red hair streamed over her shoulders like the still-brilliant center of a wilted flower. When Iris lifted her eyes to look at Milla, a flame burned inside them.

Part of Milla wanted to run away, but the greater part of her pushed forward.

"Don't be afraid," Iris said. "It's me. I'm not anyone else."

"Oh, Iris," Milla said. "I thought I'd lost you."

Iris hugged her arms around herself as if chilled, despite the full heat of midday. "I know. I thought I'd lost me, too. But it's me. You can see that, can't you?"

What Milla saw seemed to be Iris, but so much brighter. Her syrup eyes flashed. Her wheat-brown skin seemed lit from within. It occurred to Milla that perhaps Iris had been growing duller ever since she'd arrived. And maybe this Iris sitting in front of her was the same girl who'd arrived on that spring day—only fresh and unharmed, her veil lifted.

Milla should have heard Niklas approaching, but even if she had, there wouldn't have been anywhere for her and Iris to hide. By the time the sounds of crackling branches and leaves under-foot were too loud to ignore, he was there, at the edge of the clearing, taking them in with wide, confused eyes.

He walked toward them, wordless.

"She's herself, Niklas," Milla said. She turned to Iris. "Talk to him, Iris. Show him."

Iris shook her head. Milla saw sadness in her eyes, and then something else. Something unrecognizable.

"Oh, Milla," Iris said. Then she laughed and laughed. And cried. And laughed some more. And laughed and cried at the same time, her lips hitching up over her teeth in a grimace. And Milla wanted to embrace her and run from her. Both.

Iris ran from Milla before Milla could decide which she would do. Iris ran so fast—too fast—and Trude's words came back to Milla. *It was like something else was in her body making it go.*

Milla felt Niklas's hand close around her forearm. "No, Niklas." She tried to pull away from him. "We have to go after her."

She heard a bell ringing. And ringing. Mamma's dinner bell.

Niklas yanked Milla back the way they'd come. She alternated between struggling and giving in. When she struggled she despaired that there was anything she could do if she caught up to Iris. And when she gave in she loathed herself for her cowardice. And all the way home, Niklas prayed.

> *Lord, protect us from demons.*
> *Lord, protect us from demons.*
> *Lord, protect us from demons.*

8

JAKOB HAD ALREADY SAT DOWN TO EAT HIS DINNER when Milla and Niklas arrived home. At the sight of their sweat-streaked faces, Mamma's hand froze midair, halfway between her pot of stew and Pappa's plate.

"It's Iris, Pappa," Niklas said. "She's changed. Like the other girls."

Gitta dropped her spoon. She shook her head at Niklas and then stared at Milla, her eyes rounding so they showed white all around.

"I know about the girls, Mamma," Milla said.

"No," Gitta said, more breath than sound.

Jakob shoved away from the table. "Where is Iris?"

"She's run off," Milla said. "You'll never catch her. Please, Pappa, just leave her be. Let her go."

Jakob ignored her. "Where's Stig?"

"Gone after her," Niklas said. "He's planning to take her to The Place."

Gitta twisted her apron so tightly between her hands that her knuckles whitened.

"I never should have let you convince me to bring her here, Niklas," Jakob said.

"I know," Niklas said. "I'll go with you to find her."

"No. You stay here. Don't let Milla out of your sight."

"I'm standing right here, Pappa!" Milla moved in front of him, grasping his sleeves like she hadn't done since she was a small child hoping to be picked up. "Why won't you listen to me? Iris is no harm to anyone. Please leave her be."

Jakob removed her hands from his shirt and pushed them aside. "Gitta, get this child out of my sight or so help me she'll never leave this house again."

Gitta moaned. Niklas pulled Milla away and wrapped his arms around her, half embracing her and half restraining her. "You must stop this now, Milla. Iris isn't Iris anymore."

When Milla heard Iris screaming, she tore through the front door before Gitta, Trude, and Niklas could stop her. Jakob and Stig carried Iris like a long bundle—Stig's hands hooked under her armpits, and Pappa's arms wrapped around her calves, fighting to keep a firm hold of her. She was bound with rope in two places—waist and feet—and she twisted her hands and her torso bucked.

"Let me GO leeeeeet me GO let me go let me go LET ME GO leeeeeet meeeeee goooooooo let me GO let me go let me go LET ME GO let me go let me go let me go." Over and over Iris said it, sometimes wailing it low and long, sometimes barking it sharp and insistent, sometimes crying it high and plaintive.

Niklas's arms were around Milla again, and she turned to him. "Niklas, you mustn't let them do this. It's not right. You know Iris. She wouldn't hurt anyone. And I promised her. I promised her, Niklas."

Iris stopped screaming. "Milla?"

She sounded so much like herself.

"Milla? Help me."

Trude buried her face in her apron. "Lord protect us from demons Lord protect us from demons Lord protect us from demons."

Iris wept now, her long hair forming red stripes across her forehead and cheeks, covering her eyes.

Milla fought against Niklas, but his arms were tight around her shoulders and waist. "Iris, I'm so sorry," she said. "Oh, Iris."

"Gitta," Jakob said. "Take Milla inside. Niklas, ready the wagon."

"Milla?" Iris said. "Be my friend, Milla."

"Lord protect us from demons," Gitta said as she pulled Milla away from Niklas. "Lord protect us from demons Lord protect us from demons."

Milla grasped her mother by the shoulders. "Mamma! Don't let them do this."

"Help me, Trude," Gitta said, taking one of Milla's arms in two of her own. Trude did the same on Milla's other side.

"Come, Stig," Jakob said.

Iris let out a howl and she bucked so hard that Jakob nearly dropped her.

Milla felt Gitta's and Trude's hands digging into her arms like claws as they dragged her into the house and closed and locked the door behind them.

They couldn't lock out the screaming.

Milla refused her mother's supper and sobbed herself to sleep that night. Niklas had gone with Jakob and Stig to take Iris to The Place.

Milla would never forgive Niklas for that. It was just as Iris had said. He was a liar. He wasn't Iris's friend, and he couldn't possibly love her. He'd betrayed both of them.

The only person who understood her, who'd never lied to her, was Iris. And Iris was being taken away from her, brought to somewhere horrible that Milla couldn't imagine. So horrible that Iris had said she'd rather die than go there.

When Milla rose the next morning, the sun was bright and cheery, and the green leaves danced on the tree outside her window, and it was all terrible to Milla's eyes. Each green leaf was an accusation. Milla could wake up in her soft bed and drink hot tea at her parents' table. Iris was bound and dragged off in her nightdress and called a demon. All because . . . why? She'd called Trude a monster? Trude *was* a monster, Milla thought. A monster in the skin of a grandmother.

The memory of the fire that burned in Iris's eyes, and her laughing that became crying that became laughing, flashed across Milla's mind. She shoved the thoughts away.

She would have stayed in her room, avoiding her mother forever, but her bladder was full and painful. She didn't bother combing her hair. There were no men in the house to try to please. Milla never wished to please another.

She walked through the kitchen in nothing but her nightdress and bare feet, hair streaming. She felt Gitta's eyes, but she didn't speak to her mother, nor did Gitta speak to her. After she'd relieved herself in the outhouse, Milla came back into the kitchen, where Mamma had poured her tea and set out bread, butter, and preserves.

Milla ate silently, hungry and disgusted with herself for being hungry. When she'd finished, Mamma reached out her hand and placed it over Milla's. Milla felt a tremor in her chest and willed herself not to cry. Not to seek comfort from anyone who would send Iris away.

Milla looked up at Mamma. Pretty Mamma, with her golden hair shot with silver, perfectly braided around her head. She saw the fine lines at the corners of Mamma's eyes and crossing her forehead. She looked into Mamma's cornflower-blue eyes and saw the same fear there that she always had. Milla looked away.

"I know you don't understand," Gitta said.

"I don't understand because no one will explain anything to me. All I know is that Pappa and Niklas dragged Iris away like they didn't even know her. Like she was a monster. Would you do that to me, Mamma?"

Gitta didn't take her hand away from Milla's, but Milla could see her recoil, the muscles in her face shrinking. "You mustn't talk like that, Milla."

Milla pulled her hand away. "I mustn't talk like that. I mustn't act like that. I mustn't think like that. Is there anything I may do, other than wash, and cook, and clean? I'm not you, Mamma. I'm not pretty. I'm not good."

"You're just fine, Milla. Don't carry on so. You'll forget about this soon enough." Gitta stood up and cleared the table, not meeting Milla's eyes now. "You don't know how lucky you are."

"Niklas says the same."

"Niklas is a good boy. You should listen to him. He knows we're safe here."

"But you don't know that, Mamma. Do you? That's why you're always so afraid when you look at me, isn't it?"

Gitta busied her hands while Milla spoke, then glanced at Milla as if she'd been too distracted to hear her questions. "Look at you, your hair all undone. What will Pappa think when he gets home?"

"I don't care."

"Nonsense," Gitta said. "A woman's hair is her glory, that's what my father always said. Let me brush it for you. Would you like that?"

Milla felt the tremor in her chest, the one that threatened to fill her eyes and make them spill over. She couldn't speak.

"I'll just get my comb," Gitta said.

Milla sat at the table, willing herself to move, to resist her mother's attention. But she couldn't move, and the thought of her mother's hands in her hair, of that little bit of comfort, kept her in her chair, tracing the wood grains on the table with one short fingernail. It was weak to want such comfort, but she couldn't help herself. It had been so long.

Gitta returned with her comb and stood behind Milla's chair, pulling it through Milla's dense, nearly black coils of hair. Milla closed her eyes, lulled by the light pressure of Mamma's fingertips holding her head in place while the comb gently tugged on the roots of her hair, then traveled down, sometimes pausing on a tangle. Mamma worked each tangle, ever so gently. Milla struggled against the desire to rest her head back on her mother's stomach.

Then Gitta stopped. "What is . . ."

Milla felt Gitta's fingertips searching her scalp just above her left ear. Then a sharp—a very sharp—pinch. "Ouch, Mamma!" Milla clapped her hand to the spot where it felt that Mamma had pulled her hair out by the roots.

Gitta sucked in her breath. "Lord protect us from demons Lord protect us from demons Lord protect us from demons."

Milla turned around in her chair. Gitta held something that squirmed between her two fingers. A tiny, emerald green snake, the length of her pinky, with a brilliant dot of crimson blood on its tail end. Milla said, "That was in my hair?"

Gitta shook her head. "No. No. Lord protect us from demons Lord protect us from demons Lord protect us from demons." Gitta dropped the snake to the floor and crushed it beneath her heel. "It was growing *from* your head. It was . . . Lord protect us from demons Lord protect us from demons Lord protect us from demons." Gitta backed away from the snake, still shaking her head.

"Mamma?" Milla said. She looked at the bloody pulp on the floor that was once a tiny, brilliant green snake growing from her head. Her own head. That wasn't possible. "Mamma?" Milla began to cry. She didn't want to be taken over by a demon. She didn't want to laugh and cry and laugh and cry like Iris. She didn't.

Gitta grasped Milla by both shoulders. "Listen to me, Milla. You must not speak a word of this. You must not. Not to Pappa. Not even to Niklas." Milla felt her mother's nails carving crescents into her skin. "You must behave. Be a good girl. A very good girl. It's the only way to keep you safe. To keep you here. Do you understand me?"

"Yes, Mamma. I understand."

✦ ✦ ✦

Milla awakened the next morning just as night was paling into dawn. She touched the spot on her head, just above her left ear, where Mamma had ripped out the snake. She remembered the way the tail end of the snake had dripped blood. Was it hers or the snake's? Or did their blood flow together—was it one and the same?

She expected to find a sore spot there. A break in the skin. A tender place. Instead, she sensed movement that wasn't her own, and something smooth and cool and dry wrapped itself around her finger.

The snake had grown back.

9

THE FOLLOWING AFTERNOON, WAGON WHEELS ANNOUNCED the men's return from The Place. Gitta went out to meet them, but Milla didn't follow. She had nothing to say to any of them, least of all Niklas. The traitor.

She lay on her bed, staring through the window at the tree that grew so large and wide its branches brushed the house. Its green leaves were the exact shade of emerald green of the snake that grew from her head. She stroked it with her finger, felt the gentle hiss of its exhalation on the outer whorl of her ear.

She'd been terrified when she first discovered it had grown back. Even now, her heart beat faster than it should, and she felt a tension in her belly, a sense that she should be doing something but she didn't know what. She wouldn't tell her mother about the snake. Couldn't. Her mother would only pinch it off again. And the fear in her eyes would grow.

But that wasn't the real reason she wouldn't tell Mamma. The real reason was that something was happening to Milla. She was growing accustomed to the feel of that small snake wrapped around her finger. It belonged there.

The sound of Gitta sobbing roused Milla, and she sat up in bed. She felt the snake tuck itself close to her scalp, hidden in her hair. Then she ran downstairs and out into the hot, bright afternoon.

She squinted at first, unsure of the meaning of what she was seeing. Mamma knelt in the dirt in front of Pappa, sobbing into her apron. "No, no, no, no, no. Not my boy."

Stig shook his head, turned, and headed down the path that led to his cottage, where Trude waited for him.

Milla felt a stab of pain in her chest and side, and her bladder threatened to release. Niklas wasn't there. "Pappa, where's Niklas?"

Jakob pulled Gitta to standing, gripping her by the shoulders. "Calm down," he said. "Calm down, do you hear me?"

Now Gitta sobbed into Jakob's big chest, clawed his shirt. "You left him there. You left my boy."

"Pappa?" Milla said. "You left Niklas?"

"He wouldn't come, do you hear me, Gitta? He wouldn't leave Iris. He insisted upon staying and looking after her."

"Noooooooooo." Mamma's crying had become a long wail.

Jakob freed his shirt from her grip and took both of her hands in one of his. "Milla, take her. There's nothing more I can do with her and I have work to do. These horses need water and feed."

Gitta's knees buckled and Milla rushed forward to catch her before she fell. "Milla. My boy. He's left my boy." Milla wrapped her arms around Gitta's back, and the feel of her mother's flesh under her hands was startling and unfamiliar. Sweat and tears mingled on Gitta's face where she pressed into Milla's neck and shoulder, and Milla felt the snake squirm on her scalp, as if it were discomfited by the invasion.

Pappa was already leading the horses away, straightening his back as if he'd been unburdened of a heavy load.

Milla led Gitta inside. "Come, Mamma. Come."

For an hour or more, Gitta could only weep, her words barely comprehensible between sobs. When she was spent and lay on her bed silently staring at the ceiling, Milla went down to the kitchen to make tea.

Milla tried to conjure more pity for Gitta than she felt. It wasn't that she was jealous of her mother's anguish over Niklas. Milla felt it, too. There was a gaping, awful emptiness, a worse loneliness than she'd ever felt, at the thought that Niklas wouldn't be home for supper, wouldn't be there at the breakfast table tomorrow morning. That he wouldn't be there to smile at her and call her silly Milla.

While she heated the kettle she thought about Niklas and what he'd done. She couldn't make sense of it. He'd thought Iris was demon-possessed, had even helped their father and Stig take her to The Place. But then he'd stayed with her like he loved her.

For the first time since she'd learned that Niklas hadn't come home, she allowed herself to imagine him inside The Place. A place so wretched that Iris spoke of it like a waking nightmare. A place so dreadful that Iris would sooner die than be sent there. Milla gripped the table edge. The room tilted around her. She scrambled to the door and vomited her empty stomach, hot and acid, into the dirt just outside. Her sweet, smiling brother. What had he done?

Milla wiped her mouth and face. Drank some water. *Think, Milla. You say you're not a child. Stop behaving like one.* She reached into her hair and let the snake curl around her finger. Already the snake seemed longer than it had that morning. Her heartbeat slowed. The room straightened.

She brought the tea to Gitta, and got her to sit up in bed to sip it. Gitta's face was puffed and reddened, and her blue eyes were watery gray. "Why did we have to bring that wicked child here?"

"Mamma," Milla said. "Iris isn't wicked."

"You don't know what they're like, Milla. The girls who turn. You only saw Iris at the start. But if she'd stayed, she would have gotten worse. Soon she'd have been howling through the night and swearing you were a monster with the eyes of a devil."

Something wasn't right with what Gitta was saying, and at first Milla couldn't puzzle out what it was. Then she realized. Just like Milla, Gitta was only ever here, on the farm. How could Gitta know what the demon-possessed girls were like? Yet Gitta didn't talk about them as if she'd been told stories about them. She talked about them as if she knew.

"You've seen them," Milla said.

Gitta began to weep again, and Milla took the tea from her, afraid she'd spill it. "It's all my fault. My poor boy. In that horrible place with those demon-possessed girls. My child. My poor boy." She brought her knees up to her chest and rocked and keened.

Milla's heart was only half warm toward her mother, but some deeper urge in her wouldn't allow her to stand by while Gitta suffered. "Mamma. How can any of this be your fault? What have you ever done but the right thing? What's happening in the village has nothing to do with you. And Niklas stayed with Iris because he's a good boy, like you raised him to be." It was true. He was a better, kinder person than Milla would ever be. She thought of her anger toward him, her accusations, and she was ashamed.

"It's because of what we did to Hulda."

"Hulda?" Milla said. "Who is Hulda?" Milla had never heard of anyone by that name.

"The demon. We thought we could get away from her by coming here. But there's no getting away. And now she's taken my boy from me. My own sweet boy." Gitta gripped her knees so tightly that the bones in her hands made sharp lines, and her veins wove over and around them like yarn. Her mouth opened and closed, and she stared ahead of her as if she were seeing something happen right in front of her, something she couldn't stop.

"Mamma, the demon hasn't taken Niklas."

"She will," Gitta said. "She ruins everything. She always did. That's why I hated her so much." Gitta looked at Milla now as if she were confiding something that Milla should understand. "I didn't always hate her. When we were little I loved her. But she grew up wrong, Milla. She grew up all wrong."

Her mother's anguish almost made Milla want to embrace her. But she didn't. There were too many secrets sending up little shoots through the floorboards and into the room, wrapping around them, ready to bear fruit. The snake growing above Milla's ear was restless, nudging her, its tiny hiss like a whisper, urging her to ask the question again. "Who is Hulda, Mamma?"

Gitta opened her eyes, and the moment she did so she no longer looked like a child. She looked like a confused old woman who couldn't understand how she'd arrived at this place. "She was my sister," Gitta said, as if perplexed—surprised—that such a thing could be true. "She turned into a demon and she cursed the whole village. All because Jakob burned her snake."

Milla's snake hissed so loudly in her ear that Milla thought her mother must have heard. The whole world must have heard. She fell back a step and her knees went soft beneath her. "Mamma?"

But Gitta didn't reach out for Milla, to keep her daughter from falling. Instead she shrank away. Then her eyes turned cold and small. "And now you're a demon, too."

PART TWO

10

MILLA RAN INTO THE FOREST. SHE RAN TO GET AWAY FROM her mother, she ran to get away from her father, she ran to get away from what she was becoming.

At first she didn't know what she was running toward. And then she did. The spring.

It was the snake, she thought. The snake had made her a demon. So she would drown it. Even if it meant drowning herself.

She pulled off her boots and stockings and felt the coolness of the damp dirt and pebbles under her feet. She took off the apron that she hadn't stopped to hang on its hook in the kitchen. She wouldn't wear it anymore. She let it fall.

She took off her dress and dropped it to the dirt, too. She stood there for a moment in her shift, feeling the warm breeze through the rough weave of the linen, aware that she couldn't remember ever being so undressed outside. Her skin prickled, but not with chill; the day was still hot.

Then she pulled her shift over her head and she was naked. She felt the snake rising from her head, and she knew it was tasting the air with its tongue. She opened her mouth and explored the air with her own. She felt the tickling mist of the spring, but that wasn't taste. She closed her eyes, and there it was. Water mixed with moss mixed with rock. The specific flavor of the spring, forming itself on the tip of her tongue.

She had the strongest impulse to continue running. Through the forest, and on. On to somewhere else. Or nowhere else. The only destination would be the running itself, the moving, the never stopping. The never being trapped in one place.

But her fear came back to her. Her terror of the monstrosity she saw reflected in her mother's eyes. And so she pushed herself toward the water. She put a foot in, and another. She felt the cold run up her calves. She went deeper. The cold traveled up to her crotch and stomach, where it chilled the deepest parts of her. Then she went farther in than she had ever gone before, to the part of the spring that dropped away and became bottomless. She would sink there, to drown out the evil that she was becoming. To kill the demon.

Down she went. She hadn't sucked in a lungful of air, because the intent hadn't been to prolong, but to quicken. She pulled her knees to her chest, felt her hair swirl about her in the water, felt the cold in her heart like a stab. She tried to relax into the water, to let herself sink. She kept her eyes closed, willed herself to be heavy, heavy, heavy like the heaviest stone.

Her snake—and it was, she realized, *her* snake—pulled away from her as if trying to lift them both up to the surface, to save them.

She felt its panic. Its desire to live. Its will. She ignored it. She told herself no. That was the demon talking. Whether the demon was Milla herself, or the snake, or a creature that was once named Hulda—her mother's own sister . . . none of that mattered. She would not be a monster. Still her snake pulled. She put her hand there, not to smother it but to calm it. To say: I know, I know this is painful, but it's for the best.

Then, a voice.

I'm so cold.

Iris.

I'm so cold.

Iris. It was Iris.

Let me out.

Iris's voice was in her head again.

Milla opened her eyes and the pain there was piercing and immediate. The water was dark and heavy around her, but her body was light and wanted to be lighter and she uncurled herself and rose. She stroked forward until her feet touched rock, and then shallower still until she reached the edge.

She shivered and sucked in air and for a moment or more she allowed herself to bask on the rock where she and Iris had sat, to soak up the heat of the sun above her and the earth beneath her.

Then the voice again. Iris's voice.

I'm so cold.

I'm so cold.

Let me out.

Be my friend.

Milla's hand went to her head, searching. She found the snake, and relief brought tears to her eyes when she felt it curl around her finger. It was bigger than it had been even that morning. And stronger. Louder.

"I'm sorry," she said to it.

To Iris, she said, "I'm coming."

When she was warm and nearly dry, Milla pulled on her shift, dress, stockings, and boots. She left her apron where it lay. She knew what she had to do now, the promise she had to keep. She would go to the village, and she would free Iris from The Place.

First, though, she had to find it.

When Milla arrived at Trude and Stig's cottage, Trude was kneeling in her garden tending to her leeks and carrots. Wolf lay in the late afternoon shade nearby. He lifted his head and regarded Milla solemnly, then rested his head down and went back to sleep.

"Trude," Milla said, and the old woman reacted with a start.

"Oh, it's you, Milla," she said, a hand pressed to her heart. Her eyes seemed hesitant to light on Milla's face for very long, either because she didn't like what she saw there, or because she was protecting what her own might reveal. Milla wondered if she was ashamed. "How is your mother?"

"I left her weeping," Milla said.

Trude nodded. "It's a terrible thing to imagine Niklas there. That sweet boy."

"What about Iris?" Milla said. "Isn't it a terrible thing to imagine her there, too?"

Trude let out a lung full of air and her whole body seemed to deflate along with it. "Of course it is, child. She's my granddaughter. My daughter's only child. But she's lost to us."

"How do you know?"

"Hanna's not our only child, you know. We had another daughter. Leah." Trude stood and wiped her hands on her apron.

"What happened to her?" Milla said. Though she already knew.

"One morning Stig and I woke to Leah screaming like she was being murdered in her bed. We ran in to her and found Hanna crying in a corner and Leah howling at her, calling her a demon. At first we weren't sure which of them had been afflicted, but then we saw it was Leah. She wasn't right, Milla. She wasn't our girl anymore. She had this . . . this light in her eyes. There was something else in there with her, something wrong. Something mean."

Something else in there with her. Milla grew cold and then hot again, and her skin ached. Her body wanted her to leave, but she forced herself to stay.

Trude didn't sound like the woman Milla had known her entire life. She sounded like some other woman who had seen horrors, not the pleasant, chatty old lady who sat by the fire and told stories about princesses. "Hanna was just twelve when it happened. Our Leah was fourteen. The prettiest, sweetest girl she was. Never put a step wrong. That morning she wasn't herself anymore. She screamed at us. Laughed and screeched and called us monsters."

It occurred to Milla that she hadn't really known Trude at all. She didn't know any of them. She only knew a version of Stig and Trude, and of her mother and father, that they'd constructed once they came here. A version that had been cleansed of the terrors that befell the village, a version that erased all the losses. But such things couldn't be erased. They were still inside Trude and Stig, and her mother and father, and they'd passed it all on to Niklas and Milla whether they'd wanted to or not.

Now Trude looked hollowed out and shrunken. "When the

midwife came to take Leah away to The Place, I cried like your mother is crying now. But your mother is lucky. Her son will come back to her. My daughter never will. Nor my granddaughter."

Trude had called Milla a foolish little girl. Milla refused to be foolish again. She would know everything, no matter how frightening it was, or how much it hurt. "Mamma told me about Hulda and the curse. I must know. Did Niklas know the demon is Mamma's sister?" Milla wasn't sure why this was so important to her, but it was. She thought she might be able to forgive all the other things that Niklas had kept from her, but she wasn't sure she could forgive that. The truth about Hulda—about the demon—felt so tied up with her own.

Trude paled, shook her head at Milla. "Lord protect us from demons Lord protect us from demons Lord protect us from demons."

"He didn't know?" Milla said.

"No, child, no. Your mother and father would never. They don't speak of that. Speak of evil and you call it to you. That's what demons want."

Something inside Milla released at that moment, another tight little knot of resentment toward Niklas. She could cry for missing him so. She had to find him, to talk to him, to see him. "Have you ever been to The Place? Can you tell me how to get there?"

"You're talking foolishness again, Milla. You're not listening. Why would you want to go where it's not safe?"

Milla could have said, *because I hear Iris's voice in my head, telling me how cold she is and begging me to let her out.* But that wouldn't get her what she wanted. That would get her tied up and dragged off, too. "Because Iris is there. And Niklas. And I can't bear to be separated from either of them."

"Oh, child. I know you love them." Trude seemed as if about to relent, but then she said, "You'll never find it. Even if you made it all the way to the village, someone would have to show you where The Place is."

"What about Hanna? Would she show me?" The expression on Trude's face told Milla something she couldn't have imagined. "Hanna doesn't know about Iris, does she?" Milla said.

Trude moaned. "Stig couldn't bear to tell her."

Milla latched onto hope. Hanna would help her—Iris's own mother would certainly want to show Milla how to find The Place, and then they would rescue her together. "Trude, tell me how to find Hanna and Tomas, and then I'll tell them what's happened to Iris. And I'll ask them to show me how to get to The Place." Milla sensed Trude hesitate, and she took one of the old woman's hands in her own. It was knobby and thin, as light and fragile-seeming as a bird. "I'm sorry for all that's happened to you. And I'm sorry that I didn't understand. Please let me try to help Iris."

"Your mother and father would never forgive me for telling you," Trude said. "This is their farm. They brought us here, and they could send us away just as easily."

Milla closed her eyes, willed herself not to show anger. She reminded herself that she didn't know what it was like to be Trude. To have seen and lived through what she had. "Then don't tell them," Milla said. "They don't need to know. I'll leave right now. They won't miss me until supper, which is still an hour away. And they may not even miss me then. Mamma's too upset to care what happens to me. Pappa will think I'm off sulking."

Trude nodded. "Come." She led Milla inside and wrapped a hunk of cheese, bread, and two apples, then placed the bundle in a rough-woven bag and handed it to Milla. She pulled one of her own shawls from a hook and wrapped it around Milla's shoulders. For just a moment, Milla let herself remember when she was a child and Trude told her stories by the fire. Milla would sit on a low stool next to Trude and put her head in Trude's lap. Trude would rest a hand on Milla's head in the exact spot where a snake now grew. Her snake.

"You won't make it to the village before dark," Trude said. "Not on foot. Good that it's summer so you won't catch your death sleeping outside. You need only follow the road with the fresh wagon wheel tracks. It will take you straight to the village. My Hanna lives in the center of town. Tomas is the blacksmith, so you'll see the smithy and then their cottage. You'll know my Hanna. Our Iris looks just like her." Trude's eyes were damp.

"Thank you, Trude."

"Tell my Hanna that I'm sorry. Tell her I thought we could keep Iris safe."

Milla thought Trude might embrace her, but she didn't. Milla touched the spot over her left ear where her snake nestled itself, and decided perhaps it was better that way. She wasn't a creature to be embraced anymore—if she ever was.

II

MILLA'S FEET FOLLOWED A ROAD WORN SMOOTH BY
her father's wagon wheels, and it was all unfamiliar. With each
step, her fear came back to her, washing over her like a stream,
lapping. She held two thoughts in her head at once. There were
the dark things that her mother and Trude had seen. And then
there was her belief that the same hadn't happened to Iris. After
all, Iris hadn't howled at Milla or called her a monster. Maybe
she was just . . . sick. Again the image of Iris's too-bright eyes
flickered across Milla's mind and she willfully shoved it away. Her
heart thumped in her chest, and the thought that she was doing
something terribly stupid threatened to overwhelm her.

No, she said to herself. Iris was Iris. She always would be. And
Milla would always be Milla, and she would always be a friend to
Iris. Milla's mind was her own, she told herself. The voice in her
head was Iris's, and Iris was no demon. How Iris spoke to her that

way, Milla didn't know. But Milla knew so little about anything
that she was willing to believe that a great deal was possible. She
was also ready to doubt a great deal of what she'd been told. The
rules she'd grown up with made the world seem like such a small
place. And so explicable. But she had proof growing from her
own head that the world was much different from anything she'd
been led to believe. She touched her snake, which was now the
length of her hand. It settled her, and Milla felt her heart slowing
to match its coolness, its calm.

The day had been very hot, but by the time the last light of evening
turned to darkness, Milla was glad to have Trude's shawl. The moon
rose big and bright, and Milla walked long into the night, wanting to
arrive at Hanna and Tomas's as early the next day as she could.

As if it knew they were safe and alone, her snake rose up from
her head, freed from its camouflage of dark ringlets. It gently
bounced and undulated and tasted the air as Milla walked along,
and Milla felt its hunger and excitement. Milla felt both in her
own bones—and then in her belly. It would be good to eat, she
thought. She stepped off the road and sat at the mossy base of a
large tree, two roots on either side of her like armrests.

Crickets chirped around her and mosquitoes buzzed around
her face. When one landed on her cheek, her snake snapped it
up. She tasted its sweetness on her own tongue. She bit into one
of the apples Trude had given her, then stuffed her mouth with
cheese and bread, savoring fruitiness and saltiness and tanginess
mixing together in her mouth. She couldn't remember when she'd
enjoyed food this way, and then it came to her. It was back when
she and Niklas were children, when they'd gone berry picking
together and had eaten half of all they'd picked, the juice running
purple and red down their chins. That was most certainly the last

time. Since those days, meals had been about service and duty. She ate the food that she and Mamma made without thinking how she felt about it. There was no point, because there was no choice. It was what she was told to prepare, and then to eat. So she did. What was to taste?

What would her father have said to that? *A question that shouldn't be asked doesn't deserve an answer.*

After she'd eaten, she wrapped the shawl more thoroughly around her and curled up between the roots that hugged her on either side. She lay her head on the moss and closed her eyes. She felt her snake sway in the air over her, occasionally snapping up the beetles and other creatures that nudged their way into her hair or trekked across her shoulder.

She wiggled her fingers between fallen leaves and dug them into the cool, damp moss and soil, felt both accumulate under her fingernails. She imagined the dark crescents that would form there. She dug her fingers deeper. Her snake curled around her ear and rested its head on her cheek. She felt its tongue like a whisper. Like the stroke of one who loved her, but she had no memory to match with it. This was something new and restful and soothing. She felt her limbs and muscles relax into the earth. She slept.

Milla shifted, sleeping but not sleeping. She knew morning was coming, and she wasn't ready to wake. Morning should wait just a little longer, she thought, and yet some discomfort roused her. She felt as if one of her limbs were caught beneath her, but that made no sense because her arms were folded in front of her. Finally Milla gave in to wakefulness and sat up. The air was still cool and wet with dew. The bit of sky she saw through the trees overhead was a deep lavender.

Milla's first realization was that her snake was now fully grown—long enough that she could see the snake's lovely leaf-greenness where it rested its head on her shoulder. Her second realization was that another snake grew from a parallel spot just over her right ear—the side of her head that had been pressed to the ground. It was this new snake that had felt restless and stuck beneath her. Just as her first snake had done, this tiny new snake curled itself around Milla's finger when she placed her hand there—as if to say to her *hello, I'm with you, and I will never leave.*

Milla needed the comfort, because when she recalled what she was about to do, her gut clenched and she thought she might be sick. She felt a nip on her left shoulder, two sharp little teeth belonging to her fully grown snake, and then it hissed at her. Not a sweet, calming hiss. It was a hiss of anger—her anger. *All right,* she said to herself. *All right. I remember. I'm angry.* Her anger made her brave, forced her to her feet.

As she continued her walk to the village, Milla felt herself growing ever angrier. And the angrier she felt, the more her green snake lifted from her head, eager and urging her forward.

Her gut no longer clenched. It coiled and writhed. She should have been thinking of poor Iris, she thought. Or worrying for her brother. But instead she could only think of the wrongs she'd suffered. Of the lifetime she'd spent feeling never-enough and never-right.

Never-enough and never-right for her father, who mostly looked past her. On the rare occasions when she forced herself in front of him by speaking words, or spilling something, he looked at her as if flummoxed. Or worse: annoyed that such a problem should have intruded on his otherwise controllable life. Milla's value to him was like that of a tool he used on the farm. He didn't think of the axe's usefulness while he chopped wood. He only thought of the axe's failure if it dulled.

She had never been the pretty, compliant child her mother wanted, either. Oh, she'd tried. So hard. But always with Milla there would be an errant strand of hair that wouldn't bend to her mother's will. A hem that would drag. An off-kilter observation of Milla's that would cause Gitta to get that look in her eye—that look of fear. Now Milla knew why: because she was terrified that Milla would become like her sister. All her life Milla had been forced to suffer for a sin her own mother had committed: the sin of betraying Hulda. Was Milla any less strange than Hulda had been? Perhaps Milla was just better at hiding her strangeness, at pretending to be clean and free of voices. Well, she could hide and pretend no more. Her green snake hissed in agreement. Her new snake kissed her ear with its tongue. She wondered if it was as brilliant green as the other.

Then she thought of Niklas. A lifetime of resentment heated her from the inside out. She felt feverish with it. She *was* jealous that all their lives he was their mother's sunshine while Milla was their mother's dark cloud. She *was* bitter that for years he'd sat by and let Milla be the least loved in the family. He'd rested in the sure knowledge that he pleased their father and mother, that his mere presence on this earth was enough. And without a word of contradiction on his part, he'd allowed her to be less, even encouraged it. Because in contrast with her not-enoughness and not-rightness, he was always-enough and always-right. Silly Milla.

Silly Milla was dead. She died when her mother crushed her first tiny green snake under her heel. No one would do that to her again, or to her snakes. Milla touched each, and promised them aloud, "No one. Never again."

12

MILLA HAD NO IDEA WHAT TO EXPECT FROM THE VILLAGE;
all she had were fantasies. She knew there would be many more
people than she'd ever seen before. She imagined a hubbub, the
fuss and activity of a beehive. Everyone working and moving and
talking. She supposed that as she got closer, she'd first notice the
noise: the sound of all those people. But Milla walked and walked,
and there was no such sound. There were only the trees, which
were still and stolid on this already hot morning. Her boots were
loud under her feet.

Then the trees changed. No longer broad and reaching, they
seemed to give up, to give in. They drooped as if too tired, too
discouraged to continue standing much longer. Milla passed
through an orchard, and the trees were wizened, the apples
gnarled and blighted. The air buzzed with insects and the trees
crawled with them. The joints of branches were shrouded in web-

bing. Downy moth nests wrapped around leaves. Ants marched purposefully up every tree from neatly constructed anthills. Huge, threatening wasp nests hung high in branches. Milla had never been afraid of the creatures that occupied her world, but now she was. Everything was out of balance and trees that should be able to repel the assault of such tiny things were overrun with their number and losing the battle.

Black flies landed on Milla's hands and cheeks and stung, and landed again and stung again. Her snakes madly snapped back at the flies but there were too many. Milla reached for one of the small, twisted apples on a low branch, and as she pulled, it collapsed in her hand. It was the shape of an apple, but inside, it was soft and rippling with worms. Milla dropped the awful thing and wiped her hand on her skirt. She thought of the crisp apple she'd eaten just last night—hard in her hand and juicy when her teeth sank into it. It bore no resemblance to this. Ants swarmed the apple, worms and all, the moment it touched the dirt, and in seconds the pale apple flesh was black with them. Milla backed away, horrified. Then she walked on, waving her hands around her head, helpless to drive away the flies.

Still there was no sound other than the buzzing of the insects. So it was a surprise to Milla when the road widened, and there it was: the village.

And it was so . . . sad.

The village was laid out along a main street, just as Trude had described it. The houses crouched alongside it the same way the trees had—as if it was all they could do to stand up. They were tidy enough. But the green of the trees and kitchen gardens and sod roofs was less green than it should be. As if the whole place needed a good dusting.

The dreariness of the place seeped into her bones and made her feel hopeless. The fearful look she so often saw on her mother's face was everywhere here, and in every face. The town reeked of fear, like a rot. She'd so often dreamed of coming here, and part of her wanted to greedily take in all these new faces. They were all ages and sizes and complexions. All hair lengths and colors. Some round faced and some narrow, some thick browed and others thin lipped. But really, they were all the same. Each one regarded her not with curiosity but with suspicion.

Milla's snakes clung close to her scalp, hidden well beneath her hair. There was nothing outwardly strange about her, and yet each man, woman, and child stared hard at her as she walked toward them, then turned their heads to stare at her longer as she walked by them. She felt their eyes still needling her once she was past. She paused once to look behind, and she found that everyone she'd passed had stopped walking and was looking at her, eyebrows lowered, lips drawn tight. Milla told herself not to look back again. She supposed she shouldn't be surprised by their unfriendliness. It was a cursed village, after all. A village doomed to watch its sisters, daughters, friends, and cousins taken by a demon. A demon who was her aunt. Milla felt a cramp in her bowels.

These people couldn't possibly know who she was, she told herself. They'd never seen her before. But what if some family resemblance gave her away? She looked nothing like Jakob or Gitta, or even Niklas. Maybe, she thought, she looked just like Hulda. Right down to the snakes on her head. A slick of sweat formed along her hairline and ran down her sides under her shift. Oh, the many things she hadn't thought through before she set out on this journey. It was too late to think of them now.

Her heartbeat fluttered unevenly in her chest when she came to the smithy and saw a large, brown-skinned man, his shoulder-length black hair streaked with gray, holding a horseshoe with tongs. He must be Tomas, Milla thought. She raised a hand as if to wave, but then let it fall again. He watched her pass, and continued watching her as she knocked on the door of the very next house, where Trude had told Milla she would find Hanna. It was a modest place, at once clean and dismal, with a meager vegetable garden clinging to one side.

The door was opened by a woman who looked both like and unlike Iris. Like her in slim, graceful build and rust-red hair. Unlike her in that she seemed drained of the life that glowed from Iris like a flame. Where Iris's eyes were like candles, Hanna's were ash. Those eyes went round now and she grasped Milla by one shoulder and pulled her inside.

Light shone harshly through the closed windows, and inside the house, like out, was tidy but dreary. The air in the room was hot and stale. Milla felt breathless, and the more air she tried to pull into her lungs the less there seemed to be.

"Milla," Hanna said. "You're Milla, aren't you?"

"I am," Milla said.

"What's happened? Why are you here?" Hanna hadn't let go of Milla's shoulder once they were inside, and Milla felt nails digging into her flesh.

"It's Iris. Your father and mine have taken her to The Place."

Hanna pulled her hand away now and put both hands to her own mouth. "No," she said. "No, no. We kept her safe for so long." Then Hanna's eyes lost focus and her knees buckled, and Milla feared she might fall. She wrapped an arm around Hanna and led her to a wooden chair.

"I'm so sorry," Milla said. Milla had been distraught when Iris had been taken; she could do nothing but weep. Hanna was Iris's mother—how would she ever bear it? How had Trude borne it when her oldest was taken?

Hanna grabbed Milla by the wrist. "She was supposed to be safe with you. The way you've always been safe. Mamma and Pappa promised." Hanna squeezed her eyes shut and shook her head as if trying to banish a thought. "Now she's lost to us, just like Leah."

Hanna squeezed Milla's wrist so tightly it hurt, but Milla didn't pull away. Instead she put her other hand over Hanna's and held it gently. "I don't believe Iris is lost to us. She doesn't belong in The Place."

Hanna opened her eyes and Milla saw a bit of hope rise in them. "What do you mean? Wasn't she showing the signs?"

Milla hesitated, and Hanna's eyes turned hopeless again.

"She was . . . different," Milla said. "But still herself. And that's the important thing. She was *still herself.* Not lost. She was still Iris. And she shouldn't be locked away someplace awful. That's not where she belongs."

Hanna pulled her hand away from Milla and shook her head. "Oh, Milla. You don't understand. Gitta and Jakob have kept you so far from it, you don't know what it's like when the girls are taken. There's no making them better. The sooner you put them away and cease to think of them, the less your heart will ache from the loss."

The door opened, and a shaft of light scissored the room. Tomas. He closed the door behind him. Milla saw none of Iris in his face, but it wasn't a bad face. There was warmth there, and a desire to understand. Tomas's eyes searched Milla's now, but before Milla could speak, Hanna did. "Our girl has been taken." She said it blunt like that, as if there was no point in stepping up to it slowly or trying to make it any less awful than it was.

"When?" Tomas said.

Milla had to think for a moment. "Three days ago."

"Signs?" he said.

"Tomas," Hanna said. "You know the signs. Don't make me listen to them. Don't make me hear what our child has become." She put her face in her hands.

Tomas walked to Hanna where she sat and pulled her to her feet. Then he wrapped his arms around her and she sobbed into his chest. It was a moment so tender that Milla turned away from it. She had never seen anything like it—a man reaching out to a woman. A gesture meant to comfort, not to subdue. Her mother would occasionally touch her father, but only to placate a mood, to beg for calm. Not like this. And she couldn't remember her father ever reaching out to anyone—not even Niklas—with affection.

She listened to Tomas murmuring to Hanna. When there was silence, Milla turned toward them again.

"I came not only to tell you about Iris, but to ask you if you'd show me to The Place. And help me get her out."

Tomas looked at Milla, one large palm cradling his wife's head. "You don't know what you're asking. No one comes out of The Place. *No one.* And you wouldn't want them to. Our girl isn't our girl anymore. She belongs to the demon now." Hanna let out a whimper.

"But that's not true," Milla said. "She's still Iris. She talked to me. I know she's still herself."

"She talked to you? What did she say?"

Milla could tell that she'd surprised Tomas, sensed that he might be persuadable, so she kept talking in a rush. "She asked me not to let them take her there. She was frightened. She told me she was still herself. Does that sound like the talk of a demon?"

Hanna jerked her head away from Tomas. "It sounds exactly like the talk of a demon. The demon lies."

"Iris was Iris. And she never lies. I know it."

"Don't you think I want to believe you?" Hanna said. "Don't you think I want my girl back? I want my sister back, too. And my friends. All taken by the demon. All pretty and sweet one day, and the next screaming nastiness at me. Telling me they hate me. I won't see my child like that, do you hear me? Now you must leave. Get out of my sight."

"Hanna," Tomas said. "What if it's true what Milla says?"

"Tomas, ask yourself this. Why is it Milla standing here? Why is our child cursed and not this one, whose own aunt brought the curse upon us all? Why do you trust her? What if it's the demon talking through her?"

Hanna gripped Tomas's shirt in her hands while she spoke, looking him in the eyes, pleading with him. Then she looked at Milla, and Milla saw something in Hanna's face that she did not like. Not at all. Milla's snakes squirmed on her head. She felt their fear, imagined what would happen to her and to them if the suspicion she'd seen in the villagers' faces turned to accusation. She looked at Tomas. "I'll go," she said.

"Best," Tomas said.

The sun was high overhead outside, and Milla looked left and right. Then she felt a hand on her shoulder and she flinched before turning around.

It was Hanna, her face tear strewn. She pointed to her left. "Follow the road out of town. You'll pass through farmland and woods and then you'll come to a cottage. That's where the midwife lives. You'll have to talk your way past her. Or sneak around, through the forest. But I don't recommend that. Those woods are deep and once you're just feet from the road you won't know which way you've come from. Better to stick to the road and start thinking of your excuses. The Place isn't far from the cottage. There's no mistaking it."

Milla nodded the whole while Hanna talked, barely breathing. Now she didn't smile so much as open her face to Hanna. "Thank you," she said.

Hanna nodded. "You won't find Iris there. Not the Iris you know."

"But what if I do?" Milla said.

Hanna sucked air in, then out. "You think we're heartless, sending our girls to The Place. And maybe it's so. But if we are, then it's because our hearts have been taken from us. Look around this village and you'll know exactly who's lost a sister or a child or a dear friend to the curse. We all look the same, feel the same. Like we'll never be whole and happy again. When Tomas asked me to marry him I said no at first. I told him I wouldn't, because I couldn't bear to have a daughter taken from me. But. Well. I love him, and I relented. And then we had Iris, and there wasn't a day after that I woke up anything but terrified."

Milla thought of Gitta, always watching her, waiting for her to change.

"So I told Tomas, no more. I couldn't bear to have more children, not if the next might also be girl. When your father asked my father to work for him, and he and Mamma went to live there, I felt abandoned. My own mother and father leaving me for somewhere better. But they told me it was for Iris's good. That someday they'd bring her there to live with them, where the crops were always healthy and the trees still grew tall. And then Iris would be safe."

The words were out of Milla before she could stop them. "Iris would be safer here at home than in The Place, wouldn't she? How can you leave her there?"

Hanna's face closed up. Hardened. "I was like you once," she said. "I had ideas about how things should be. I hoped. I visited my sister there and told her I loved her and missed her. And each time I saw her there she was less and less my Leah. Then one day she only screamed when she saw me. She said I wasn't her sister, I was a demon come to drag her to hell with the other demons. I tried to touch her, and she hissed at me like a snake. After that, I never went back. It's too hard, Milla. Too hard. You'll see. Now go on with you. And don't come back here. You're not welcome."

Hanna turned away from Milla and walked into Tomas's arms. He looked at Milla over his wife's head, two stones where his seeking eyes had once been.

13

MILLA WALKED DELIBERATELY PAST THE VILLAGERS, keeping her eyes on the ground, hoping that if she didn't look at them, they might not look at her, either. When she'd passed the church, and the cemetery, and the market square that she'd so often dreamed of visiting with her brother, the homes grew sparser. Milla felt that she might soon be safe.

Farmland rolled on either side of her, the wheat stunted and shriveled, nothing like her father's fields. Why had Hulda cursed the village so, but allowed Jakob and Gitta their healthy fields only a day's walk away? An answer came to Milla. The torture was in the waiting. That was how Hulda cursed Gitta and Jakob. Their punishment was to wake each morning wondering if that was the day the aphids would come and suck the life out of their wheat, the day the demon would come and swap their daughter for their greatest fear—a demon just like Hulda herself.

Fields gave way to forest. The temperature dropped with the shade of the trees, and Milla's snakes peeked out of her hair. Milla was used to woods that felt alive—tree life, insect life, birds and animals all pecking and crawling, flying and scurrying. The drip of damp and soft rustle of leaves. But these woods were dying. There were no birds to drive back the onslaught of fat caterpillars and ants, grasshoppers and beetles that feasted upon the papery leaves and ate the trees from inside out. Milla felt queasy moving among the diseased roots and branches.

Milla felt a kiss of snake tongue on her left ear, and another on her right. She touched the snake over her right ear. It was so much bigger in just a day; it circled her wrist, not just her finger. She caught a flash of brilliant red, so beautiful. She was amazed by it, how it was part of her and yet not. How it moved of its own volition, and yet she felt what it felt. Its alarm was her own, its thirst was her own as well. Thirst. She was terribly thirsty. But if there had been water here, she wouldn't want to drink it. Even the air smelled wrong.

The sun was halfway to the horizon, the light just turning golden, before the forest turned green again. She caught the homey scent of wood smoke and soon she arrived at the midwife's cottage. It hugged close to the side of the road. Next to it was a barn and paddock with a single horse standing outside looking back at Milla with mild curiosity.

A dark-haired woman peered out from one of the cottage's two front windows. If Milla had wanted to slip by undetected, she'd failed. She could try to keep walking, but if the midwife didn't want her to pass, she'd only come after her. The woman nodded at Milla, then moved away from the window. Within a moment she'd opened the door.

Milla could see that the woman was older than Gitta, but beyond that she couldn't tell how old she was. She stood tall and straight-backed. A slender, perfect streak of white sliced across her dark hair, which was thick and unbraided, and swept over her right shoulder. Milla hadn't thought what to expect of the midwife, but upon seeing her in the flesh she realized she'd assumed her to be ugly and craggy, with a face to match what was surely the blackness of her heart. She wasn't expecting a woman so striking, so interesting to look at. The midwife seemed strong and capable, alert and intelligent. She smiled. Her lips were full and her teeth were straight and white. "What are you doing so far from the village, and so late in the afternoon?"

Milla had prepared herself for questions, and she forced herself to breathe evenly, not to betray her lies with shaking, and not to tell more lies than she absolutely had to. Not because lying to this woman troubled her, but because she was afraid she wouldn't be very good at it. "I'm looking for my brother," Milla said.

True.

The midwife raised her eyebrows. They were full and arching. "And who might that be?"

"Niklas."

True.

"Ah, Niklas. He came with Iris and didn't want to leave her, is that right?"

"Yes," Milla said. Also true.

"Come inside." The midwife stepped back and to one side, inviting.

Milla's snakes hissed softly, so softly. A warning that only Milla could hear. "I . . . I shouldn't. I need to get to Niklas. Before . . . before it's too late."

The midwife's eyebrows shot up again. "Oh my. That sounds serious. Well. All the more reason to come inside." She smiled again, closed-lipped now but not unkindly. Milla tried to remember Iris's warnings. Iris was terrified of this woman, and Milla knew there were good reasons for that. And yet Milla felt herself drawn to the midwife. Admiring her, even. She seemed like the kind of woman Milla might want to grow into being—so sure, so certain. She didn't seem like a woman who ever tried to puzzle out what would please someone else. She simply knew what was right. And not the way Gitta knew the right way to serve Jakob's dinner or to feed the chickens. Milla sensed a deeper sort of knowing in this woman, and underneath that, something else. A lack of concern. Of trepidation. There was only solidity where Milla so often trembled and shook. This was not a woman who said sorry. Or felt regret. What must that be like, Milla wondered.

As the distance closed between her and the midwife's door, Milla looked down at her feet and wondered at the strangeness of knowing that she shouldn't be doing this—even feeling that she didn't want to do this—while her feet continued to carry her forward. Soon she would be in the midwife's cottage and the door would close behind her. She felt like the stupid girl in a story that Iris might have told her.

Still Milla's feet carried her forward. As she moved past the midwife and stepped inside the cottage, the warmth of the woman's hearth met Milla's face and perspiration chilled her temples. The chill traveled to her snakes and down her spine. Then the midwife closed the door and Milla saw that she wasn't alone.

There was a girl in a chair by the fireplace. She seemed to be hugging herself so closely that her hands disappeared behind her, which Milla thought odd. Then Milla saw that the sleeves of the girl's dress were twice again as long as they should be and had been used to bind her arms to her torso. The girl's hair was parted down the middle and pulled smoothly behind her. It shone blackly as if wet. Milla couldn't tell how old she was. She seemed tiny, the shelf of her collar bones forming a straight line that was visible through the drab gray wool of her strange dress. Her eyes were a deep brown. She looked at Milla and blinked once, twice. She pressed her lips together, just enough that Milla could detect the effort. Milla recognized that expression. It was the same one Gitta turned to Milla every day. Fear of what might happen, combined with willing oneself to remain silent. The girl looked past Milla to the midwife.

"Milla, this is Asta."

So the midwife knew Milla's name. But of course she did. Milla had said her brother was Niklas. Which meant that the midwife also knew the demon was her aunt.

"Hello, Asta," Milla said. The girl said nothing in response, though she looked at Milla again and blinked. Once. Twice. Milla looked at Asta a beat longer, a question in her own eyes. Still the girl said nothing.

Milla looked around the room. It was about the size of her mother and father's cottage. It had all the same features. A kitchen, a table and chairs. But it all felt too close. And there was no scent—not of apples or bread or stewed meat. Panic tightened her belly and Milla wanted to shove past the midwife and run. "And your name?" Milla said to the midwife.

The midwife raised one dark eyebrow. "Ragna."

"Thank you for inviting me in, but I can't stay," Milla said. "I need to take a message to my brother. To tell him that our mother is ill."

"Is she dying?" Ragna said.

Milla felt herself pale. It would be a terrible thing to say her mother was dying, like bringing a curse down upon her. But Milla reasoned that the midwife wouldn't let her see Niklas if the news weren't very bad. The contents of Milla's stomach rose up, stinging the back of her throat. She swallowed. "Yes."

"There's nothing to be done then," Ragna said. "You'll only upset him if you tell him. He'll want to see her and even if I allowed it, which I won't, by the time he got home she'd be dead. No. You may stay here the night, but you go back home first thing tomorrow. And I hope your mother is still alive when you get there. It was foolish of her to send you here. I'm surprised Gitta would do that." Ragna's voice was drained of emotion. Unyielding. Challenging.

Where Milla had felt only panic a moment before, anger bloomed. She felt the quick flicks of her snakes' tongues against her scalp. Ragna was so sure she knew what was right and that Milla would do as she was told. And if Milla didn't . . . then? Milla looked at Asta, so quiet and so still on the outside. Yet Milla saw how her stillness cost her. The restrained terror in her eyes.

"Sit," Ragna said. "Are you hungry?"

"Not a bit," Milla said.

"Well, sit anyway."

"It will be dark soon. I should go," Milla said.

"You'll stay here," Ragna said. "I told you."

Milla's anger unfurled some more. It didn't make her stupid, though; it made her sharp. "Why doesn't Asta speak? And why is she bound like that? Is she ill? Is she your daughter?"

Milla could see that her last question caused a flicker of unease to pass across Ragna's face. "She's my daughter, in a way. All the girls are my daughters."

"She's from The Place?"

"I'm helping her," Ragna said. "The girls say bad things sometimes. Cruel things. Asta says especially bad things. She upset her mother and father very much when they visited her yesterday. So we're having a talk. And when she's ready to be a good girl I'll take her back."

"Back home?"

Ragna's eyebrows formed two soft crescents over her eyes, rough imitations of kindness. "Oh, aren't you a sweet child. I know it's hard to understand. But these girls are stricken. Cursed by the demon. They can never go home. The best I can do for them is to keep them safe and calm." She smiled. "See how safe and calm Asta is. She's feeling better already."

Asta blinked. Once. Twice.

Milla imagined Iris in that chair, and she thought she might be sick.

Ragna crossed her arms over her chest and cocked her head. "You look like her, Milla. Has anyone ever told you that?"

"I don't look like anyone in my family," Milla said. Her snakes coiled tighter around her head and she felt an ache in the bones of her face, tears about to form and spill.

"So much like her," Ragna said. "Hulda was never pretty like Gitta. There was always something strange about her. And then we found out why. It's a miracle you haven't been taken. Isn't it?"

Ragna's eyes were on Milla, enjoying her agony. Milla couldn't bear to look back at Ragna, so instead she looked at Asta. And that was how she saw the silent word that formed on Asta's lips. *Go.*

By the time Ragna had finished feasting on Milla's pain and had turned her attention back to Asta, the girl's expression had once again stilled to barely controlled terror.

A thought entered Milla's head then. It was her own but also not. *The secret to lying well is to give them what they want.* Lying to Ragna, Milla realized, was no different from lying to Niklas, or to her mother or father. What Ragna wanted was sweetness and obedience to her wishes. So Milla would give that to her. Or at least the appearance of it. Milla allowed her bottom lip to tremble, but ever so slightly, as if she were trying not to. "I've made a terrible mistake," she said. "You're right. Mamma was foolish to send me here, but she loves Niklas so. I should go home to her. If I leave now I can stay the night with Tomas and Hanna and I'll be that much closer to home in the morning. Maybe they'll even lend me a horse so I can get home faster. Would that be all right? I feel that I'm intruding here . . . while you're so busy helping Asta." Milla made her eyes as round and innocent as a hare's.

She thrilled a bit. It was a very different thing to lie simply to please someone than to do what she was doing now—to lie to get something she wanted. Or it felt different, anyway. This felt like a game that she could win.

Ragna looked at Milla as if measuring her, and Milla tensed inside while exerting every bit of will she possessed in order to relax herself to soft compliance on the outside.

"Stay to the road and walk straight back," Ragna said. "It will be dark in a few hours and these woods are thick. You'll be lost before you've taken a step."

"Oh, I would never step into the woods," Milla said. "Mamma and Pappa wouldn't allow it. And anyway, I'd be frightened." Milla moved toward the door, not too fast, she told herself.

"As you should be," Ragna said. "Fear will keep you safe."

Milla reached to open the door while smiling at Ragna in a way that was at once sad and grateful and apologetic. "Thank you, Ragna." Once the door was open, Milla turned back to look at Asta. "Good-bye, Asta." She wanted to say to Asta, *I won't forget you.* She wanted to rush past Ragna and pick up that slight, frightened girl and save her. But in that moment Milla had no idea how she would keep herself safe, much less Asta. And Ragna loomed over Milla, strength of purpose and conviction rising off her like a threat—a reminder of the fate that would await Milla if she didn't do as she was told. Milla made her smile a lie but kept her eyes honest for Asta. Then she blinked at Asta once. Twice. Asta did the same.

Milla didn't breathe while her legs took her back to the road and pointed her toward town. She didn't breathe while Ragna followed her out to the road and stared after her. Milla's snakes stayed close to her scalp as if they, too, could feel Ragna's eyes. Milla took in her first breath only once she'd passed Ragna's barn. She kept walking without looking back until her snakes began to move in her hair and she felt them peek out and lick the air. Only then did Milla look behind her to see that Ragna had disappeared.

14

THE WOODS WERE SHOWING THE FIRST SIGNS OF INFES-
tation when Milla left the road. It was revolting to pick her way
through the caterpillars and webbed leaves. She'd traveled well
past Ragna's cottage before doubling back again. She was certain
Ragna hadn't followed her, so the trick now was to conceal herself
should Ragna be keeping watch on the road. Milla wasn't afraid
of the woods. She never had been and she wasn't now. She felt
certain that no matter how thick the forest, she'd find her way
straight. Her greater fear was that Ragna might take it upon
herself to go to The Place tonight—and that she'd be waiting for
Milla when she got there. But Milla had to hope she wouldn't
be, not with Asta there to look after. Milla shuddered to think
of what that might mean. Maybe, somehow, she and Iris—and
Niklas, too, if Milla could convince him—could save that poor
girl. But first, Iris. Iris was the one she'd made a promise to.

As the woods grew healthier and thicker and wetter, the air was sweeter to breathe but the traveling was harder. So as not to find herself moving farther and farther from the road, she clambered over rocks and branches rather than around them. When she drifted left, her snakes rose up and leaned her right, closer to the road.

A breeze rustled through the leaves, sending a chill through her dress. Then the rustling became whispering.

Let me out.

I'm so cold.

Let me out.

Iris. Wasn't it? But not only Iris. Not one girl. Many girls. And women. All whispering together.

Let me out.

Milla turned abruptly right, heading for the road. She had to be well past the midwife's cottage by now. And those voices told her she was close.

The woods were so thick that darkness seemed already to have fallen, but as she drew closer to the road and the trees thinned, Milla saw that the sun hadn't yet dipped below the horizon. When she emerged from the woods, the whispering grew louder, as if showing her the way. Her snakes were on high alert, tasting the air over her head. She felt their excitement and her pace quickened. The road made a soft turn and she reached a wide meadow, blue-green in the twilight and dotted with yellow flowers. It might have been beautiful.

The Place rose up in front of her, a curved wall of stone so covered with moss that it looked like a flat, green hill.

The whispering that had sounded pleading before had become howls. The wind carried them to Milla's ears in screeches and shrieks.

LET ME OUT.

Milla's snakes retracted into her hair and she felt them tremble. Her bravery dissolved. The Place was so big, and she felt so small and alone. The only thought that calmed her terror was that Niklas was within those walls. He would help her, she told herself. He must. Maybe she could even tell Niklas what was happening to her, make him understand that though Iris had changed—and though Milla was changing, too—that they were still themselves. If she could get him to believe that, then he would have to help her free Iris. He would know that Iris didn't belong there. And then they could all leave here and find someplace where the curse couldn't reach them.

Darker thoughts crept in, pestering her and giving her no peace. Did she really think that she and Iris weren't cursed by the demon? Did she think that once away from The Place, Iris would get no worse, or for that matter that Milla herself wouldn't become a demon like Hulda, snake by snake? Then Milla wondered: If she continued to transform, would she merely look like a monster—which would be horrible enough— or would she actually become one, as well? Would her brother be safe with her? Would anyone?

She was a coward. She looked down at her feet, once again willing them to stop carrying her forward, into something that terrified her. *Stop, Milla. Turn around. Leave. Go somewhere safe, to a village where no one knows you. Cut the snakes from your head and pray they never grow back. Keep cutting them off if they do. You can't help Iris or Asta. You can't even help yourself.*

Her snakes rose up in protest, and Milla felt the sting of tears in the corners of her eyes. All she wanted in the world was for her brother to call her silly Milla and to tell her that everything would be all right.

Silly Milla is dead.

Was that her voice, or Iris's, or the demon's? Milla didn't know anymore. Were they all the same?

The howling grew ever louder. So many voices, each singing her own song of misery but using the same words.

Let me out.

I'm so cold.

Let me out.

The sun was fully down when Milla stepped through the open, arched entrance of The Place. She could see that it had once been a ring fort. Trude had told her stories about them, safe places where farmers took shelter from marauders. The stone wall was thicker than a grown man's arm span. Milla felt swallowed by it, made even tinier and less significant. Inside was a broad dirt yard with a large bell hanging atop a stone pillar. Beyond it was a wide well, also stone. Around it the dirt was muddy and puddled with spilled water. Clinging to the outer wall of the fort there was a stable with an attached corral where five horses stood dozing, and a chicken coop, and a small barn—all made of ash-gray wood. She might have heard the clucks of chickens or bleats of sheep if it hadn't been for the howling.

Let me out.

I'm so cold.

Let me out.

The Place was a building at the center of the ring fort—two stories high and made of stone. The second story had windows that overlooked the yard, too small to bring in much light or air. The wooden doors of the entrance also seemed too small for such a large structure. Milla walked to the doors and rapped twice. She waited.

The door opened slowly and a fair-haired boy appeared in

the opening. Milla thought of him as a boy, because he was as long-limbed and awkward as a colt, but the beginnings of a beard sprouted from his chin. His eyes opened wide.

"I'm here for my brother," she said. "Niklas. I . . . I have a message for him. From home."

The boy peered past her into the night.

"I'm alone," Milla said. "It's just me."

"I'm not supposed to let anyone in," the boy said. "It's not allowed. Midwife said so."

"What's your name?" Milla said, attempting to smile brightly. *What does he want*, she reminded herself. *Give him some of that.*

"Petter," he said.

"And do you know my brother, Niklas? He would have arrived just three days ago. Sandy hair. And tall?"

"I know him," Petter said.

"I could wait right here, and you could go get him for me, and then he and I could talk?" It was all Milla could do not to scream. To say, *You oaf, I haven't time for your wide eyes and your surprise—I need to talk to my brother.* Instead she kept smiling.

Petter nodded. "All right. But you can't come in."

"Oh my goodness," Milla said. "I wouldn't. I'd be frightened to." She arranged her face while imagining this boy was someone she very much wanted to make happy. She stood off to the side of herself and marveled at her cunning. Here she was, a girl who'd grown up with just one boy, her brother, and she was unmoved by talking to another boy, a boy she didn't know. His good opinion of her felt so . . . unimportant. Which was a surprise to her after all the stories Trude had told about magical first meetings between boys and girls. She'd assumed when it did finally happen to her that the expected response would churn up inside her. She'd feel some measure of what Trude had described as the most potent kind of joy. Milla looked at this tall, gangly boy. His face was nice enough, she supposed. But it certainly wasn't magic.

He nodded again, closed the door and left Milla alone. She tried to calm her desperation to see Niklas. She'd have to be careful not to make a fuss when he came. She shouldn't draw attention to herself in a place where any sign of oddness, of excitement, might get her locked up along with Iris.

The air was cooler here than at home. She thought about Trude's shawl and then realized she'd left it in Hanna's kitchen. Well, she thought. Just as well that Hanna should have her mother's shawl. Milla wrapped her arms around herself.

Her back was to the doors when she heard them open, and she stayed where she was, fearing what she'd feel, or do, if Niklas hadn't come. If he told Petter to send her away.

"Milla?"

A box inside her that she'd kept tightly closed since she'd set out from home opened in that moment. So much climbed out of that box—fear, relief, sadness, joy, regret, love, guilt—that it was all she could do not to sob. Instead she turned around and threw herself into her brother's arms.

"Oh, Milla," Niklas said. He wrapped his arms around her and she felt his size and strength and she wanted to stay there. But after a moment he gently held her away from him and said, "What are you doing here? And all alone? Where are Mamma and Pappa?"

"At home. They don't know I'm here. They wouldn't have let me come, and I had to. I had to see you. And Iris."

"Oh, Milla," he said again. In just three days he had become a different boy. There were angles in his face she hadn't seen before. Purple half-moons under his eyes where before there'd only been cream dotted with freckles. She waited for him to admonish her, to ask her why she must worry their parents so. Why she couldn't behave. Instead he brought her to him again, and she pressed her cheek to his chest and felt a tremor there like he might be crying. After a moment he pulled away and looked up at the dark sky, taking in a deep breath. He wiped both eyes with the back of one hand. "All right. We need to figure out what to do with you. You can't stay here. It's not safe. I'll tell Petter that I'm taking you to the midwife. You can stay the night with her, then go home tomorrow."

The snakes on Milla's head hissed so loudly that she thought Niklas must have heard them. *"No,"* she said. "No. Please, Niklas, don't make me leave until I've seen Iris. I've come all this way."

Niklas breathed out heavily. "I suppose you can sleep on my cot tonight. But, Milla, are you sure you want to see her? She's not as you remember her. And it will only upset you to see her here."

"How terrible is it here, Niklas?" She looked up to the small windows in the second story, where the howling spilled out in waves of agony and begging. "Why do they complain so of being cold? What does the midwife do to them?"

Niklas looked at her without blinking. She could see in his eyes that he was making a decision, and she knew him well enough that he didn't need to speak the words once he had. He was going to take her inside.

Niklas led her past Petter, who sat on a stool leaning against the wall of the fort's open central courtyard. From the way he startled, she thought he must have been dozing.

"My sister is staying here tonight, Petter. It's too late to send her home."

Petter looked at Milla with narrowed eyes. "You're sure she's all right?"

All right, Milla assumed, meant that she wasn't possessed by a demon. She almost laughed. Her snakes squirmed.

"She's my sister," Niklas said. "I'd know if she weren't."

Petter shrugged and closed his eyes. Not bothering to open them again, he said, "You can explain to the others. And the midwife."

"I'll have her out before the midwife comes in the morning." Niklas looked at her as if to say, *and no argument from you.*

Milla thought to herself that he needn't worry that she'd want to stay here. It was the dreariest place she'd ever seen. Worse even than the blighted village. Bad things happened here.

"The only time the girls are allowed out of their cells is when they're brought here to the courtyard," Niklas said. "That's because the ground is covered in stone. The midwife says the demon comes from below, from deep in the earth, and so the girls mustn't touch earth or else the demon will get an even tighter hold on them. Make them stronger and impossible to control."

"What's that?" Milla said. She pointed to a stone slab in the center of the courtyard, five empty buckets lined up next to it.

"When the midwife thinks a girl is being troublesome, she has the boys tie the girl up and lay her there. Then we're to douse the girl with water. The midwife says demons are made of hellfire and hate the cold. Water subdues them."

"I saw a girl named Asta at the midwife's cottage."

"You met Ragna? You didn't tell me. So she knows you're here?"

"Not . . . really."

Niklas frowned. "That's not good, Milla. You don't want to make an enemy of her."

"If she douses the troublesome girls here, what was she doing with Asta at her cottage? She said Asta told her mother and father terrible things."

"I don't know. I tried to find out, but the other boys wouldn't tell me. They're all so miserable, Milla. Most of them don't want to be here, but they're forced to be. And the few that do want to be here are the ones you want to stay away from. The midwife chooses what boys come here to be guards and there's no saying no. It's the deal every villager makes in order to be kept safe from the girls. And the oldest boy isn't allowed to leave until there's a younger boy to come in to replace him."

"That's horrible."

"It is. But, Milla, it's so much worse for the girls." His eyes traveled to the stone slab.

"Have you seen it happen?"

"Once," Niklas said. "It's awful. I haven't had to help tie up any of the girls yet. But it takes four boys just to tie up one girl and carry her down here. The girls buck and scream so. And it's no wonder. The water is icy and once the dousing is over they're wearing nothing but their soaking wet shifts. Then Ragna sends them back to their cells to shiver."

Milla thought of that happening to Iris. No. She couldn't let it. And she didn't believe Niklas would either. "No wonder they howl so."

"I feel sorry for them," Niklas said. "It's not their faults. It's the demon who deserves to be punished. Not them." In that moment he looked to Milla like the sweet Niklas she played with in the woods when they were children—the boy who didn't want to believe in any of the dreadful things that Milla could make up in her head. As dear as he was, and as much as she knew he loved her, he'd surely never want to know that his sister had snakes growing from her head—and that most of the time she rather liked the company. She despaired that she could ever tell him.

"Come," he said. "I'll show you the rest. Then I'll take you to Iris."

Niklas led her back through the stone tunnel that led from the courtyard to the corridor that circled the entire first story of The Place. The first room they came to was a large, dank chamber lined with ten straw-padded cots and lit by hanging oil lamps. Small windows high in the walls opened out onto the courtyard they'd just left. Four boys sat or lay across the cots, not talking, only staring, as if too spent to do anything else. Niklas said to them, "This is my sister."

All four looked up at once, like dogs catching a scent. One of them, round-faced and dark-haired, said, "Are you mad, Niklas? You think we're allowed visitors here?"

Petter walked in then. "I told him he'll have to explain to Ragna. I'm not getting blamed for this."

Milla could tell that Niklas didn't like this Petter. Neither did she. "And what's Ragna going to do to Niklas if she finds out I'm here? Make him leave? Good!"

Milla saw two of the boys exchange looks between them as if to say, *she has a point.*

Niklas, for his part, looked at Milla in horror—as if he could see the snakes on her head.

Petter, who for all his gangly dimness clearly did not like being bested by a girl, narrowed his eyes at her. "I think this one's showing the signs. She's got a demon light in her eyes."

Milla sensed the other boys shifting behind her.

Niklas stepped in front of her. "Milla is overtired from her journey. But she's as meek as a mouse, I promise you."

Bile rose in Milla's throat at being dismissed so. She wanted to let the snakes rise from her head and attack Petter with her nails. Let him see the signs of her claw marks then. Let him release his bowels with fright at the sight of her green and crimson snakes, jaws wide and ready.

Then Milla wondered if maybe Petter really had seen the demon light in her eyes.

"Come, Milla," Niklas said, pushing her out of the room. When they'd walked five paces he turned on her. "You must be more careful or I can't keep you safe here. These boys would sooner lock you up right now than worry that you'll turn demon-possessed by morning."

"I'm not as meek as a mouse, Niklas. And I was defending you. You should be thanking me."

Niklas searched the ceiling, as if for strength. "Milla, if you have any love for me at all, then you will stop defending me."

She smiled at him. "You didn't say that when the forest witches were after you. Then you made sure I didn't leave your side until we were all the way home."

"You are a strange girl, Milla."

She wrapped her arms around him and put her head on his chest. "But you love me."

He sighed. "I do. Though you'll be the death of me." He let her rest against his chest for a moment longer, then he pushed her gently away. "Are you hungry?"

Milla thought back to when she'd eaten last. Had it really been a full day since she'd had Trude's apple, bread, and cheese? "Starving," she said. "And so thirsty."

Niklas took her to the kitchen, a large room with a massive, cold hearth at the opposite end, and a long wooden table and benches in the center of the room. Against one wall there were shelves with baskets of apples, cabbages, and potatoes, also a bowl of eggs and some cloth-wrapped cheese. He poured water into a cup and she drank it so greedily that it ran down her chin.

"A village woman cooks dinner for us once a week. The rest of the time we fend for ourselves." Niklas handed her an apple, then tore off two large hunks of brown bread. He handed her one and tucked the other and a second apple into the pocket of her dress. "Give those to Iris."

Milla devoured the food without tasting it.

"I'll take you to Iris now. But, Milla, you must prepare yourself. I can see the hope in your eyes, and I'm sad for you."

"There you go again talking to me like you're so much older and wiser." Her snakes twitched. "You don't know what I've seen. Or what I know." She saw Niklas withdraw from her, and she calmed herself. This wasn't the way to get what she wanted. She breathed, settled herself. "Niklas, if there's something I don't understand, then help me understand it. Right now I can't think of a single reason that you and I shouldn't take Iris out of here tonight."

"You don't know what you're asking, Milla."

Her impatience flared again. She wanted to shake him. Why should she have to pretend to be settled in her heart and mind when he was the one in the wrong? "You're just like Tomas and Hanna. They said the same thing to me. But I *do* know what I'm asking. You can't let them do this to Iris. She's our friend. We love her." Milla gripped Niklas's rough linen shirt in her hand.

He closed his own hand over hers. "You don't know what you're asking because you haven't seen the girls, Milla. Come. I'll show you."

15

Niklas led Milla to a wooden ladder that went up to an opening in the stone ceiling. He climbed up first, and she followed. As she climbed she was struck by how quiet it had become. No howling or crying. She wondered if the girls were sleeping. When she'd climbed all the way to the second story, the moment her face was just above floor level she was hit with the overpowering scent of sour milk. It was so strong she could taste it in her mouth. She let out an involuntary grunt of disgust.

Niklas reached out a hand to help her all the way up. "Another of Ragna's ideas. The girls get cups of milk every four daylight hours. It's supposed to calm them. From what I can tell it just makes them angrier. None of them drink it and half of them throw it back at us. I've only been here three days, and I don't think I'll ever want to drink milk again."

Milla didn't think she'd ever wish to, either. They paused

before continuing on. Milla realized that as badly as she'd wanted to see Iris, there was now a tremor of hesitation in her. A fear of how Iris might have changed. "Is it always so quiet at night? Do they sleep?"

"I've never heard it quiet like this since I've been here. It's . . . strange." Niklas looked worried. She supposed that if howling seemed normal to you, then the absence of howling might be a cause for concern. "Come. Iris's cell is toward the middle." He held her eyes. "I think it would be better if you didn't look in the cells, Milla. Keep your eyes forward, on me."

Milla nodded while knowing it was a promise she couldn't possibly keep.

The stone hall circled the courtyard, just as the one beneath it did, and was lit by oil lamps that hung from iron hooks sunk into the walls. Milla felt the damp chill of the place in her flesh, and she thought of those poor girls, soaked to the skin and then left to huddle alone in their cells.

A whispering rose along the hallway. Milla could tell by the way he faltered for just a moment that Niklas had heard it, too. It sounded like wind through leafy branches, only sharper, crisper. Then she thought, *No, that's not what it sounds like at all. It sounds like hissing.*

Then the hissing became words.

She's here.

She's here.

She's here.

Niklas held one hand behind him, quickly squeezing one of hers. "Remember what I said. Don't look. And . . . don't listen, either. They'll say things to you. It's the demon talking. Remember that."

Milla noticed he hadn't prayed the way they'd been taught to do whenever anyone mentioned the demon. Nor was there salt around doors and windows. Come to think of it, there was none in Ragna's cottage, either. She wondered if everyone who spent any time here realized it was pointless. The demon was already here, and would do as she wished.

Milla could see the iron bars of cells, one after the other, curving along the outer wall of the corridor, and as they passed the first, hands shot out at her through the bars, fingertips grazing her arm and nearly catching hold of her sleeve. Niklas threw an arm around Milla and jerked her backward until they both leaned against the corridor's inner wall, beyond the reach of the girl.

Though she was not a girl at all. She had a woman's shape beneath the rough burlap she wore—more sack than dress. There were lines cobwebbing the corners of her eyes, and her cheeks were hollow, her lips thin. She stood pressed up against the bars, a smile across her face from ear to ear exposing her teeth, yellow with age. She laughed and hissed—laughing on the intake of breath, hissing on the exhale—and gripped and shook the iron bars. "She's here! She's here! She's here!"

More hands and arms emerged from the iron bars along the corridor and the whisper-hissing grew louder and constant.

"I'm taking you out of here," Niklas said. "It's not safe."

She turned to him, calmed her face and willed herself to be convincing. "I'm fine, Niklas. They're all locked up. They can't get out. And I've come this far to see Iris. Please don't make me leave until I do."

Niklas took her hand, less with affection and more, she felt, out of a desire to keep her close. Then he turned and led her on. Milla made no pretense of not looking at each woman and girl that they passed, their faces lit up by the oil lamps. She saw that there seemed to be two kinds of prisoners here. Those who smiled and whispered and held the bars as if waiting for something to be brought to them. Their faces were bright with expectation, from the oldest to the youngest. One of these women, old enough to be her mother, had hair and eyebrows that looked as if they might once have been the same rust-red as Iris's. She wondered if it was Leah, Iris's aunt. These women frightened Milla—their smiles were so wide as to be grimaces. They seemed to have teeth too numerous, too large. They were frenzied.

But there was another kind of prisoner here, too—girls who didn't whisper or grip the bars. In their faces Milla saw what Asta would become, whenever Ragna was finished with her. These girls huddled in the dim of their cells, only staring, the fight gone out of them.

Niklas stopped in front of one of these cells. Inside, on a low cot covered with dirty hay, sat a girl, her knees pulled up to her forehead, her arms wrapped around them.

It was Iris.

Niklas stepped up to the bars. "Iris. It's me. Niklas."

Iris lifted her head from her arms, and Milla was overcome with relief and anguish—both. Relief because here was Iris. Anguish because here was Iris. *Here.* And in this way. She wore the same rough, dirty burlap sack that all the other girls and women wore. Milla rushed to the door of the cell and thrust her arms through the bars. Iris leapt up and reached for Milla before Niklas could pull Milla away.

"Oh my dear. My dearest. I'm so sorry they've done this to you." Milla held Iris through the bars, felt the bones and muscles under the skin of Iris's back. Iris seemed at once thinner and stronger than she'd been just a few days before. Milla wanted to push her face through the bars and press her cheek, wet with tears, to Iris's. But the bars were too close together. She looked at Niklas. "Let me inside. Let me sit with her."

"Oh, Milla," he said. "Don't you know how I'd love to let you? But it's not safe."

"Niklas, please," Iris said, in a voice that was all her own. "I'm me. You know me. I would never hurt Milla. She's like my own sister."

"Iris," he said. "You know that won't keep her safe from the demon."

What he meant, Milla knew, was that Iris's love for Milla wouldn't keep Milla safe from *Iris*. "Niklas, what is the worst that could happen if you let me inside? What is the worst these girls ever do? Say bad things? Look at her, Niklas. She's just as she ever was." What Milla thought, but didn't say, was that Milla herself bore far more proof of possession than any of these girls. If Ragna knew there were snakes growing from her head, they'd build a new prison, just for her.

Niklas raised an eyebrow at her. "Milla."

"I know Iris. All you have to do is let me in and lock the door behind me. And if anything happens I'll call to you. Anyway, I'm hardly going to sleep in a room with all those boys looking for their proof that I'm demon-possessed. I'm safer here than there. Then you can come get me in the morning and let me out before Ragna arrives."

"Petter's on guard duty tonight," Niklas said, "so he'd be the first to hear you if you called. Not that I imagine I'll be able to sleep a wink knowing you're in here."

"You could stay with us, Niklas." Iris smiled at him, and

something in the brightness of her smile gave Milla pause, but then she told herself that she was being silly. It was just Iris's usual smile. Wasn't it?

"Yes, Niklas," Milla said. "Do that." She looked to Niklas hopefully, realizing with shame that she'd welcome his company. As the damp chill of the stone walls settled into her and the whispering circled and circled the corridor like a creature prowling, Milla felt suddenly afraid to be here alone.

Niklas thought for a moment. "No. It will make the other boys suspicious, and that will be no good for you. Besides, I can only lock the door from the outside. And . . ." He looked at Iris. "Leaving it unlocked wouldn't be a good idea." He pulled Milla away from the iron bars. "Milla," he said quietly. "You must listen to me now. And believe me. Trust that I love Iris, too, and I wouldn't lie to you. Do you trust me?"

Milla nodded. She did. Didn't she?

"Then trust me when I say that Iris isn't always like this. I know she seems like herself now. But I've seen her act just like the others. She hisses and laughs and throws her milk back at me like she doesn't even know me. She says terrible things. Things Iris would never have said to me before."

Milla wanted to protest, to say it was no wonder—after all, look what they'd done to Iris. Shouldn't she be angry? But something in Niklas's face told her that he'd seen things she hadn't. That arguing with him now would be unkind. That he was frightened for her, and trying his hardest to do right by her.

"Promise me that you'll scream your loudest if you need me," he said. "I don't trust some of those other boys. I see how they act with the girls. So far I've kept them away from Iris. And I'll keep them away from you. I'll stay awake in there with them, and I'll keep an ear out for Petter, too. You call me if you need me, do you hear?"

Again, Milla nodded, then put her arms around him and squeezed tight.

"All right then," Niklas said. He walked toward the door to Iris's cell and unclamped the wooden bar that held the iron-barred door closed. "Iris, you'll take care of Milla tonight, will you? Don't let anything happen to her?" He lifted off the bar and pulled the door open.

Milla squeezed Niklas's hand one last time and then she walked inside Iris's cell.

"Milla is my friend," Iris said. She put a gentle arm around Milla's shoulder and smiled at Niklas, so brightly.

16

ONCE NIKLAS HAD LEFT THEM, MILLA FELT SHY AND uncertain. She pulled away from Iris and circled the cell, touching the cold, rough stone of the walls, looking up toward the small window—more an opening than a window, too high and tiny to offer much light during the day, but big enough to let in the night chill. The moon shone weakly through it now. The only other light came from the oil lamp that hung from the wall outside. Milla looked around the floor, at the bucket in the corner where she supposed Iris must relieve herself—the stench rising from it revealed as much—and then, finally, at the cot with its layer of old straw. Clearly Iris wasn't the first girl who had lain upon it. And if she wasn't the first, then what had happened to the others?

"The girl who was here before me died," Iris said.

"How did you know I was wondering that?"

Iris shrugged. "I know you, Milla. I read the question in your eyes. It's natural enough to wonder. I did, too. It's the first thing I thought when they put me in here. I could smell her in the straw. I could smell her in the bucket."

"How did she die?"

"Fever."

Milla imagined a girl curled up on that straw, sweating and shaking, all alone. Ragna did that—she was responsible for that poor girl's death.

"I found out this morning what the girl's name was. Her name was Beata. My dearest Beata. She glowed, Milla. Like a flame. And they put her out."

Milla heard a whisper. Iris went to the door of the cell and crouched down, pressing her face to the bars. "It's Milla," she whispered back. "Niklas's sister. She's come to save us. I told you she would."

Whispers hissed up and down the corridor then.

shesheresheshereshesheresheshereshesheresheshereshesheresheshere

Iris stood and turned toward Milla. Milla groaned and put her hands to her face. How would she save them all? The most she could hope to do would be to convince Niklas to let Iris out. But even that seemed remote. She saw the fear in his eyes when he looked at Iris. He didn't trust her.

Iris stood there, thin and dirty, barely dressed, and still she looked so strong, so alive with certainty. Iris walked toward Milla and put her arms around her. "Milla, dearest. I knew you'd come. I knew you'd hear me. And you did."

Milla had never felt so uncomfortable to be embraced by Iris. She pulled away. "How can I possibly save all of them? I'm not even sure I can save *us*."

Iris looked at her oddly, as if she weren't listening to Milla's words at all. "Why do you hide them from me?"

"Hide what?" But Milla knew what Iris meant. What chilled her gut now was not that Iris knew. It was *how* Iris knew.

"Your snakes." Iris reached out both of her hands as if to cradle Milla's head, and then turned them palms up, the way you would to reassure a dog. Milla felt her snakes emerge from their hair nest and watched as they rested their heads on Iris's hands and tasted the salt of her skin with their tongues. Milla's crimson snake was now as fully grown as her green, both of them as slender as her little finger, elegant and beautiful, and long enough to rest their heads on her shoulders. "You're so lucky," Iris said.

"Lucky," Milla said. "How can this be lucky?"

"The demon gave you snakes but left you this." She tapped Milla's forehead with a finger. "You're still you. You're not taken."

"You're not taken, either," Milla said.

"No? Then why do I hear her voice in my head?" Iris gripped her skull in her hands, squeezing as if she would crush it if she could. Her face crumpled like a dry leaf. "She's always in here. I want her out, but she won't leave."

And there she was. There was Iris, Milla thought. Her Iris. This time, Milla was the one to embrace Iris, and neither of them pulled away.

They sat on the old straw of the cot while Iris ate the bread from Niklas and told Milla about The Place. And about how Stig and Jakob had left her with the midwife. By then, Iris said, she'd so exhausted herself with crying and begging and terror of what was to come that she no longer tried to escape. When she was led to her cell she walked meekly by the other girls and women, who stared at her, blinking. Once. Twice. She sat on the dirty cot and obediently changed out of her nightdress and into the burlap she now wore.

"You say the girls blinked at you," Milla said, thinking of Asta.

"When we're not alone but can see each other, that's our way of talking."

"What does the blinking mean?"

"Anything. Everything. *I see you. See me.* There's a lot you can say with your eyes when you can't use your mouth. And there isn't time for anything more than that, because the only time we're out of our cells is when one of us is taken out for punishment or on visiting days. And most girls never get visitors. At night, when Ragna's gone and there's only a boy on guard, we talk to each other in whispers, from cell to cell to cell. The woman next to me is Agnetha, and she's the youngest of four sisters, all taken. Agnetha will give me a message for her sisters and then I pass the message to Rebekka in the next cell. And then she passes it on. It's how we spend our days, whispering to each other. They like my stories. Sometimes we get loud. We howl." Iris wrapped her arms around herself and looked around at the grimness of her cell as if seeing it again for the first time. "It's so cold here, Milla. And lonely. So lonely. It's only been three days and already I feel that I can't survive another. The last woman to be doused was my mother's sister, Leah. I heard her screaming, then crying. It hasn't happened to me yet, but it will. Agnetha says there's no rhyme or reason to when they come for you. You could be sleeping in your cell and next you know they're dragging you away."

"Oh, Iris," Milla said. "I can't bear to think of them doing that to you. I won't let them." Then Milla remembered the blinking. "I was in Ragna's cottage and saw a girl there, named Asta."

Iris nodded. "I heard about her. From the whispers. She made Ragna angry."

"How?"

"Her mother and father came to see her on visiting day. It's only the newer girls who get visitors. Their families still miss them. The older ones, their families have given up. Can't bear to see them here, I suppose." Iris's face changed, became all planes and edges, and she seemed to go somewhere else in her head. "Or maybe those mothers and fathers didn't love their daughters much in the first place."

"Asta," Milla said, wanting to bring Iris back to her, frightened of the sudden distance she felt between them. "What did she do that angered Ragna?"

Iris spoke urgently, as if she thought she'd be stopped even though she and Milla were alone and there was no one to interrupt them. "The thing you need to understand, Milla, is that not all the girls here are the same. Some of the girls aren't taken by the demon at all. They swear they can't hear her voice in their heads."

"Then why are they here?"

"They just misbehaved. Some only once, some more than once. But they say it wasn't because the demon was making them do it. They just got . . . angry."

"That's all?"

"The villagers are so frightened their daughters will turn on them that some of them, if their daughters make the tiniest misstep, they'll send for Ragna. And the thing is, Ragna never examines a girl and says she's *not* possessed. Once Ragna is sent for, the girl is doomed. That's what happened to Asta. She slapped another girl and that girl told her mother and father, and they insisted on sending for Ragna."

"Asta's mother and father should have taken her away before Ragna could get her. She doesn't belong here."

Iris cocked her head at Milla. "And I do? And these other girls who hear the demon's voice in their heads? Do they deserve to be here?"

Milla felt hot with shame. "No! No, that's not what I meant."

Iris smiled at her. "It's not? Then what did you mean?"

"I meant . . . I meant . . ." But what had Milla meant, really? She'd meant what she said. She could make an exception in her head for Iris. She knew Iris and loved her and didn't want her to be here. But those other girls, the ones who smiled too wide and hissed . . . she could understand why their mothers and fathers were frightened of them. She was frightened of them, too. She knew she was wrong to make such a distinction. To make allowances for the known while shutting herself off to the unknown. Did Milla think she herself deserved to be here? What made her better or different? She had snakes growing from her head, and hadn't she heard Iris's voice in her head? Why did anyone deserve this? There was no good reason. No one did. "I'm sorry."

Iris patted her hand, but looked away.

"Please finish telling me. Why is Ragna keeping Asta at her cottage?"

Iris turned back to her. "It's only the girls who insist they're not possessed who are taken there. And when they come back they don't insist anymore. They give up. When Asta's mother and father visited her, she told them that she didn't belong here, that she'd just been angry with that girl she slapped. And I suppose she must have seemed quite herself to them, and maybe that got them to thinking. They must have gone to Ragna."

"And then Ragna took Asta," Milla said.

Iris nodded.

"What's she doing to her?"

"Ragna has a way of getting in your head. Of making you give up. It's like she's a demon herself. Kari, one of the girls who came back from Ragna's, said that after being forced to listen to Ragna for days on end, she wished she *were* demon-possessed. She said she would prefer it to having Ragna's voice in her head, telling her things about herself that weren't true. She said Ragna talks and talks until you start to wonder if you really aren't who you think you are—if you know yourself at all. She said Ragna's voice was worse than any demon."

"Ragna. Hulda," Milla said. "They're the same, aren't they? Putting their voices where our own should be."

"But now you've come, Milla. And you'll get us all out."

"How can we get everyone out, Iris? Niklas wouldn't agree to it. And even if he wanted to, the other boys would stop him."

"It must be tonight," Iris said. She stared past Milla, as if watching her plan unfold. "You'll call to Niklas, tell him that you want out. When he comes to let you out, we'll lock him in the cell here and then we'll let the other girls out. And then we'll all escape."

"We can't lock Niklas in here, Iris. He helped me. And he wants to help you. No, the only way is to tell him that we need to get you out. And then he'll help us."

"You said yourself that he won't let the other girls out, and I won't leave without them. Milla, how could you expect me to after everything you know now? And can you imagine what Ragna would do to them if I got away? How much worse it would be for the rest? Anyway, if Niklas let only you and me out, we'd still have to get past the other boys. And that Petter.

He's a nasty one. We need the other girls to help us if we're to get out."

"But locking up Niklas, in here?" Milla looked around her and couldn't imagine it. She'd never forgive herself.

"I've survived it for three days. It would be a few hours for him. Ragna or the other boys will let him out by daybreak, if not sooner."

"How can you be so sure he won't help us, Iris? Why can't we explain to him?"

"Have you shown him your snakes, Milla?"

"No."

"And why not?" Iris's voice was mocking.

"Because he wouldn't understand. He'd be frightened. But maybe he'd come to understand. Someday."

"Someday, of course." Now Iris was soothing, stroking Milla's arm. Something inside Milla recoiled from Iris. The feeling she'd had when she first walked into the cell had returned to her. The fear that maybe Iris wasn't entirely Iris anymore. "But someday isn't right now," Iris said. "And right now, Milla, I promise you. I will not leave here without the other girls. And if I don't leave here, I'll die. Just like Beata."

17

"WHEN SHOULD I CALL TO HIM?" MILLA HOVERED AT THE iron-barred door to the cell, peering into the dim passageway. Now that she had decided, she wanted to get it over with. To get past the horrible disappointment she'd see on Niklas's face when he realized what she was doing.

"Not yet. Wait a bit longer. Petter is supposed to stay awake all night, but he won't. Let him get good and sleepy. Then you'll call to Niklas."

"And Petter won't awaken at the same time?"

"He won't come up here. He's a brave bully during the day, but when night falls he stays well away." She smiled. "We tell him the demon is coming for him."

Iris's smile chilled Milla. "Does the demon really talk to you?"

Iris looked troubled for a moment, then her face cleared and recomposed. "I told you she did."

Milla wanted—and didn't want—to know more. She worried that asking more about the voice, how it felt in Iris's head, what it sounded like, might somehow make it worse. Might even conjure the demon. "After we leave here, how will we get her out of your head? And how do we stop her from turning me into a demon, too?"

Iris looked at the wall, wouldn't answer. Milla couldn't tell if she was hurt, or angry. Milla sat down next to her. "I'm sorry. I didn't mean to make you sad. We'll figure that out later. There must be a way." Iris smiled back at her vaguely, patted her hand. Milla looked down at Iris's slender brown fingers, the delicate weave of blue-green veins just under the surface, and she thought of something else. "How will you and I lock Niklas in here? He's twice as big as either of us."

"I'm stronger than I look," Iris said. Milla believed her. There was a hardness to Iris now that was new. And Niklas might be far bigger than she, but he was also far softer. Iris tugged on a lock of Milla's hair, and Milla's crimson snake peeked out. "Let me play with your hair," Iris said. "It will calm me."

Milla sat on the floor, her back to Iris, and Iris sat behind her, running gentle fingers through Milla's hair, softly tugging on the ends. Despite herself, Milla's eyes drooped closed and she allowed herself to be soothed for a moment, as if she and Iris were back home, and not in this cell. If it weren't for the chill and the smell, and the snakes rising from her head, preening for Iris, she might have believed it.

"Tell me a story," Milla said.

"Oh . . . a story. All right. Let me think."

Iris continued to comb Milla's hair with her fingers, and Milla's snakes rested their heads on her shoulders as if they wanted to listen as well.

"There was a young man," Iris began. "A beautiful young man whom everyone loved. He was as sweet and gentle of disposition as he was handsome of face. Oh, and he was also a prince, which meant he was rich, and of course all the girls in the village wished to marry him. But the prince was sad. There was only one girl the prince could love, and she was dead. She was his childhood sweetheart and they had loved each other long before either of them thought anything of beauty, or gold, or marrying well. For this reason, the prince knew that she was the only one who would ever truly love him for himself. The prince carried on despairing and making everyone around him miserable as well, until finally the prince's father told him to go out for a walk and not to come back until he was in a better mood."

"No one likes a moody prince," Milla said.

"Indeed. So the prince walked and the sky was blue, and still he despaired. He said aloud, if only I could see my beloved one more time, maybe I could be happy again. And just as he said that, who should appear but a small, wizened woman who looked very much like the witch in all the stories that the prince had ever been told. And the witch said to him, I can take you to the smoothest, glassiest pond where you can see the face of your beloved in the water. You can even talk to her. But you mustn't try to get her back or you'll die, too. Will you promise not to try? The prince was so overjoyed that he agreed. When they arrived at the pond, the prince saw that the pond was so glassy that when he leaned over it, he saw his own face as if looking into a mirror. But then he wasn't looking at his own face anymore. He was looking at his beloved's face, just as he remembered her, so fair and full of love. His beloved said to him, my dearest, how I've missed you. And he said the same back to her. He told her how lonely he'd been for her and how he didn't think he'd ever be happy again. But, he said, perhaps now that he'd been able to see her one last time, maybe he could find a way. His beloved wept, and her tears bubbled the surface of the pond. My darling, he said to her, why do you weep so? And she said, because I have never stopped loving you, but you have stopped loving me, and now you are going off to love another. So the prince promised her that he would never love another, not as long as he lived. His beloved stopped crying and once again her beautiful face shone up at him smooth and unperturbed. And then she said, now come to me, my darling."

Milla tensed, and Iris laughed a little. Then Milla laughed a little, too. "Poor, silly prince," she said.

Iris continued. "This gave the prince pause, because of course the witch had told him that he mustn't try to get his beloved back, or else he'd die, too. And he told this to his beloved, and she said, but, my darling! You're not getting *me* back, I'm getting *you* back. Because you'll be coming to me and living with me forever and we'll never be parted again. So you see, she said, you'll still be keeping your promise to the witch. And this caused the prince to pause just a bit again, because *had* he told his beloved that he'd made a promise to the witch? He wasn't sure that he had. But in any case, if his beloved told him it would be all right, then he believed her. And so he dived in. As soon as the prince broke the surface of the water, he realized his mistake. His beloved wasn't there, and he wondered if she ever had been. Instead of his beloved, there were water snakes. Hundreds and hundreds of water snakes. And even as they ate him, the prince wondered if he might ever see his beloved again."

As she neared the end of the story, Iris had stopped combing

Milla's hair with her fingers and she rested her hands on Milla's shoulders instead. Now Iris's fingers gripped Milla there, and Milla felt Iris shaking. She turned and found Iris weeping, tears streaking her face, her mouth in a pained, tight line.

Then Iris began to laugh.

Then she began to cry again.

Laugh.

Cry.

Laugh.

Cry.

Milla rose to her feet and backed away from Iris, not entirely meaning to. But perhaps meaning to, a bit.

Iris's face went still, and she wiped her nose with one long swipe of her forearm. "Do you know what the moral to the story is, Milla?"

"What is it, Iris?" Though she was afraid to ask.

"The people you love are dead and want to kill you." Iris sobbed with an anguish so deep that Milla would have gathered Iris in her arms if she hadn't been so frightened. Then Iris stood up abruptly, stopped crying, and looked around her in expectation. A smile hitched up the corners of her mouth—ghastly, all wrong. Up went the left, then the right, then the left. "She's here."

"Who's here?"

"The demon," Iris said.

"Hulda?" Milla said.

"Oh no. No, no, no, no. No, it's you. You're the demon, Milla. You've always been the demon." Iris's face was lit up from the inside, her eyes bright and wide. And that hitching, twitching smile.

Cold sweat slicked Milla's forehead, her skin burned and prickled. "No. I'm not. I'm me."

"Even with those snakes on your head? Come out to play . . .
snakes."

Iris pulled back her lips and hissed between clamped teeth.
Milla fell backward away from Iris and cowered in a corner of
the cell. Iris went to the bars of the cell and shook and howled.
"Come get her, Niklas! Come get your sister!"

The shaking of the bars grew deafening as every girl and
woman shook the bars of their cells, too, and hissed and howled,
"Come get her, Niklasssssss. Come get your sssssisssssster! Come
get her before the demon comes for her. She'ssss coming, Niklas.
The demon is coming."

Milla had thought her worst fear was to be a demon herself.
But now she knew what her worst fear was. It was this. Locked
in this cell with Iris, the demon who was eating Iris up from the
inside coming to make a meal of Milla, too. She'd lost all her
bluster, all of her belief in herself and in Iris, and it was all she
could do to keep from emptying her bladder in her dress.

"Are you afraid, Niklasssss?" Iris shouted. "Afraid of me? Is
that why you never touch me, Niklassssss? Because you're afraid?
Is that why you put me in this cell, Niklassssss? Because you're
afraid? You've always been afraid, Niklasssssss. That's what Milla
told me. I know eeeeeverything about you, Niklassssssss. How
you used to cry when she told you stories. Because you're such a
big baaaaaaby, Niklassssss."

Milla's terror turned to shame. Things that Milla had confided
in Iris were coming out of her as poison. Nasty and cutting and
bitter. Milla hadn't intended to hurt Niklas by telling his secrets,
had she? Milla had only been lonely, had only wanted a friend—
someone to love her. To *see* her. But now Iris was using Milla's
words to hurt Niklas, and Milla knew it was her fault. All her

fault. She had betrayed Niklas, and Iris had betrayed her.

"Stop it! Stop it, Iris!" Milla jumped up from her crouch and tried to drag Iris away from the door. "Don't say those things!" Iris shrugged Milla off, her back to Milla. Milla grabbed back on, pulling at Iris's dress, her arm. "Please, Iris. Please. Come back to me. I know you're in there."

Iris stilled for a moment. Milla allowed herself to hope. Then Iris turned around to her, and Milla's shame and hope dissolved and fear and abandonment rushed into their place.

The face that looked back at Milla wasn't Iris. Her eyes were the same amber, her skin the same wheat-brown. But something else moved under the surface of her skin, altered its shape. And the voice that passed between her lips wasn't Iris's at all. It belonged to someone else. Someone older and filled with a hate that had been festering for years upon years.

The face that was Iris and not-Iris was so close that Milla could see the bones bulging and reforming themselves as if something had climbed into Iris and was wearing her body as its own. This thing—Iris and not-Iris—smiled at Milla. "Iris is mine now."

18

MILLA HEARD NIKLAS'S BOOTS POUNDING ON THE
stone floor as he ran down the corridor.

When he came to the door Iris backed away from it.

"Let her out, Niklas," Iris said.

"No, Niklas," Milla said. "I'll stay in here. Don't open the door."

Niklas's face was tight with worry, his eyes blinking fast. "Milla, are you all right?"

"I am," Milla said. "I'm fine. But if you open that door, Iris is planning to lock you in here and release all the other girls."

"Why would you tell him that?" For a moment Iris looked like Milla's dear friend whose feelings had been hurt. Her face was her own face, not the demon's. Then the moment passed, and Iris's face turned hard and strange and horrible again. Iris walked toward Milla and pinned her against the wall of the cell, one hand around Milla's throat, leaning in so close to Milla that their foreheads touched. Iris squeezed, and Milla's snakes rose from her head and snapped at Iris's face, but didn't break skin. Milla tried to push Iris away, leaning into Iris with all her strength, but Iris was like stone. Immoveable.

Iris was calm in a way that was more dreadful than her laughing and crying had been. "I'll kill her, Niklas." Her voice was a chorus, Iris mixed with not-Iris.

Milla heard the clank of metal and then the crack of wood hitting stone and the door crashing against the wall as Niklas opened it. And the moment he did, Iris released Milla, and she turned on Niklas and shoved him so hard that his head knocked against the stone wall behind him and he sank to the floor.

"Niklas!" Milla screamed, and she ran to him as Iris dashed through the door.

The girls and women raised such a din of hissing and clanging metal that it was as if the noise were inside Milla's head and chest. She held Niklas by each shoulder. His eyes were closed and his skin was more gray than cream. "Niklas, please. Please be all right, Niklas." She felt tears in the corners of her eyes and panic rise in her belly. She could hear Iris opening the doors of the cells one by one, and the slaps of the girls' bare feet as they ran down the passageway, a quick and excited pitter patter. Niklas's eyes fluttered and then he opened them. "Niklas!" Milla let out a moan of relief.

"Milla," he said, and touched his hand gingerly to the back of his head. It came away with a slick of shiny red on the fingertips.

The clanging had stopped and now Milla could hear the girls' whoops and shouts and hisses as they taunted the boys.

"We're coming to get you, Petter." They shouted down to him.

"We're coming to get all of you. Time for your dousing!"

Milla struggled to calm herself and think through how best to keep Niklas safe. If Iris—her Iris—could threaten to kill Milla, if she could do this to Niklas, then what might the rest of them do to him? To them he was just another boy, like the others who'd tortured them. She hoped for those other boys' sakes that they'd run off. Then again, she was hard pressed to feel sorry for them. "Can you get up? We need to leave, Niklas." Milla rose and held him by the hands to help him stand. He wavered on his feet at first, but then steadied himself. "Can you walk?"

He nodded, and she picked up one of his arms and brought it around her shoulder. She looked outside the cell and saw the corridor was empty, then she led Niklas out and toward the ladder. She looked down at the girls and women in burlap running below, hair streaming around them, laughing and hollering like children playing a game. One stopped and peered up at her. Faded red eyebrows, faded red eyelashes and hair. Leah. She smiled wide and sharp. Then she ran off.

"All right, Niklas," Milla said. "Can you climb down?"

Niklas nodded at her, but looked troubled. "I saw something. But I couldn't have seen it."

"What?" she asked, even though she knew already what Niklas meant. Her snakes had hidden themselves away again, under her hair. But Niklas had seen them rise up when Iris's hands were around her throat, had seen them try to fight off Iris.

"There were . . . snakes. Coming from . . . there." He pointed to her hair, like a small child pointing at something he didn't know the word for. "I saw them. But I couldn't have."

Milla couldn't lie to him now. She didn't have the will. She loosened her hair with her fingers, encouraging her snakes to show themselves. They rose up to greet her brother.

Niklas stared openmouthed. Then he took a step backward, just as she had done with Iris. Milla didn't think she had more heart left to break, but as it turned out, she did.

"I'm still me. I'm Milla." Her snakes hid themselves away again. "Please. Come with me."

As she climbed down the ladder, she looked up at him all the while, begging him with her eyes to follow.

When Milla reached the bottom, Niklas paused one moment longer, leaving her to wonder if he'd stay where he was rather than go with her, a girl with snakes on her head. But then he started down, and Milla scanned the passageway for signs of danger. The girls had all run out, it seemed, and there were no signs of the boys, either. Perhaps they'd had the sense to get away. Milla hoped it was that.

She stepped away from the ladder to make room for Niklas. At the bottom, he turned toward her and then he took one of her hands in his. "Let's go home," he said.

Milla knew they had no time to waste, but she threw her arms around him nonetheless. They held onto each other one moment longer than either of them needed to, and then they both turned toward the doors that led to the outer ring of the fort. Milla could hear the screams and laughter of the girls. She hoped they were so consumed by their escape—by the joy of breathing in clean night air after so long crouched in dank, airless stone—that they wouldn't notice or care that Milla and Niklas were making their own escape. She took Niklas's hand as they emerged into the moonlight.

To their left, most of the girls and women were gathered, hissing and laughing and undulating like one creature with many heads—Iris's coiling, rust-red hair a bright spot among them. After traveling all this way to save Iris, Milla felt sick with defeat and self-disgust. Was she really going to leave here without Iris? Milla's eyes lingered on Iris, willing her to look back, to show her the eyes of a friend and not a demon.

"Come, Milla," Niklas said.

Milla looked back at him. "Iris," she said.

"She's a demon girl now," he said.

Demon girl. Is that what the boys called them? Did that not make her still a girl? Or did the girl part of her no longer matter? Once again she looked at Iris, willing her friend to look back, to show Milla some part of herself that was still Iris. As if in response, Iris threw her arms up in the air and hissed. Then all the demon girls did the same, their arms rising up together, then weaving and interlacing.

Niklas grabbed Milla's hand and pulled.

The arched passage to the outside of the fort was directly in front of Milla and Niklas, and they both looked at it, measuring the distance between them and it. She and Niklas began to walk toward it slowly, purposefully, silently agreeing that a frantic sprint would only draw the girls' attention. Milla wanted to believe that the girls wouldn't hurt her—that they sensed in her someone as afflicted as they were, someone who would never wish to hurt them. But then she thought of Iris's hand tightening around her throat, of the blood darkening Niklas's hair, and of the howling and the frenzy, and she knew she couldn't be sure of what any of them might do. They weren't girls with thought and reason of their own anymore; they were all Hulda. Single-minded and furious.

Milla and Niklas walked. Each step caused her heart to tighten painfully, anticipating the moment that the girls would turn on them.

The hissing was terrible, but it was a different kind of eerie when the hissing stopped. As one body, the girls fell silent and stared at Milla and Niklas as they walked past.

Halfway between the door to The Place and the arch in the outer wall, Niklas halted. Milla looked at him, confused. Was he faint? Was he unwell?

Niklas looked to his right, and in an instant Milla knew what he was looking at. The bell.

She shook her head, horrified that he'd even think of it. "No, Niklas."

"Milla, I have to ring the bell. Then Ragna will know the girls are out. She'll warn the village."

"Warn them of what? Those girls won't go back to the village. That's the last place they'll go. Those are the people who sent them *here*. Besides, the boys have all run off. Surely they'll have warned Ragna."

Niklas gave her a skeptical look. "Milla, they *hate* her."

Milla was painfully aware of the stares of the girls, the passage of time, everything slipping away. She could feel them behind her, their interest ever more aroused. "Niklas. *Please*. Do not ring that bell." She looked at the horses in the paddock. "When we ride by Ragna's cottage we can warn her." She would say anything to get Niklas out of there, to get out of there herself, and she reasoned that the girls would still have plenty of time to scatter. Ragna couldn't go after all of them by herself, and by the time she'd gotten to the village, the girls would be safe somewhere else. Iris among them.

Niklas nodded and they walked to the horses. Then Milla saw them: five more girls, crouched on the far side of the paddock. Milla's lungs tightened and she grabbed Niklas's arm. The girls blinked at Milla. Once. Twice. Milla saw in their eyes and how they clung together that they were as frightened as she and Niklas were. Milla moved toward them, her hand cupped in front of her as if she were approaching a wary, possibly dangerous animal. "Come with us," she said to them. "We'll take you home. You're safe." Were they, though? How could she promise them that? They were so thin, like girls made of sticks. Like Asta, bound and mutely suffering in Ragna's cottage. Milla wondered how these girls could have the strength to move, but when they saw that Milla and Niklas meant to help them leave, they scrambled to their feet. Milla and Niklas handed the girls the reins to three of the horses and together they led the horses through the outer arch of the fort, the demon girls behind them still silent and watching.

The moon washed the meadow in shades of blue and darker blue. The strongest of the girls mounted one of the horses; the other four mounted horses two by two, their burlap dresses hitched up around their legs showing their livid bruises and scraped knees. The girls were all knobs and angles, but they looked fiercer now, the night air expanding their lungs and ruffling the ends of their matted hair. Milla and Niklas each mounted the two remaining horses. They would go to Ragna's, but not to warn her, as Niklas wished to do. Milla knew it was evil of her—and she could taste the nastiness of her loathing on her tongue—but she didn't care whether Ragna survived this night. The girls could have the midwife and do what they wanted with her. There was only one reason to visit Ragna tonight, and that was to save Asta.

19

LIGHT FLICKERED IN THE WINDOWS OF RAGNA'S COTTAGE, though Milla could tell by the angle of the moon that it was now well past midnight. Then the light shifted and Milla saw Ragna's tall, strong outline.

Milla and Niklas dismounted, but the girls stayed on their horses. "Asta is in there," Milla said to them. "Will you help us get her out?" She looked at the girls' shadowed faces, at the way memories of this place passed across each one, the pain still fresh.

As the girls all dismounted, Niklas whispered to Milla, "They're so small and worn out, Milla. I don't think they'll be much help."

"We're stronger than we look," one of the girls said. Her voice came out hoarse, unused. She was Milla's height but half her width. Still the girl shoved between Niklas and Milla, sending each of them stumbling to one side, and she slapped barefoot up to Ragna's door. "Open up, you witch! And give us Asta!"

A girl's voice called from inside the cottage. "Ellinor! Is that you?"

"It's me, Asta!" Ellinor looked over her shoulder at Milla and Niklas. "I'm getting Asta out of there if I have to burn this cottage down, and Ragna with it."

"There won't be any need for that," Milla said, walking toward the window where Ragna stood, staring back. "Will there, Ragna? Open up. We want Asta and then you can stay or leave as you please."

Milla saw Ragna's eyes widen, circled with white. Ragna retreated backward from the window, and then Milla saw why. Two of the girls were dragging something between them toward the window. An axe. Niklas started to run toward them, but Milla put herself in his way.

The girls lifted and swung, and Ragna's front window shattered inward.

"Milla, this is wrong," Niklas said.

"Ragna had her chance to open the door. They just want Asta. They won't hurt her if they don't have to."

Niklas tried to move past Milla, but she put herself in his way again. While Ellinor and the other four girls cleared the window of glass and climbed into the cottage, Milla grabbed Niklas by the shoulders. "*Go.*"

"Home? Without you? No!"

"You don't belong here, Niklas." This hurt him. She could see it in his eyes.

"Milla! You don't know what you're saying." It struck Milla how strange that phrase was, and how often she heard it, or some variation. *You don't know what you're saying, Milla. You don't know what you're doing, Milla. You don't know what you're thinking, or feeling, or wanting, Milla.* Anyway, when people said that to her they didn't really mean that she didn't *know*. Of course she knew. They meant she was wrong. But she wasn't wrong.

Milla placed a hand on either side of her brother's face, which was hopeful even in this moment, and so different from her own.

She felt full of knowing. The knowing rose to her throat; she tasted it in her mouth. It tasted of grass and dirt and the undersides of damp rocks. This knowing had been growing inside her ever since her mother pinched the first snake from her head.

"Look at me, Niklas." She took her hands from his face and ran them through her hair, encouraging her snakes up and up. "What do you think Mamma would say when she saw me? What do you think Pappa would *do*?"

Niklas's open face collapsed. "No, Milla. No. Please. I can't leave you. I won't."

She wrapped her arms around him, pressing her cheek to his chest, feeling his heartbeat in her ear. She listened for two beats, three. She memorized the sound. Then she looked up at him, and she had to blink to see him clearly. "If I can ever come home again, I will."

Niklas's face changed, and he wasn't looking at her any longer, he was looking past her, over her. His mouth slid open.

Then she heard it: the sound of breath forced between many sets of teeth. The demon girls.

She turned around and her own mouth gaped. The moon had set, and she felt the chill of predawn. But that wasn't what raised the hair on Milla's arms. The demon girls surged toward Ragna's cottage—they flowed, they *snaked*. They were still minutes away and yet their hissing sizzled through the air like meat hitting a hot pan. "Iris is with them," Milla said. "I can't leave now. I have to try to talk to her one more time. But you must leave, Niklas. They'll hurt you. They're so angry. I can feel it in my bones like . . . like it's a part of me, too." And she did feel it in her bones. Like a hum. She looked up at Niklas again, took his shirt in her fists and shoved him backward toward the road. "Go." Her snakes reared back and snapped, hissing in chorus.

Niklas looked at her—all of her, girl and snakes—and then behind her at the surging, roiling, hissing mass. "You'll come home Milla. Someday. I know you will."

She blinked at him. Once. Twice. *I see you. See me.*

Niklas mounted his horse and looked back at her. She held up a hand to match the one he held up. She hated herself for wanting to catch his hand in her own, for wanting to say, *You're right, Niklas, I don't know what I'm saying. Tell me what to do, Niklas. Tell me this doesn't have to be so hard, Niklas. Tell me how to go home.* But she didn't do that. Instead, she watched as he turned away from her and kicked his horse forward toward the village. Milla's snakes wrapped their cool bodies around her neck, rested their heads on her shoulders, and hissed softly, reassuringly. She hated herself again for half hoping Niklas might still turn around. But he didn't, and she told herself that she didn't really want him to.

20

THE FRONT DOOR TO RAGNA'S COTTAGE OPENED, AND Ellinor emerged with her arm around Asta's waist. The other girls trailed behind. Milla didn't have to tell them the demon girls were coming. They all turned toward the sound of their hissing. "We have to leave. Now. Or they'll make us stay with them," Asta said.

Milla said, "Why?"

"Because the demon will tell them to," Ellinor said. "It's not their fault. They can't help themselves."

Asta's legs wobbled under her, and Ellinor urged her forward toward the horse she'd ridden there. The girls all mounted their horses, two by two, but Milla hesitated, stood staring down the road. She could see Iris. She could call to her if she wanted. What if Milla could talk to Iris, she thought. What if there was still hope for her? For them? She remembered back when she'd first met Iris. Iris had said that the two of them could leave, could go . . . anywhere. Maybe she could get Iris to go somewhere, anywhere, with her now. Now that she was free.

"You go," Milla said to them.

Ellinor's eyebrows came together. "You think you'll be able to talk to her. But you can't. You'll see. For a moment she'll seem like your friend, but then the demon will snatch her back."

"I have to try," Milla said. Asta reached out, and Milla took her hand for just a moment, felt the bones under her skin, and the sinew holding them together. "Good-bye. I hope . . . I hope you find home again."

Asta looked over Milla's head and her face filled with loathing.

"There's no home for them." It was Ragna. She stood in her open doorway, her arms crossed over her chest.

"You're not in our heads anymore," Ellinor said. Then she smiled. "They're coming, Ragna. They're coming for you."

The other girls laughed. Repeated what Ellinor had said in singsong voices. *They're cooooming for you, Ragna.* Even after the girls were off, Milla heard their laughter carried back on the dawn breeze, chiming like bells.

Ragna took a step backward. Whatever certainty had remained in her after the girls shattered her window, it fell away from her now. Milla said to her, "You should have opened up when we asked. You still had time to get away. Now your only hope is that your shutters hold."

Ragna slammed her door, and by the time she'd closed and locked the last shutter, Milla and her mare were surrounded on all sides by the demon girls. She remembered the first one she saw in The Place, and how she realized that the girl who stood in front of her was no child; she was a woman whose life had been taken from her. But since the girls had left The Place, even the oldest among them looked like a girl again. They might have lines on their faces, and even touches of silver in their hair, but their eyes were bright and they crackled with energy, like fires that had just caught, their flames licking high and thirsty.

Iris, though, was calm, as if something in her had been quenched. She stepped out of the mass of girls that circled Milla, and Milla could see in her eyes that the only light in there belonged to Iris. Her face was its familiar heart shape. "Iris?" Milla said to her, turning her friend's name into a question.

Iris took her hand. "It's me," she said. "For now."

Milla looked around her at the other girls, not hissing now, but staring and quiet, as if waiting for a signal—or an order. She kept her voice low. "Leave here with me," she said. "We can climb on this horse and go."

"Go where?" Iris said. "You with your snakes growing from your head, and me with the voice inside mine. Where would we go that people wouldn't run us off or lock us up?"

"We don't need people," Milla said. "We can take care of ourselves."

Iris cocked her head. "Chickens don't grow on trees. And nothing grows on trees in the winter."

"What else can we do?" Milla said.

"Come with us." Iris squeezed her hand. "To the mother."

Spark. There it was. The light that wasn't Iris, and yet inside her. Getting brighter by the second.

"The mother? You mean your mother? My mother?"

"Not them," Iris said, her lips thinning. "They don't want us. They never did. No. *Our* mother," Iris said. "*The* mother. We're going to her. She loves us, and she's going to take care of us. But first"—Iris looked over her shoulder at Ragna's cottage—"the mother is going to take care of *her*."

The anger that Milla had felt humming in her bones now vibrated so powerfully that her teeth chattered. It was all around her—under her as well. She felt it from her feet to the tips of her hair. A spot of heat bloomed in her belly so suddenly that Milla looked down, but there was nothing there, and the heat expanded through her torso like a live coal in a pot. Milla scanned the landscape around her to find a source of the humming, but there were only the demon girls, quiet, still, and waiting, and Ragna's cottage, shut up tight, and the clear dawn sky, all pink except for a few soot-black clouds.

Something about those clouds held Milla's attention. Her snakes stretched high, straining even higher, as if trying to get a closer look. The clouds were moving, spreading, changing shape faster than any clouds Milla had ever seen. It was as if the clouds were gathering together overhead—pulled to this spot from north, south, east, and west. Then it seemed to Milla that the humming was even louder and the quality of the sound was different, more jagged. It was no longer a humming; it was a buzzing.

Milla's eyes widened and she sucked in air and she realized those were no clouds at all. They were swarms upon swarms of wasps, pulling together, forming a funnel pointed directly at Ragna's chimney.

The girls were no longer silent; they were giddy. They giggled and clapped. They danced. Milla thought she might be sick. She grabbed Iris by the wrist. "What's happening?"

"It's the mother," she said. "She sent them to punish Ragna. Now she'll never hurt us again." Iris smiled.

The demon girls had lost interest in Milla, they were so over-joyed at the sight of the vicious cloud of wasps filling the air overhead, pouring now into Ragna's chimney.

Milla heard screaming inside, and she clapped her hands over her ears. The girls circled the house as if about to sing and play a child's game. They held hands and looked up expectantly. The sky was turning more golden than pink and the light shone down on their faces and Milla might almost have thought them beau-tiful if it weren't for what she imagined was happening inside Ragna's cottage—just the midwife and all those angry wasps.

Iris had left her side and joined the other girls, her joy as thorough as theirs. Milla put her hand on the mare that still stood patiently beside her. She didn't paw or stomp the ground. Her ears were up and alert and she looked back at Milla. Milla's father had trained her not to view animals as anything but what they were. Creatures to be worked, or eaten. Or worked and then eaten. They weren't people. They didn't have thoughts. But if Milla were looking for something or someone to tell her what to do, she saw it in her own mirror reflection in the mare's wet eyes. Milla looked like a lonely, terrified child who didn't belong here. She pulled herself into the saddle, and then she buried her head in her hands and wept. She didn't belong here, but she had no idea where else to go.

Milla felt the earth move beneath her, but it wasn't the earth, it was the mare, walking. Milla gathered the reins in her hands but she didn't attempt to direct her, because the mare had ideas of her own. She wasn't taking them back to the village; she was headed in the other direction, toward The Place. Milla had no desire to go back there, but nor did she want to go back to that sad, suspicious village. Milla's snakes circled her neck. All that mattered to Milla at that moment was that the mare had made a decision and Milla didn't have to. She was taking them away from the midwife's cottage, the demon girls, and the swarming wasps. If there was anything else that Milla might hope for—in this moment or the next or the one after that—she hadn't the strength to imagine it.

PART THREE

21

MILLA HAD EXPECTED THE MARE TO TURN TOWARD The Place once they came to the open meadow that led there. That would make sense—for her to return to the last place she'd been fed. But instead the mare kept walking. Milla let the reins go slack and the mare continue to lead the way.

The sun was high overhead and the day was hot when the road passed through another lushly green meadow and the horse veered off. At first Milla thought the mare planned to gorge on clover, but she continued on. Through the meadow they went until they came to a path wide enough for the horse, and with only the occasional branch hanging so low that Milla needed to duck. It seem to be an old cow path, grown over but still passable. The mare took her time, careful of her footing, and Milla fell into a thoughtless trance. Then the path widened into another hard-packed road.

"Well, aren't you smart," she said to the horse. Milla felt a pang for Niklas at that moment. He would have liked this horse. Iris would have, as well.

Except for stops at streams, where both the horse and Milla took long drinks, the horse walked on until afternoon became evening became night. Milla's eyelids were so very heavy, and her empty-hearted exhaustion, combined with the gentle rolling gait of the horse, lulled her dangerously close to sleep. More than once she jerked herself awake having nearly fallen off the horse.

The night air grew chill again, and for the first time since the horse had led them away from Ragna's cottage, Milla allowed herself to feel frightened for herself. Perhaps the horse had no more sense than she did, and they were simply wandering. Perhaps they'd both starve. Milla had no idea if another village lay down the road. She was hungry, and she was cold, and she was scared. And then she cried. Her snakes caressed her cheeks, licked her salt tears, and she felt comforted by them. Once she stopped crying, her panic was replaced with a hollowed out feeling, a desolation. A sense of aloneness so profound that she couldn't imagine it ever ending.

When she thought she couldn't possibly go any farther, whether this mare continued on or not, Milla noticed that the forest on either side of the road was thinning to scrub. Then scrub became meadow, which became pasture and then farmland. Farmland meant a farm. A farm meant a house, and a barn, and people. Milla sat up straighter in the saddle. If there was a farmhouse nearby, it was hidden in the dark—too late for a lamp to be burning. Milla struggled to make out a darker mass among the trees. Then the horse turned off onto a smaller road and Milla smelled the familiar scents of home—a place where people lived.

People who made fires, and baked bread, and chopped wood. People who milked cows and spread hay in barns. Then a barn and paddock rose to her left, and beyond it Milla made out a cottage, a bit larger than Jakob and Gitta's. The horse didn't take them to the cottage. Instead she stopped suddenly at the gate to the paddock, and Milla got the distinct sense that the mare felt they'd reached the end of the road.

Milla slid off the horse and unlatched the paddock gate. The mare followed her through the paddock and then into the barn, which softly vibrated with the rhythmic night noises of heavy, deep-breathing animals. The mare made straight for the manger, and while she ate, Milla sat down on the straw-strewn floor. She might have been sitting in manure for all she knew, and she couldn't begin to care. The night spun around her and her ears closed to sound, and then there was nothing.

"Pappa! Fulla is back! And there's a girl with her!" The voice was young, high-pitched, and excited. Then it was gone.

Milla sat up and looked around her. The mare stared at her, still in her saddle and bridle. Not knowing what else to do, Milla stood and took the mare's reins in her hand. The barn door was open, early morning light catching dust so it sparkled in the air. In walked a girl who looked to be about nine. Her hair was a mass of black curls that sprang from her head like living things, and she had bright, lamp-lit amber eyes. Milla thought instantly of Iris. Not because she looked like her, but because there was the same restlessness sparking inside her.

The girl held the hand of a man whose hair was a shorter, neater mass of black curls. He didn't spark the way his daughter did. "What's this now?" he said.

"I'm sorry," Milla said. "It was late, and I was tired. I thought it would be all right if I slept here."

At first she thought she read suspicion in his eyes, but then she realized it was simply puzzlement. "Why were you out in the middle of the night all alone? Where's your home?"

"I don't have one." Her first answer was her most honest. "I lived with my grandmother. But she died." Milla didn't know where the words were coming from, but she let them flow and decided to see where they led her. "So I left the village and decided to find somewhere I might work. You wouldn't need help around here, would you? I can cook and clean. Tend a garden and feed chickens. I work hard, and I'm never sick." Words, words, and more words, and she wasn't even sure what she was angling for. Did she really want to stay here and work on this family's farm? How would that be any different from the life she'd always led? But hunger and the craving for a bed were powerful things, and she thought she might tolerate more of the same for a while—till she got her bearings and formed a plan for what to do next.

The man cocked his head at her. "You're hungry, I expect. Liss, take her in to your mother." He nodded to the mare. "Fulla, you found your way home." He removed her bridle, stroking and patting her, then he unsaddled her.

Liss smiled at Milla so wide that her oval face went round. She grabbed Milla's hand. "Come. It's time for breakfast. Mamma will take care of you."

The girl's words caused Milla to bristle and lean away from her. Milla didn't want a Mamma to take care of her.

Liss's smile shrank. "What's wrong?"

Milla struggled to control herself, to make her face placid and pleasant. "Nothing," she said, closing the space between them again. "It's just that I've never been away from home before."

"Oh," Liss said, her face serious and thoughtful. Then she brightened again. "But you'll like it here. You'll see." Her tone turned confiding. "And just so you know, Mamma needs help with my brother. Babies are terrible. Anyone who tells you otherwise is lying."

When they reached the log cottage, the front door was open to the morning breeze. The cottage's grass roof was brilliant green and sparkled with damp. Everything here was healthy and bright and untouched by the insects that marched in lines under the doors of the village and turned the surrounding fields and forest to dust. Maybe Milla had truly left it all behind. Maybe the worst was over now that the girls had been freed and the midwife was surely dead. Milla wanted to believe that, but then her snakes squirmed.

Milla's hope was a delicate creature, and it bruised at the lightest touch.

22

MILLA SAT AT KATRIN AND OTTO'S WOODEN TABLE
breakfasting on bread with butter and jam, and slices of cheese
and cold chicken. She tried not to look as wild as she felt. The
moment Katrin had set the food before Milla, it was all she could
do not to tear it apart and stuff it in her mouth by the handful.

Katrin's face had made an O of surprise when she first saw
Milla at her door, but then she smiled and welcomed Milla to
her table as if it were a typical sort of thing to have a girl awaken
in your barn. First though, Katrin led Milla to the well in back
and handed her a washcloth and a bar of soap. Milla saw Katrin's
eyes travel to Milla's hands. Her nails were black with dirt. Milla
flushed with embarrassment, and Katrin smiled wordlessly and
touched her arm before leaving her alone.

Milla scrubbed her hands, face, and neck with soap and crisply
cold well water, and the cloth came away brown. Her filth was

something she hadn't thought about in days—not since she left home for The Place. It was disconcerting to be doing this routine thing in a place that looked like home, but wasn't home. Milla wondered if she should drop the cloth right there, fetch Fulla, and keep going. Then she thought that Fulla would be very unlikely to want to go with her. Nor could Milla blame her. The mare had done enough.

In any case, Milla knew that she wasn't going anywhere. At least not right now. She was starving. And so tired it was an effort to breathe. For the moment she needed food and shelter. That was all she could think about. All that made sense.

So she sat at the breakfast table like a good girl, and after she'd eaten enough that she could concentrate on something other than her hunger, she began to examine her surroundings. Liss was a chatty one. A little sly, but well-behaved. She made faces at her baby brother, Kai, who was just old enough to walk and babble nonsense. He sat in a high chair scooping up fistfuls of oatmeal despite Katrin's attempt to guide the food to his mouth with a spoon. This made Liss laugh. Katrin was gentle. Motherly. She smiled.

Milla took this in: Katrin smiled at Liss. A mother smiled at her daughter. She didn't look at her with fear.

Then Milla scanned the rest of the room. There were no streams of salt across the window frames or doorways or hearth. Katrin and Otto lived like people who didn't expect to lose their daughter to a demon. Who might not even know what a demon was.

Otto chucked Kai under his chin and the baby cackled and sprayed oatmeal. This caused Liss to laugh harder. Katrin wiped drool and milk from Kai's chin and handed her husband the spoon. "Here, you take it. And just so you know, the idea is to get the oatmeal *inside* the baby."

Otto took a big spoonful of the oatmeal, started for Kai's mouth, but then reversed the spoon and began to steer it toward his own. The baby's mouth and eyes opened with anticipation and Otto held the spoon just outside his mouth, held it, held it, and waggled his eyebrows at the baby. The baby screamed with laughter and reached for the spoon, and then Otto ate the oatmeal himself. Then he handed Kai the spoon and said, "All right. Now you."

Kai took the spoon in his hand and Otto looked at Katrin triumphantly. "See," he said.

Kai slapped the spoon down on the surface of the oatmeal, sloshing and spraying it over the sides of the bowl. Slap, slap, slap.

Katrin raised an eyebrow. "Yes," she said. "I see. Very smart."

"Kai, you rascal!" Otto scooped him up.

Liss looked at Milla. "I told you. Babies are terrible."

Milla smiled despite herself.

Katrin stood and wiped Kai's face and untied his bib. "You," she said to him, and kissed him on his round, sticky cheek. Then she kissed Otto's cheek as well. "Liss, take your brother out to play while we talk to Milla."

"But, Mamma," Liss said. "I want to talk to Milla, too. You'll let her stay, won't you?"

"Liss." Katrin looked at her daughter, and Milla sensed unspoken communication. An understanding. Trust between them that there were reasons for what mother was asking daughter.

Liss sighed and took Kai from her father.

The baby looked at Milla. Then he made a sound that caused Milla's hair to rise all the way from the nape of her neck down to the small of her back.

"Ssssss. Sssssss. Ssssssssssss." He hissed. Right to *her*. To Milla. Had the rest of them heard it? She looked around the room frantically, searching for proof that they'd all heard it, seen it, and would also stare at her and point and call her: *Demon. Snake girl.*

Liss laughed, oblivious to Milla's panic. "That's what he calls me, Milla, isn't it funny? Say my name, silly. It's not Sssss. It's *Liss*. Say it, silly. *Liss*."

"Ssssssss. Sssssss. Sssss."

"You sound like a snake," Liss said. "Mamma, I wanted a baby brother, not a snake. Send this one back and ask for another."

"Liss," Katrin said.

"All right. All right, I'm going. Come, Snake."

"Snnnnnn. Snnnnnn. Snnnn."

"Oh heavens, Liss. You'll have him thinking that's his name. Off with you." Otto waved her toward the door.

Liss held Kai in front of her and looked over her shoulder at Milla on her way out. She smiled. "Come find us in the meadow. Kai likes to try to catch butterflies. But don't worry. He never can."

Katrin placed a mug of tea in front of Milla. "How did you happen to come by our Fulla? We were sad to sell her, but she's one more than we need, and she's getting old for pulling."

Milla couldn't think what to say, so she stalled. "She's a wonderful horse. Took me right here. And now I know why."

"Sweet old thing," Katrin said.

"The woman from the far village who bought her from me," Otto said. "I can't remember her name, but she said she was a midwife. Any relation?"

"No," Milla said. She felt her snakes tighten around her head, insulted by the suggestion. "How long ago was that?" Milla wondered what he'd thought of the village. If it was as sad and threatening a place then, Otto would have to say so. It was too glaring a thing not to mention.

"Oh, let me think. Had to have been a year ago," Otto said. "No one in the near village wanted our Fulla. At least not at the price I wanted. So I took her to the spring market in the far village. I hadn't been to the far village in years. It always felt . . . unfriendly to me." He shrugged. "Liss insisted on going with me, and I should have said no. Oh how she cried when I sold our Fulla."

"She gets attached to the animals," Katrin said. "A dangerous thing for a farm girl to do. Our horses aren't pets. But she doesn't have much company here," Katrin said. "She gets lonely. She looked forward to Kai coming, but then once he was born she realized that he wouldn't be much of a playmate for a few years yet. In the meantime, he's just more work for her."

"Yes," Milla said. It occurred to her that Otto and Katrin were so chatty that she could let them talk and maybe she'd never have to say anything at all.

Katrin looked at her with gentle eyes, her thick dark eyebrows knit together in the center. "You must miss your grandmother. And you've really no other kin?"

"No," Milla said. "They're all dead."

"It happens," Otto said. "I lost all of mine when I wasn't much older than you. But at least I had the farm." He looked at Katrin and raised his eyebrows. She nodded.

"Milla," Katrin said. "We really could use your help. We haven't much to offer. But you'd have your own bed, and we'd treat you as one of our own. We'd ask no more of you than we'd ask of Liss if she were your age."

"Oh," Milla said. "Oh. Yes. I'd be most grateful." Milla felt a combination of relief and dread in her belly. Now that she had been offered what she'd hoped for, was this really the right thing? How could she possibly know? Not for the first time, she wished there were a voice in her head to say, *yes, yes, Milla, exactly right, stay there*. But when she needed it most, there was no voice. There was just her own trembling, uncertain heart. She told herself that for today, this was the right thing. When it was no longer the right thing . . . then she would figure out what was.

Katrin smiled at her. "Good," she said. "Good."

Otto smiled, too. "It's settled then. To the fields with me. I'll see you at dinner." He kissed Katrin on the forehead and ran a hand over her tightly braided hair.

Once he was gone, Katrin led Milla up to a pleasant room with a peaked ceiling, a window looking out over the garden, and two narrow beds. "You'll share with Liss." She ran her eyes over Milla's dress. "You're slimmer than I am, but taller. I have a few dresses and night shifts I'll give you."

"Oh," Milla said. "But not if you need them."

Katrin smiled at her, touched her arm. Milla was learning that this was Katrin's way of saying, *I understand, and we don't need to speak of it.*

"And an apron, too."

An apron. Milla remembered the apron she'd left in the mud next to the spring back home. She felt overcome with weariness and the recurring, heart-numbing fear that she was making a terrible mistake. If she wore Katrin's clean apron, would that change her back into the sort of girl who did such things? Would her snakes shrink away to nothing, or possibly worse: rise up in protest? Her green snake nipped her scalp.

"You must be tired," Katrin said. "Rest. I'll wake you for dinner."

"I can help with dinner," Milla said. "I should help."

Again Katrin smiled, touched her arm. Then Katrin left and quietly closed the door behind her. Milla looked at the bed that was now hers. She lay down on it, and her aching body sank into its softness. What a weak-willed creature she was. Defiant one moment, and crying with relief the next. She reached her hands into her hair and gave each of her snakes a long stroke. "You must keep us safe," she said. "These people are kind, but they won't understand you. So. Please. Keep us safe."

Milla closed her eyes, and her snakes settled in, hidden away in her thick, black hair. She slept.

23

IN THE SLENDER MONTH BETWEEN SUMMER AND WINTER, there was more work than could be done by Otto and Katrin even with Milla's help. Two men from the near village helped Otto with the harvest, while Milla helped Katrin preserve jar upon jar of vegetables to hold them through the frozen months. Milla fell into the familiar rhythm of working alongside another woman, doing the things that must be done to keep a family fed and clothed and clean.

Once that fall, Milla visited the near village with Otto and Liss. She hadn't wanted to. Katrin was being kind in encouraging her to go, thinking she might enjoy the distraction, but Milla would have preferred to be left alone. That was when she felt most comfortable, most herself—when there was no one around to please. With Katrin and Otto she felt the need to be sweet and grateful—and in truth she was grateful—but the effort involved in showing it all the time made her feel trapped. Milla thought of all those people in the village—so many people to try to be well-behaved for—and sweat dampened her hairline. She felt cramped and breathless.

This village hugged the road, same as the other village had, but the people were more curious than suspicious. And the market was full of ripe, healthy apples and unblemished potatoes and fat livestock. There was a din of haggling and sociable chatter and shrieks of children chasing each other among the stalls. Otto bought her and Liss sweet buns studded with raisins.

Milla was only half in her body all that day. She felt the curious eyes on her, the strange girl whom Otto and Katrin had found in their barn. She'd taken care with her appearance, wearing an old dress of Katrin's made of moss-green wool. She combed her hair. She no longer worried that her snakes might show themselves; they knew better. But still she felt like an oddity. All around her there were people, their mouths perpetually wagging with words. Milla couldn't imagine having that much to say to anyone anymore. The only people she'd ever been able to talk to that way—never running out of things to say—were Niklas and Iris. And just the thought of how much she missed them turned the doughy bread in her mouth to sand.

Liss chatted and pointed and laughed, filling the too-wide space between her and Milla. Milla had a feeling that Liss did this on purpose, that she knew how Milla struggled with words. Beneath Liss's easy smiles, there was a bright intelligence—the snap that Milla had sensed in her that first morning in the barn. Milla wondered if she'd buzzed the same way when she was that age. She remembered how easily stories had come to her as a child, but it was as if her desire to make words had died at The Place. Now she just wanted to be quiet. Still, despite herself,

Milla felt herself warming more to Liss every day. She told herself not to get too attached, not to let her guard down. She imagined what Liss's face would look like if she ever saw Milla's snakes. Best not to get too close, Milla told herself. Not even to Liss. Especially not. If Liss ever looked at her the way Gitta had, Milla didn't think she could bear it.

Then there was Katrin. Milla sensed Katrin's desire to be motherly with her, and it was a struggle for her to be kind in the face of it. Why must a mother's love come with so many rules? Katrin was warmer and easier with Milla than Gitta had ever been, but still Milla felt the judgment in her eyes. The gentle nudge toward the wash basin. The reminders that she probably meant to be subtle, but weren't subtle at all. And always the observations about Milla's appearance. Katrin seemed to think it a nice thing to tell Milla that she would look pretty with her hair braided. But what Milla heard was that Katrin didn't approve of Milla's hair the way it was. Too wild, too unkempt. Once Katrin had offered to show Milla how to braid her hair around her head the way Katrin wore hers. When Katrin lifted her hand as if to touch a lock of Milla's hair, Milla flinched away from her. Katrin's face showed hurt and surprise.

"I'm sorry," Milla said. That old, familiar word. She was using it again, so often. "I'm just tender-headed. I wouldn't even let my grandmother touch my hair." Then Milla smiled in a way that she hoped said, *let's forget all about this*. Katrin smiled back in a way that said, *you're a strange girl and I certainly won't try to touch your hair again*.

The air had smelled like snow all day, and the clouds were so low and heavy that they seemed to settle on the treetops. Just before supper, the first snowflakes fell. By supper's end, the world outside the cottage was frosted white.

Once dishes were cleared and washed, Milla and Katrin worked on a pile of mending, while Otto rubbed grease into his boots. Liss rolled a wooden ball across the floor to Kai, who was supposed to roll the ball back to her. Instead of rolling it, though, he cackled louder each time and carried the ball back to Liss, dropping it at her feet. Then he waddled away from her as fast as he could.

Liss put her hands on her hips. "Kai, that's not the way you play the game."

"Apparently it's the way Kai plays the game," Otto said, and winked at Liss.

Liss walked over to Kai and picked him up like a sack. "All right, you. Time for a story." She sat at her mother's feet with Kai in her lap.

Katrin set down her mending and ran her fingers through Liss's springy curls. "Such beautiful hair you have, Liss." She lifted up a curl and wrapped it around her finger.

"She's getting to be as lovely as her Mamma," Otto said.

Milla kept her hands moving—needle through fabric, needle through fabric—and her eyes on her work.

"Once there was a little snake," Liss said. She tickled Kai.

"Sssssss. Sssss. Sssssss," Kai said.

"And that little snake thought himself very smart and very beautiful. And also very big. He went around quite puffed up, as a matter of fact. He slithered by an anthill and said, you're all so very little. I could eat every single one of you with just a lick of my tongue. And the ants all said, oh please, don't eat us. We're too small to be much of a meal. A big snake like you wants something big to fill his belly. And the snake agreed that the ants weren't at all a worthy dinner for him, so he moved on. Then he saw a ladybug, and as he passed her, he swished her with his tail. The ladybug called after him, saying, well that wasn't very nice. The snake looked back at her and said, you shouldn't say such things to me because I could eat you. I'm a very big snake. And she said, oh, you wouldn't want to eat me. I taste very bad. And the snake thought he'd heard that about ladybugs, so once again he moved on. He passed all kinds of creatures after that. Flitting moths, busy grasshoppers, fierce dragonflies. And to every single one he bragged about how big he was and how he could make a quick meal of them. And every single one talked him out of it, flattering the snake that they were much too unimportant and not tasty enough for such a pretty, smart, big snake as he. And the snake agreed with every one of them. By the end of the day, the snake was feeling so pretty and so smart and so big, that he slithered right up to a . . ." Liss stopped her story and tickled Kai. "What do you think he slithered up to, Kai? Do you remember?"

"Goose! Goose! Goose!" Kai clapped his hands.

"That's right! The snake slithered right up to a goose, and he very proudly said, you look like a plump, tasty meal for a snake as big as me! Well, that goose was so amused by this that she laughed and laughed. And the snake was quite offended at first, but something about the way that goose laughed and stomped her quite large goose feet, made the snake think that perhaps he wasn't *quite* as big as he thought he was. So the snake said to the goose, yes, ha ha ha, that is very funny. And you are a very big, very handsome goose, and I think I'll be going. Well, the goose looked at him with two black, beady goose eyes and said, oh no, I don't think so, little snake. I think I shall be making a meal of *you.* Well, now our smart little snake needed to be a fast little snake, and he slithered right between the goose's legs and down a tiny little hole that only a very tiny little snake could fit into. And when our snake was safe down that hole, he heard the goose above him go snap snap snap with her beak." And here Liss stopped to snap at Kai with her thumbs and index fingers like little jaws. Kai squirmed and giggled. "And our smart little snake thought that really, after all, it was a very fine thing to be quite tiny."

Otto and Katrin clapped. "Liss, you tell a very good story," Otto said.

"Silly snake," Katrin said. "I'm glad he learned his lesson. Best not try to be something you're not."

Milla resisted the temptation to reach into her hair, to remind herself of what she was. Instead, she kept her eyes on her sewing. Needle through fabric. Needle through fabric.

That night, when Milla and Liss climbed into their beds, Milla thought of Iris and her stories. "That was a good story," Milla said.

"Kai likes it. Mamma and Pappa, too. My favorite is one about two children, a brother and a sister, who get lost in the woods. But Mamma doesn't like that one."

"Oh? What happens to them?"

The room was dark, but Milla could hear Liss turn on her side. "They meet a witch. But they don't know she's a witch. And she offers them wishes."

"Wishes never go well, do they?"

Liss laughed. "No."

"So what happens to these poor doomed children?"

"The witch eats them, of course."

"Of course," Milla said. "They must have broken the rules. That always happens with wishes."

"Not in my story," Liss said.

"No?"

"No. In my story, they get eaten *because* they follow the rules."

"That's a twist," Milla said.

"All those stories about doing what witches tell you are silly. Why would you do what a witch tells you?"

"Hm," Milla said.

Silence fell between them, and Milla knew Liss's night noises well enough now to recognize the moment she'd drifted off.

It was only at such times that Milla's snakes emerged from her mass of hair and rested their heads on her shoulders. She looked forward to these moments. She closed her eyes and stroked their cool, smooth skin and thought, *I wish I knew your names.* It didn't occur to her to name them herself. She felt certain they had names already.

Then she heard two soft, smooth, distinct voices in her head. And two distinct words to go with those voices. The first voice said, *Sverd.* The second voice said, *Selv.*

Milla lifted her hands so they hovered just above each snake. "Sverd?" The green snake over her left ear raised its head and tasted her hand. She stroked him and said, "Well, hello."

Then she said, "Selv?" The red snake over her right ear did the same. Milla smiled—genuinely, widely. *It is right to know their names*, she thought. *Only a stranger is nameless.*

24

AT FIRST IT WAS PLEASANT TO BE COCOONED IN THAT warm place. For much of the winter, Milla spent the few daylight hours sitting in one of the cottage windows, looking out at drift upon drift of snow. There were days when the sky was so blue and the sun on the snow so bright that it hurt to look at it. But mostly the sky was a pale gray, and snow became more snow, became even more snow. Only the sharp, dark spikes of the evergreens broke the sea of whiteness.

Then the cocoon grew too tight, and Milla felt suffocated. She envied Otto strapping on snowshoes and venturing into the woods to lay his rabbit traps. He'd come back with his beard frosted with ice, his cheeks bitten red, and Milla could smell the forest on him as he blew into the door. She was so desperate for air, for rough bark, for the sky over her head, that she asked him if she could go with him to check the traps. Katrin laughed at this. "Oh, Milla," she said. "You don't want to do that. You'll freeze to death." Milla nearly said that she'd take her chances, but she stopped the words before they could spill out. She sensed it would mark her as even stranger in Katrin's eyes. Then once again she grew resentful of the effort not to appear odd.

Finally, when even Liss grew blank and prickly and tired of telling the same stories, the snow turned to mud. Rivers of mud. Which meant oceans of laundry, but Milla never thought she'd be so happy to be scrubbing until her hands bled. Soon, she thought. Soon she could walk in the woods. She felt the need for it in her bones. In her snakes' bones.

Once the first wildflowers poked through the last of the melt, Milla had begun to notice a change in Katrin. She seemed heavier, slower. Tired all the time. Then Milla noticed how Katrin filled out her dress, and the round of her belly under her apron, and she knew: Katrin was expecting another baby. Milla said nothing, knowing this was news that you waited to be told.

One morning as Milla and Katrin were cleaning up from breakfast and Liss played with Kai, Katrin sat down in a chair at the kitchen table and said, "Milla, I don't think I've ever been so tired."

Sunshine poured through the windows and the trees were budding. The air was fresh and just barely cool. It wasn't a day to be tired. Katrin was pale with exhaustion, and Milla nearly touched her arm, but didn't. "Why don't you nap?" Milla said.

"No, no," Katrin said. "It's time to knead the bread for dinner. And you must tend to the goats while I do that. And the chickens. There's too much to do." Katrin rested her forehead in her hand for just a moment. "There's always too much to do."

"Liss and I can do it all. Not as well as you, but it will get done. You rest."

Katrin nodded and pushed herself up to standing. "You're a good girl, Milla. Thank you."

Milla scattered a handful of flour on the table, and fetched the bowl of risen dough. She plopped the dough onto the floured wood, and just as she was about to begin kneading, she saw that the surface of the risen dough was alive with weevils, spread out over and through it like seeds. She opened Katrin's crock of flour. It was crawling with tiny, pale brown worms.

Milla told herself that these things happened. Weevils got into flour. It was nothing more than that.

"Liss," Milla said. "Why don't you take Kai outside? He'll like picking some flowers for your mamma. I'll find you when I've finished here."

"I can help you," Liss said.

Milla covered the dough with her hands, wishing away it and the dread that was growing in her belly. "No. Go out, Liss." Her tone was sharper than she meant it to be, and Liss looked hurt.

After Liss had dressed Kai in boots, she turned back to Milla at the door, and said, "You'll come when you've finished?" Her face looked so hopeful and eager to be loved and attended to. Milla felt a mixture of tenderness and revulsion.

Milla conjured a smile that she hoped carried an apology as well. "Yes, of course."

Liss smiled back, her face opening up like one of the crocuses dotting the meadow.

Milla tossed out the infested dough and flour. She fetched another crock of flour and the sourdough starter. She ran her fingers carefully through the flour and saw nothing amiss. There, that was proof, wasn't it? Weevils had gotten into one crock of flour. It was nothing more than that.

She set to mixing more dough. She'd tell Katrin that the first batch hadn't risen. Such things happened, and no sense worrying her. That was the right thing to do, Milla thought—for Katrin's sake, because she was so tired. She practiced what she would say, the lie forming on her lips.

Once Milla had set the dough to rise, she fed the chickens and milked the goats. She told herself to ignore the busy anthills in mounds around the paddock, the trails of ants that marched row upon row, single file into the barn. *They're just ants,* Milla told herself. *This is what ants do.* They hadn't been there yesterday because this was the first truly dry day.

It was nothing more than that.

She also ignored Sverd and Selv, who'd grown unusually restless. She tried not to notice their whispers in her ears. She told herself that it wasn't they who whispered warnings to her. It was just the ghost of a memory of something terrible that had happened but was over now. In the past.

It was nothing more than that.

As the sun was nearing its peak, she remembered that one of Katrin's hens had gone broody the day before. The hen had pecked Katrin's hand when she'd tried to come close, so Milla knew to stay well away from her, but she wanted to look in the coop to see if the chicks had hatched. It would be a little surprise she could offer Liss, something to make her smile.

Milla reached the yard to find the chickens in a frenzy of pecking. Milla swatted something black from her arm. Then from her other arm. Sverd and Selv hissed.

Termites. They swarmed up from the ground, an oozing mass, thick and black like smoke. Milla swatted more from her skirt, kicked them from her boots. The chickens pecked and pecked at them. Then, as quickly as the termites had risen, they subsided again and the yard was back to normal, the chickens calm and incurious. Among them, Milla realized with a start, was Katrin's brooding hen. The hen shouldn't be in the yard with eggs still to hatch. Perhaps she'd given up on them. That would be a shame.

But nothing more than that.

Sverd and Selv hissed at her again, impatient.

Milla walked toward the coop telling herself that she'd find a clutch of unhatched eggs.

Instead, she found six eggs that had hatched, and six chicks lolling inside, all dead. Their pale yellow feathers crawled with ants; their eyes were gone, and in their place were more ants. Milla backed away, her hand to her mouth, willing herself not to scream.

The curse had followed her. It was here.

When she dropped her hand from her mouth, she sucked in her breath so hard the intake burned her lungs. The skin on her palms was a pale, shimmery, grassy green. Cool and scaled. She dropped her hands to her sides.

Milla walked into the kitchen, her mind turning and turning but unable to settle on a thought or action.

Katrin was placing a round of cheese and a plate of cold meat on the table. "There you are," she said. "Where are Liss and Kai?"

Milla tried to create order on her face, to arrange her mouth and eyes in a way that wasn't horrifying to behold. Katrin had asked her a question, but the effort required for Milla to compose her face and string words together was too much. She opened her mouth and nothing came out.

"Milla? Is something wrong?" Katrin's eyebrows knit together. "Where are Liss and Kai?"

"The meadow. Playing."

Katrin cocked her head at Milla. "Would you go fetch them for dinner? It's a cold meal today. There isn't time for anything else. Take Fulla. She could use the exercise."

"Of course," Milla said. She heard how flat her words were. She willed herself to walk calmly to the door, to keep moving her feet, and perhaps soon thoughts would form out of the sick panic that was rising inside her.

25

Milla rode Fulla toward the meadow while words screamed in her head. Her panic had turned to anger, and that had turned to speech.

Why, she demanded to know. Why was it not enough that she'd been forced to leave her home, that she had these snakes growing from her head? That the girls had all been freed and the midwife was dead? Everyone who had betrayed Hulda had been forced to pay in some way. And their children—and their children's children—they had paid as well.

Why was it not over?

Sverd and Selv whispered to her. *You know why.*

The delicate hope that Milla had just barely sustained since she arrived on the farm was now gone, choked and breathless. The curse had followed her, because the demon wasn't finished with her yet. Milla had become a half-thing. Herself inside, and yet something else on the outside. Demon-like and yet not a demon. And everywhere she went, she would bring the curse with her, causing anyone she touched to suffer as well. She should have drowned herself in that spring. She remembered how Sverd had kept her from killing herself then. She'd thought of Sverd and Selv as her snakes. But maybe they were really Hulda's. Maybe she should rip them from her head.

Sverd and Selv rose up from her head, whipped themselves downward, each staring into one of her eyes. *We are not Hulda's snakes,* they hissed, *we are yours.*

She reached out to them, stroked their leafy-green and crimson heads, wanting to believe them, wanting their comfort. "I'm sorry," she said. "Help me. I don't know what to do." She touched the palms of her hands, as scaled and beautiful as Sverd and Selv. And yet so wrong. She was fascinated by herself and disgusted at the same time. She wanted to look and also to look away.

Liss and Kai weren't in the meadow. The sun was high overhead and though it was still early spring and Milla wore a winter wool dress, her riding trousers underneath, and a coat of Katrin's, she could feel a hint of warmth on her shoulders. Maybe, she thought, they'd sought shade.

The orchard.

It was a voice in her head, and not her own. It was a voice so familiar and dear to her that despite everything that had happened, she was too grateful to be frightened. Milla looked around her, scanning the meadow and the forest beyond. She caught a flash of movement and color—the color of rust. The color of autumn leaves. The color of Iris's hair.

The orchard, Milla.

Then the flash of color was gone, and the voice was, too, and

Milla turned Fulla toward the orchard. She squeezed her legs tighter around Fulla's belly. "Faster, Fulla. I know you'll do just as you please, no matter what I do. So please go faster."

She could hear the buzzing over her own heartbeat and breath and it grew louder and louder the closer she and Fulla came to the apple orchard. She saw the orchard ahead of her—neat rows of slim trees separated by lanes of green.

The apple trees should have been white with blossoms, but instead they were white with the webbing of moth nests. Where there should have been fresh, new petals there were chewing caterpillars. The buzzing was now loud in Milla's ears, but there were no flies, and the deeper Milla walked into the orchard, the more intense the buzzing grew and yet there was no sign of where the buzzing came from. Then, amidst the slender tree trunks she saw a large, round mass of black and livid yellow, like a storm cloud that had settled to the ground.

In the center of that mass were Liss and Kai.

Milla slipped off Fulla and ran toward the black and yellow cloud, and the angry, eager buzzing was all she could hear. The cloud was made of wasps—so many wasps. It was as if every wasp that had funneled into Ragna's cottage had come here, now, and all were circling their prey. Milla stood just outside the cloud—so close she could feel the air shift around their vibrating wings. The wasps ignored her, their focus trained on the children caught inside. Liss sat on the ground, Kai pulled into her lap. She wrapped her arms around her own head and his.

"Liss!" Milla screamed over the buzzing. Liss didn't move.

Milla screamed again, a sound that started out as a word— *why*—and became a howl. She screamed at nothing, at everything. At Hulda. At Iris. *Why*. Why her? Why these children? Why must hurt breed more hurt, pain breed more pain? What sense did any of it make? She alternated between anger so bitter she could taste it in her mouth and despair so deep she wanted only to sink to the ground and sob. But she couldn't, because those children were in that cloud of wasps, and it was her fault. And she would not let them suffer for what someone else had done.

Sverd and Selv rose from her head and hissed at the cloud, and Milla saw a parting open in front of her, big enough to put an arm through. "Again," she said. "And louder." Another hiss, and the opening grew larger, as big as a window.

"Liss!" Milla called to her.

Liss looked up. "Milla!" She started to stand, and Kai squirmed in her arms.

"Don't move," Milla said. "Keep holding Kai close to you." Milla saw Liss take in Sverd and Selv, but she didn't scream, only grew open-eyed with wonder.

Then Milla spread her arms wide as if they too were snakes, and from deep in her belly, a place where there was nothing but gut and anger, she hissed. She hissed her anger and her demand that those wasps disperse and leave those children. Her hiss was louder than the buzzing, it was louder than the wind. In response, the cloud widened and widened, and grew, and thinned, and Milla felt the wasps pass her, withdrawing and withdrawing.

Then they were gone. Liss remained crouched over Kai, their faces and eyes hidden, just as Milla had told her to do. Sverd and Selv tucked themselves away in Milla's hair, and Milla went to Liss and touched her shoulder. She felt Liss's trembling, and she said, "They're gone, Liss." She wanted to say *you're safe*, but that would have been wrong. Because they weren't.

Kai struggled out from beneath Liss, and Liss stood. Red-faced, his dark curls matted to his forehead, Kai looked at the air around them. "Fly! Fly?" Then he tugged on Liss's hand. "Ssssss! Sssss! Fly!"

Milla said, "Wasps, Kai. Very mean wasps."

Liss looked at Milla with round eyes. "You saved us. I knew you would."

"How did you know I would save you, Liss?"

"She told me."

Milla felt as if she'd pitched forward off an unexpected step. "She?"

Liss tapped her forehead. "The voice in my head."

"What did the voice say to you, Liss?"

"It said, *she's here.*" Then Liss smiled, her eyes alight.

26

MILLA'S EYES SEARCHED THE SPACES BETWEEN THE trees. The voice Liss heard in her head could have been Iris's. But Milla feared it wasn't. The blight, the cloud of wasps, the brightness in Liss's eyes . . . there were too many signs that the *she* who was here—who was nudging her way into sweet Liss—was not Iris.

It was Hulda.

"Come, Kai." Milla scooped him up and handed him to Liss. "Go straight home. Tell your mamma and pappa about the wasps, and the moth nests. Tell them I told you I've seen it before—that it's what killed . . . my grandmother. Tell them I was afraid that I'd caused it, and so I needed to leave. Tell them all of that."

Liss nodded. "I will, but I don't want you to leave." Liss's bright eyes were wet and shiny.

"I have to, Liss."

"What if they don't believe me? What if they think it's a story?"

"They won't. You're so smart and so strong. And your mamma and pappa love you." Milla's voice broke. "They'll believe you."

Kai struggled to get down. "Sssssss! Home!"

"All right, Kai, all right," Liss said.

For the first time, Milla took it upon herself to embrace Liss. She held Liss close and kissed the top of her head, her curls tickling Milla's nose. Then she released Liss and walked away from her fast, looking back just once and seeing that Liss was doing the same.

Fulla stood her ground stolidly. Imperturbably. Milla thought the mare would follow Liss and Kai back home. Fulla had become more dog than horse to the family. But she didn't. She stood there staring at Milla, waiting. "Really, Fulla?" Milla said to her. "You know we're not going back." She reached for Fulla's reins and tugged gently, expecting the horse to finally resist and turn around. But instead Fulla followed Milla out of the orchard and into the mossy evergreen forest. What she would do with Fulla, Milla had no idea. But the mare had a mind of her own, and whenever she wished to turn around and go back home again, she no doubt would.

Anyway, the mare calmed her. Sverd and Selv rose up and craned forward, as if they knew the way. As Milla had done before with dear old Fulla, she allowed her snakes to lead them, trusting that they could taste Iris in the air the way Fulla had tasted home.

The forest was so thick that the sky was just a sliver of blue above her head, and Milla felt a chill even under all her wool. Evening would fall soon, and she hoped Iris would show herself before then. The forest floor was soft with evergreen needles and Milla was tempted to curl up between two tree roots and rest her head.

Rustle. Flash.

Milla looked quickly to her right and there she was—Iris.

She wore a man's shirt over pants that she'd rolled up over leather boots that looked at least a few sizes too large for her feet. Her eyes were syrupy amber, no brighter than they should be. She smiled at Milla. "I'm happy to see you," Iris said.

Milla wanted to run to Iris, to embrace her, but this was the same girl who'd threatened to kill her, who'd hurt Niklas. Who'd hissed and writhed under a full moon, who'd held hands with the other demon girls, who'd tried to get Milla to join them. "You seem like yourself, Iris. But you seemed like yourself before. And you weren't. Or you weren't for long. I want to trust you, but how can I?"

"Because you love me. And I love you back."

Milla sighed. She wished it were so simple. But everyone she loved most had hurt her. Or she had hurt them. She thought of the moral to the story Iris had told her in her cell at The Place. *The people you love are dead and want to kill you.*

But Iris wasn't dead. Niklas wasn't, either. And sweet Liss hadn't ever hurt anyone. Liss deserved so much better than whatever fate Hulda had in store for her. "If you really do love me, will you take me to Hulda and help me end this?"

Iris led Milla and Fulla deeper into the woods. She dug into her trousers' deep pockets and handed Milla an apple, and she ate one herself while Milla asked her question after question. They gave the cores to Fulla. Often they paused while Fulla stopped to chew on the leaves of low-hanging branches and shrubs.

"How do you live?"

"You'll see," Iris said.

"Where did you get those clothes?"

"Hanging on a line." Iris smiled. "I'm awfully quiet when I want to be."

"Do you see the other girls?"

Iris's face closed and she seemed to recede. "Sometimes. They frighten me. Only the girls who hear Hulda's voice are left. The ones who were never possessed in the first place have run off. I stay away as much as I can, but sometimes Hulda calls to me, and I have to go."

"Why do you have to?" Milla struggled to understand, but she couldn't. Why couldn't Iris resist? Shut out that voice, and refuse to do what the demon said?

"Because she's the mother. And when she's in here"—Iris tapped her forehead—"I have no choice."

"What does she want from you and the other girls?"

"She wants us to hate everyone. She wants to punish our families and the people who hurt her. But each time she curses another girl, it doesn't ease her pain. It only stokes it. Makes it hotter. Nastier. So then she sent the insects after the village's harvest. And then that wasn't enough, either. When we all escaped from The Place, and she sent the wasps for Ragna, even that wasn't enough."

"What does she want from me?"

Iris looked at Milla with pity in her eyes, and Milla's heart went cold. The chill seeped outward, wrapping tightly around her rib cage, squeezing the air from her lungs. She looked down at her hands, the scales pale green and spreading to her wrists. "I suppose I already know, don't I? She's turning me into a demon like her. But why?"

"She hates your mother and father most of all. She's punishing them for what they did to her by turning you into a monster, too."

"If only Hulda knew how little Mamma and Pappa care for me she wouldn't have bothered. It's Niklas they love."

"Don't tell Hulda that. You saw what she did to Ragna. You don't want Niklas catching her attention. She'd kill him if she knew, and make Jakob and Gitta watch. That's why I keep you and Niklas in a special place in my head. A place she can't touch. She can fill the rest of my head with her pain, but not that place. That place is mine."

"Why didn't you come find me before now? I've missed you so. I've felt so lost."

"I haven't been right, Milla. I knew you were out there, and I wanted to find you. But I remember what I did to you at The Place. I remember my hand around your throat. I remember wanting to squeeze, and squeeze harder, and I didn't know if it was all a trick or if I really would hurt you then. Or if I might hurt you if I saw you again."

Milla reached out and held Iris's hand. She tried to imagine the pain of a head so torn in two. She thought she could. A bit. Sverd licked her cheek. But no, her snakes weren't like that. They didn't make her do things. Or think things. "And now? Your head is more your own? And that's why you came to find me?"

"No," Iris said. "My head isn't more my own. It's mine right *now*. Right at this moment. But I never know when she's going to take it."

"Now that I'm with you, maybe we can keep her out of your head for good. Maybe we can find a way."

Iris stopped walking and her face rippled, the outlines of not-Iris reforming the planes of her face. "No . . ." Iris said. "No . . .

I . . . I don't think so." She shook her head, hard, as if she were trying to shake something out of it. Then she smacked the side of her head, harder still. "No. No. No." *Smack.*

Milla let go of Fulla's reins and took Iris's hands firmly in her own. Iris struggled against her, but Milla wouldn't let go. "Iris, no, please, dearest. You mustn't hurt yourself. And you're here now. With me. Yes?"

Iris nodded. Her muscles were hard under Milla's hands, as if flexed with the effort to hold herself together. Slowly her face reassembled itself again, and she was wholly Iris.

Milla gathered Fulla's reins and they continued walking, quiet for a time. Then Milla said, "Why do you suppose I can hear your voice in my head?"

"I don't know," Iris said.

"I think I do. I think it's because I want to, so badly."

"But I don't want to hear Hulda's voice in my head, and yet I do."

"True," Milla said. "But that's different. You didn't invite her. The moment I met you I found the person who'd never let me be lonely again. The person who really saw me, all my strange parts, and loved me all the same. I invited your voice into my head and you never left. And I never wanted you to leave."

"That's a nice story," Iris said.

"Shall I tell you another?"

"Yes, please."

"There was once a girl who loved to lie in the grass and let it tickle her skin. She liked the feel of dirt under her fingers. She didn't like aprons or making dinner or washing dishes. She didn't like being told to behave. She didn't like feeling that no matter what she did her mother and father looked at her with disappointed eyes. She could never be pretty enough or sweet enough or pleasantly talkative enough. And she grew angrier and angrier and angrier that all anyone wanted her to be was an idea they held in their head that had nothing to do with her. And this anger became bitterness, and this bitterness turned her into a monster. And the monster that she became wanted to hurt everyone that had hurt her. So she did. She punished everyone until there was no one left to punish. No one at all."

"That's a sad story," Iris said.

"It is."

"It has a bad ending."

"It does," Milla said. "But I think maybe it hasn't ended yet."

Iris stopped walking and looked at Milla. "I'm afraid it will go on and on, Milla. The punishing. The anger. The sadness. I feel Hulda's sadness inside me, her resentment. It's growing stronger, and it's making me weaker. What if I leave you again, and what if I never come back? What if I'm gone for good?"

Milla took Iris's hand. "Iris, I promise you this. I will never abandon you. I don't care what you say to me. What you do. What Hulda makes you say or do. You're my sister as much as Niklas is my brother. My mother couldn't be a sister to Hulda, but we are not them. We get to choose. And I choose never to leave you." Milla's voice was shaking now, tears rimming her eyes and spilling over. "And I will get Hulda's voice out of your head. Because no matter how deep her pain, no matter what she's suffered, she doesn't get to take my sister from me."

Iris threw her arms around Milla and Milla held on tight. Milla swore to herself: No demon above or below would ever separate them again.

PART FOUR

27

IRIS LED MILLA AND FULLA UP THE LEDGE OF A LOW
rock slope and into a cave. "This is where I come when I can
shake Hulda's voice from my head."

There was a battered basket of clothing. Another of apples,
and yet another of potatoes and onions. Everything stolen. Iris
gave Fulla an apple and then knelt in front of a circle of stones
where she built a fire. The ceiling of the cave was black with soot.
Milla looked around, imagining how many long nights Iris had
spent here, alone and dreading when Hulda's voice would return.

After a supper of berries and hazelnuts, Milla and Iris slept
cocooned in blankets that smelled of damp and smoke. Whenever
Milla woke in the night, which she did often, she sensed that Iris
was just as awake beside her. Sverd and Selv squirmed, restless.
Fulla slept so deeply she snored.

As soon as the sky was light, they set off to find Hulda. Iris was quiet as they walked. Milla sensed Iris's fear, her worry that the closer she was to Hulda, the greater her risk of losing herself. The same fear twisted in Milla's belly. If Iris became that other version of herself, Milla would have to face Hulda alone.

They hadn't gone far when Milla felt Iris tense beside her. "What is it?" Milla said.

"Listen." Iris eyed the woods around them.

Fulla nosed the back of Milla's head when she stopped walking. At first she heard only the horse's breathing and the shushing of air through evergreen needles. But then she realized it wasn't shushing, it was hissing. Soft and low. Then there was a flash of movement through the trees and a woman leapt in front of them wearing only an apron and a man's trousers. Her hair and eyebrows were faded russet-red.

Leah.

She hissed at them, her breath a sizzle between her teeth. Sverd and Selv rose from Milla's head and hissed back.

Iris extended an arm in front of Milla. "Let us pass, Leah. Milla is here to see Hulda."

"She's here," Leah hissed. Then she leapt and slithered through the trees—over rocks and roots, weaving out and in among the tree trunks.

The words *she's here* were picked up and passed along in urgent whispers, and then more demon girls emerged from the woods like gathering fog. First there were only tree trunks, and then there were girls and women, some still wearing the rough burlap dresses they'd worn in The Place. Others wore odd combinations of rags and clothing, knotted and sewn together. All had bright, lamplit eyes. All hissed.

She's here.

She'ssss here.

She'sssssssssss here.

Iris led Milla on, her eyes fixed forward. "Talk to me, Milla. Remind me who I am."

Milla reached for Iris's hand, held it tight. "You're Iris. And you're my sister. And I'm yours."

"Yes," Iris said. "That's right. Tell me again. Keeping telling me."

And so Milla did. Over and over. *You're Iris. And you're my sister. And I'm yours.* Each time Milla said it, Iris squeezed her hand more tightly, as if she were holding onto herself, as much as to Milla.

They came to a clearing with an evergreen tree larger than any Milla had ever seen. Its grooved trunk was as wide as a cottage, with a jagged opening in the front. The tree grew so high, and its thickly needled branches spread so widely, that it seemed endless, like the tree from which all other trees had sprouted—like something that had existed forever, and would exist forever.

Iris let go of Milla's hand and slapped her hands to her ears. Milla was losing her. Iris was being shoved aside, and something else was taking her place.

"You're Iris," Milla said. "You're my sister, and I'm yours."

Iris dropped her hands from her ears and smiled at Milla. "She'ssssss here," she hissed. Then she ran into the woods to join the other demon girls.

Milla threw Fulla's reins over her saddle, then pushed her fat rump. "Go on, girl. This is too much even for you." Fulla let herself be driven off, and Milla knew that if any animal could find her way home, that one would.

As the girls moved around her through the trees, Milla was reminded of the cloud of wasps that had surrounded Liss and

Kai. Now she was the one surrounded, only there was no one outside the cloud to save her. If it hadn't been for Iris's hair, Milla wouldn't have been able to pick her out of the swarm of girls.

Then, from the jagged opening in the tree, Hulda emerged.

She was a woman made of snakes—constructed of snakes. Instead of hair she grew countless snakes, all of them lifting from her head, eyes forward, tongues out and tasting. The snakes shimmered black, blood-red, brilliant green and yellow. All were longer and thicker around than either Sverd or Selv, who hissed and whipped the air above Milla's head madly, frantically. Hulda's shoulders and arms were woven with snakes where a woman's muscles should be. Even her fingers were slender snakes. She had snakes for veins, snakes for ribs. She wore no clothing, so Milla could see the snakes that corded her chest and belly, her thighs and legs. When Hulda moved toward Milla, the snakes that made up her legs spread out, slithering across the ground and carrying her forward, so her motion was more like undulating than walking.

Hulda's face, like the rest of her body, was both beautiful and terrible. Her skin was the texture of snakeskin and brilliantly colored. Her forehead was grassy green, her cheeks blushed red-orange, her lips were the blood-brown of clay. They drew back over fangs that were long, sharp, and starkly white.

Milla's voice came out high and childlike. Querulous. "I'm here to give you what you want," she said. She'd wanted to sound strong and sure, but looking at Hulda made that impossible. Ridiculous.

Hulda opened her mouth and every snake that made up her body seemed to hiss as one. "What isssssssss that? What isssss it you think I want?"

"An apology," Milla said.

Hulda's snake legs swirled and whipped the ground, lifting leaves and dirt in violent gusts. "An apology? An apology? An apology?" Hulda rolled forward and wrapped her snake arms around Milla. She pulled Milla so close that Milla could look into her lidless eyes, her slender, black pupils encircled by amber that quivered yellow and green. Where Hulda should have had eyebrows, her scales arched upward, blackberry-purple. "Can there be an apology for thisssss?"

Milla struggled to speak and not whimper. "I know you've suffered."

"You don't know *what* I've suffered." Hulda's breath hissed hot and acid between her fangs. "How my own sssister betrayed me. Gitta, my love. My best love. How I wished she could love me back. How instead she despised me. How they buried me in the snow. How they left me there. Alone. How I shook and froze and cried out for my snakes to comfort me. And how then . . . I became this."

Hulda unwrapped her arms from Milla and she stretched them out and the snakes that made up her body moved and shifted and her snake arms whipped the air around her. Her face became a grimace, and the hisses that made up her voice vibrated with sadness. "Will an apology make me a girl again? Will it give me back my life?"

The demon girls hissed in response, a chorus of abandonment so profound that Milla felt it vibrating in her chest.

Then the air around Milla grew thick with bitterness. The scent of it kissed the tip of Milla's tongue and it tasted like bile. She despaired. "Hulda, I would give you back your life if I could. Instead I'm begging you. Please let the curse end with me, and then you can let these girls go. Let them have their lives back."

"Why do you care about these others?" Hulda hissed. "No one cares for you. Silly Milla. Loveless child."

Milla felt Hulda's hatred rising from her, burning Milla from the outside in. Milla was overcome by Hulda's desire to hurt her, to make her suffer, and it made her stupid; it opened up her mind to Hulda's words and they latched onto her like thorns. Milla's years of isolation, of being called *silly Milla* by the one she loved the most, heated her up inside. She felt on fire, would have doused herself with water if she could.

"You can't know that," Milla said.

"But I *do*. I know because the one you call *friend* told me. She'ssss telling me right now. She'ssss telling me you're the least loved. That your brother shines like the sun. Your brother makes everyone happy. And you . . . you are the one they wish had never been born."

Milla looked around her for Iris. Then she spotted her, russet-haired and hissing. Traitor. She said she'd keep Niklas and Milla in a safe place in her head, but she hadn't. Sverd and Selv writhed and nipped at her cheeks, sensing her resentment toward Iris rising, her feelings of betrayal making her stupid and incautious. *Stop*, they hissed. *Stop*. But Milla couldn't stop.

"Iris lies," Milla said. "None of that is true."

Hulda rolled and writhed to Iris, who cowered away from her now, whimpering. Hulda wrapped five snake fingers around Iris's neck and dragged her to Milla. She held Iris in front of Milla, the tips of Hulda's snake fingers all snapping and hissing around Iris's throat. Her eyes were round and panicked, the eyes of Milla's friend. More than friend: sister. And Milla had betrayed her in a heartbeat. Milla had thought herself so much better than her mother, but now, overwhelmed by shame and self-loathing, she knew she wasn't.

"Milla?" Iris said.

Milla lurched toward Iris, but Hulda jerked her out of Milla's reach. She squeezed Iris's throat, and the air around Milla was coal-hot. Milla felt it scorching her cheeks. Then there was no air, only burning. Milla felt that she was suffocating, surely turning to ash.

"Iris can't lie to me, Milla. She *belongsss* to me."

Iris screamed, slapped her hands to her ears. "Get out get out get out get out get out get out get out."

Then Milla screamed as well. "Stop it!"

Hulda smiled, triumphant, and she dropped Iris to the ground. Iris sobbed and covered her head with her hands.

Milla wanted to pick up Iris from the ground, to tell her that it wasn't her fault. Milla had thought she'd understood Iris's pain. But she hadn't had any idea what Hulda was really like. Milla had really only thought of her own pain, her own resentments. She was worse even than her mother; Milla felt no less a bitter, hateful monster than Hulda was.

"Please, Hulda," Milla said while pulling up one sleeve and showing how the pale green scales had spread to the crook of her elbow. "I'm a monster already. You've gotten your revenge. Let this stop with me."

Hulda wailed from her belly, not a hiss but a howl. "I CANNOT."

Iris scrambled away from Hulda on hands and knees.

"But you can," Milla said, trying to make her voice sound calm and certain. "You're the demon. It's your curse."

Hulda's snakes rose from her head and froze in midair, staring.

"You think *I'm* the demon?" Hulda said. "I'm not the demon. The snakes brought the demon to me, and then she turned me into"—she looked down at her own slithering body—"*this*. A monster."

Milla tried to imagine a demon that wasn't Hulda—a demon more powerful and horrible than Hulda was. She couldn't. Milla's thoughts couldn't stretch that far. "But you cursed us. So you can lift the curse. Can't you?"

"The demon has all the power," Hulda said. "It was her voice in my mouth when I cursed the village."

"Then you must ask her to lift it," Milla said. "Go to her and tell her that it's enough. Or take me to her, and I will ask her myself."

Hulda whipped her snake arms and legs so wildly that Milla stumbled backward to avoid being flattened. Hulda's words came out in panicked hisses.

cannot . . .

frightened . . .

the demon . . .

terror . . .

terror . . .

terror . . .

The girls responded to Hulda's wild panic with their own, hissing and writhing.

terror . . .

terror . . .

terror . . .

Hulda rolled back and back, a swirl of snake hair, snake legs, snake hands, snake fingers, and back and back and back until she disappeared into the jagged, dark opening in the tree.

The hissing of the girls grew louder, and Milla saw that they were closer than they had been before, and closer all the time. Iris still crouched on the ground, her arms over her head. "Iris," Milla said. "We must leave. *Now.*"

Milla reached for one of Iris's hands to pull her to her feet. Iris snatched her hand from Milla while twisting up and hissing. Iris was gone again. "Terror," she hissed at Milla. "Terror. Terror."

Milla backed away from Iris, looking around her for a path through the writhing, hissing, encroaching swarm of Hulda's girls.

Then she ran.

28

EACH TIME MILLA TURNED HER HEAD TO SEE HOW close the demon girls were, they were too close, and so she kept running. The girls slipped and slid through trees and over rocks and branches as if they were no barrier at all. All the while they hissed. *Terror.*

Then, in an instant, the girls' hissing stopped. Milla turned around to find them gone, the woods quiet except for the scurrying of small animals and the calls of birds. She was alone. Strangely alone. Hadn't the girls been there just a moment ago? It was as if they'd vanished. Milla should have been grateful, but instead she felt unnerved. She wondered if they might be hiding, waiting for her to stop running so they could surround her.

Sverd and Selv tasted the air, alert to danger. "Which way should we go?" she said to them. There was no answer. She felt herself crying and that made her angry. She said aloud to herself,

"Stop it, Milla. Since when has your crying gotten you anywhere?" She didn't want to be the stupid, frightened girl in a story. "Think, don't cry," she told herself.

Then she knew: She would go to Niklas and warn him that Hulda was coming for him. That was the only thing to do. It was already late afternoon, and if she was going to find her way back to familiar ground today, then it must be before nightfall. The forest canopy was so thick here that sunlight only trickled through in slender beams. At night, the way ahead would be black and treacherous.

Milla had been walking for some time, when she heard a sound like humming. Not a buzzing. Not the humming of wasps. The humming of a person. A woman, Milla thought.

Her snakes strained forward, as curious as she was. If this were a story, Milla thought, the girl wandering in the woods and hearing a song would find a witch at the end of it. But this wasn't a story. And if a woman lived here and might give Milla food and shelter for the night, well . . . it was worth at least a peek.

Milla walked toward the humming, and as she drew closer she smelled wood smoke and something more pungent. Then Milla saw light shining into a clearing ahead and she dropped to a crouch. She moved from tree to tree peeking around each to see what she could glimpse until she was nearly to the edge of the clearing. From there, Milla saw a ragged little cottage at its center—and the humming woman. Or rather: witch.

Because that was what she must be—a witch out of stories. Her long white hair was in a tangle atop her head, her eyebrows were as woolly as caterpillars, and her face was as creviced as a walnut shell. She appeared so impossibly old, and her pallor so gray, that had Milla seen her lying down she'd have thought her dead. Her lips were as cracked as her cheeks, and were puckered as if stitched into a knot. And the tip of her long, warty nose nearly met the tip of her long, warty chin.

Milla sucked in a breath.

The witch was puttering around a kettle hung over a fire, out of which curled a stench so vicious that Milla's eyes teared and she feared she'd sneeze. Hanging from two posts held together by horizontal pieces of wood were three bloody animal carcasses, scraped of most of their flesh and drawing flies. The cottage looked more like a loosely constructed pile of sticks than a house, and was topped with a high-pitched, thickly-grassed roof. Chickens pecked about the yard, the one thing about the place that made it look at all homey.

Sverd and Selv hissed in Milla's ears, then tucked themselves into her hair as if to say, *if you don't have the sense to avoid a witch, then we certainly do.*

Milla backed away over soft evergreen needles that she hoped muffled both her scent and her sound. Gradually the witch's humming grew softer and the clearing was just a spot of brightness behind her, and Milla allowed herself to breathe.

She stopped for a moment, looking forward, left, and right. Which way? She was more lost than ever and the only thing she knew for certain was that she should leave the witch as far as possible behind her. Finally deciding that straight ahead was the likeliest route back, Milla took a step forward and her foot sank into soft needles. Then she felt herself sink farther and farther, and then she was crashing down and down and grasping at branches, but the branches weren't holding and before she'd reached bottom she knew: She'd fallen into a trap.

Her fall was mostly broken by damp, rotting leaves, but she landed stomach-first on a bowl-shaped rock that knocked the wind out of her. She rolled off it and lay there for some moments feeling stupid.

Sverd and Selv tasted her cheeks and nudged her neck and shoulders. "Yes," she said to them. "I'm all right." She sat up and her hand brushed the rock, which wasn't a rock at all, she realized. It was a skull—a man's, judging by the size of it. She held it up and centipedes oozed from its eye sockets. She tossed it away. She stood and felt along the sides of the pit, looking for something she could hold onto. She scraped and clawed until her hands bled, but any root she grabbed pulled free. She dug her hands into the earth, finger deep, and tried to climb up while kicking footholds, but she could manage to lift herself no more than three feet from the bottom before the soft earth gave way and she lost her grip. It was hopeless—the top of the pit was a good five feet above her head.

Milla sat down on the floor of the pit. In the dim she looked around for what else might be down here with her—some sign of what this pit was used for, and how recently. The poor fellow whose skull she'd fallen on had clearly been down here a long time. The bone was smooth and picked clean. She searched about with her hands, brushing away leaves and evergreen needles, and she found more bones, some person-sized. Some deer-sized. Some tinier. This accounting of the dead things that occupied the pit with her kept Milla's brain from spinning into panic. If someone had gone to the trouble of making this pit, she thought, and then covering it over, then that someone would surely come back and check what they'd caught. Surely Milla wouldn't be left here to starve, she told herself. Her very next thought was that perhaps whoever dug this pit intended it for unsuspecting wanderers like her and was content to leave them here to die—however long that took. Hence the skull Milla had landed upon. Milla thought of the humming woman. Wasn't that just the kind of thing a witch would do?

Sverd and Selv hissed to her. *Sleep.*

"How can I sleep?" Milla said. "I'm in a trap. With bones."

It's the only thing to do, they hissed back at her.

Milla gathered wet leaves together, cushioning a spot under her head. She lay down, looking up at the darkening trees. Sverd and Selv rested their heads on her shoulders, and she stroked them.

There was a soft crackling of life and movement around her. Bats fluttered above, dipping into the pit and circling her head. She looked at them through the darkness with wide, curious eyes, and they looked back at her with their own. Her panic subsided, and she felt strangely at peace here with these crawling and flapping things. She would sleep tonight, she told herself, and tomorrow someone would come for her. And then she would get out of this pit and go find Niklas.

Just as her lids grew heavy, Milla felt something shift beneath her—deep beneath her. Something dark and endless. Something that was waiting . . . waiting to be called. Milla hadn't said her prayers in such a long time, but in the seconds before sleep the words came back to her.

Lord, protect us from demons.

Lord, protect us from demons.

Lord, protect us from demons.

29

MILLA SENSED LIGHT THROUGH HER EYELIDS, AND morning damp in her hair. She opened her eyes and looked up to see two faces staring down at her from opposite sides of the ditch. One was long and familiar: Fulla, the dear. If not for the other face that looked down at her, Milla might have smiled. But the other face—cackling and hideous—belonged to the humming witch.

"That is one nasty curse you've got on you, girly." The witch slapped a knee. "I haven't seen a curse that nasty in . . . well, since the last time I cursed someone myself!" She slapped her knee again.

Milla looked up at the old woman. She knew her first request should be that the witch throw her a rope, but she was more curious about something else. "How do you know I have a curse on me?"

"I can see it," she said.

"Do you mean my snakes?" Milla said. "Anyone can see them."

"No, I don't mean your snakes," the witch said, rolling her eyes as if affronted. "I mean I can see your curse all around you. And the demon who did *that*? Well, there's not much I'm afraid of, but she's a doozy."

Milla sat up. "You know what demon did this?"

"I'm a witch, girly."

"I need to find her. Can you help me?"

The witch scratched her nose. There was a lot of nose to scratch. "I can. Are you sure you want me to? She's not one you sit down and have a chat with. Not without coming away more cursed than you already are."

"It's really not possible to be more cursed than I am," Milla said.

"You're wrong there, girly," the witch said. Then she walked away.

Milla waited, staring at the wall of the pit and the beetles that scuttled in and out. Then, in front of her eyes dropped a thick rope.

The witch's name was Hel. She led Milla to her yard and offered her a stump to perch on, then handed her a cup of something hot. Milla looked at it suspiciously. Her snakes tasted the air over the cup. "Smell it, girly," Hel said. "It's tea."

Fulla had refused to step any closer to the witch's cottage than the forest's edge. She'd simply stopped in her tracks, immovable as a mountain. Her mouth full of leaves, the horse hadn't look frightened, merely decided. Milla had patted her neck and said, "Smart, Fulla. Very smart."

Milla sniffed the cup. It seemed like tea. Smelled like tea.

Still, she didn't take a sip. She'd heard too many stories to sip the first cup of tea a witch had handed her. This witch seemed kind, though, if that was the right word for her. Strange, yes. But she didn't look at Milla as if she were a monster, and for that Milla was grateful.

Milla peered around the witch's yard. The animal carcasses still hung there, flies feasting. The witch tracked the direction of Milla's gaze. "My maggot farm," she said. "There's not a potion I know that isn't made better by maggots."

Milla nodded as if this made perfect sense. The steam from the tea wafted up, warming her face. She was so tired and chilled from the night spent in the ditch. She took a tiny sip from the cup. It really was tea.

Hel narrowed her eyes at Milla. "What do you know about demons?"

"Nothing, really," Milla said. "I only know that my aunt, Hulda, used one to curse me and my family and her whole village. And I'm trying to break the curse. My aunt says she can't do it, that only the demon can do it."

"Hm," Hel said. "I think your aunt is lying to you."

"How do you know that?"

"Because I know her demon. She's my demon as well."

"Does she have a name?"

"She does," Hel said. "She's the oldest of the demons, the original. You don't want to tangle with her, girly. Like I said, she's a doozy. Always hungry. Never satisfied."

"But *you* tangled with her," Milla said.

Hel smiled, lips puckered over teeth that crossed over each other like fingers, and were so yellow they were brown. "Keep drinking your tea."

Milla looked down at her cup. What was that floating in it?

Hel laughed and slapped her knee. "Taking tea from a witch, girly! Taking tea from a witch!" And she slapped and laughed until she coughed and spit into the dirt.

What Hel spit up was black. It squirmed. Milla blinked her eyes at it and watched as the black mass crawled across the yard and into the grass. She felt the world shift just slightly around her. She wasn't dizzy, or disoriented. But what she saw around her was different. Clearer. Colors were brighter and sounds were louder, and when she looked at Hel she saw something forming over the witch's face, like a mask. Every one of Hel's already exaggerated features became more so. Her nose was so long it curled under her chin. Her eyebrows weren't just woolly *like* caterpillars, they *were* caterpillars. The largest wart on her nose puffed and curled mushroom-like, then began to vibrate. It burst open and out oozed a nestful of tiny gray spiders that spread across her face.

"Do you see it yet?" Hel asked her.

"What is happening to you?" Milla said.

"Oh, it's not what's happening to *me*. It's what's happening to *you*. I gave you something to help you see. We don't just cast our curses, girly. We become our curses."

"Who did you curse? And why?" Milla hoped that it was worth it, and that whoever was on the receiving end of something so ugly deserved it.

"Years and years ago, I was pretty," Hel said. "Would you believe that? I was a pretty farm wife with a husband and no children. And then one day my husband died. He left me with the farm, but no sons to protect me, and no daughters to take me in. But I didn't think I needed sons or daughters, because I had a farm, and that was enough. I was wrong, though. Of course I was." Hel laughed, but it didn't sound like a laugh. It sounded like an axe striking wood. "My husband's brother arrived on my doorstep and told me the farm was his. I could live there, but he'd run it. Well, I was always mouthy, and I wasn't interested in having that man run my farm, so I went to the village elders to complain. My husband's brother didn't like that, and so he and his wife spread it around the village that I was a witch and that I'd poisoned my husband. The elders never liked me anyway, and they had no trouble believing I'd done such an evil thing. So they let my dead husband's brother take my farm. And then I cursed all of them. I cursed their harvests and their children's harvests and their children's children's harvests."

"And did it work?" Milla asked.

Hel leaned forward and smiled, and a shiny green beetle raced across her front teeth. "They all starved."

Black smoke curled from Hel's nostrils, so sharp and biting that it caused Milla's own nose to curl and her eyes to sting. Then the smoke filled the air around Milla and the scent took on meaning, and Milla felt that she knew the name of Hel's demon, and of Hulda's. The smoke had told her the name. "Vengeance," Milla said. "Your demon is Vengeance."

Hel laughed, and her face reconfigured itself into something a shade less hideous than it had been. "And a fine demon she is. She's done right by me all these years."

"You don't . . . you don't feel . . . sorry . . . for all those people who starved?"

"Did they feel sorry for calling me a witch and taking what was mine? They got what they deserved. They wanted a witch, and I gave them one."

Milla wanted to believe that Hel was weakened by her curse.

But she didn't seem weak. Twisted, yes. But not weak. Milla wondered if the strength Hulda drew from Vengeance was as unbending as Hel's, then why would she ever let it go? "You said you saw my curse on me. Can you show me?"

"You've drunk the tea. You only need look at your reflection." Hel went to the well and drew a bucketful of water, then placed it in Milla's lap. "Look. You'll see."

Milla stared into the water and saw only her own unkempt hair and serious face staring back at her. Sverd and Selv rested their pretty green and red heads on her shoulders. Then something formed around Milla. A cloud. A dark cloud, shot with flashes of yellow. No, not a cloud at all. A swarm.

A swarm of wasps. Thick and hungry. Tireless. Buzzing. And they were all over Milla. In her hair, her eyes, her mouth. Laying their eggs in Sverd and Selv, their larvae growing plump and eating her snakes alive.

Milla cried out, dropping the bucket to the ground, sloshing water over her boots.

"*That* is Vengeance," Hel said. "I told you not to tangle with her."

30

"THERE MUST BE A SPELL FOR LIFTING CURSES," MILLA
said. "You must know one?"

"There isn't," Hel said. "Else it wouldn't be a curse. Curses are
powerful magic, and only the one who casts a curse can lift it."

Milla thought about the curse hanging over her like a swarm
of wasps—the same curse that also hung over Iris and now Liss.
Milla had made the mistake of thinking she could escape it, and
instead she'd brought it to Katrin and Otto's door.

"Maybe Hulda doesn't realize she can lift the curse," Milla said.

"Hm," Hel said. "Doubtful. More likely she's a liar."

Milla knew Hulda was a monster, and yet she struggled to
believe she was a liar. She'd seen the torture Hulda inflicted on
the girls and everyone who loved them. But the part of Milla that
felt rejected and abandoned by Gitta was drawn to the part of
Hulda that felt the same way. Milla remembered the anguish in

Hulda's voice when she said, *Will an apology make me a girl again?* *Will it give me back my life?* The demon Vengeance had kept Hulda alive but at the cost of almost everything else. At the cost of any impulse other than the desire to punish.

Milla shook her head. "I don't believe she's lying. I think she's in pain, and the pain is all she can think about or feel." Milla thought for a moment. "Hel, I'm not the only one Hulda has cursed. She's cursed many girls, including my friend. Hulda gets inside their heads. She makes them feel what she feels and do things they wouldn't do ordinarily. She's not inside my head, not yet. But I'm afraid she might do that to me."

"And you want to stop her from doing that? You want some sort of potion for that? Don't think there is one."

"No. Not a potion for that. I wonder, is there some kind of spell that could put me inside Hulda's head?"

Hel crossed her arms over her chest and squinted at Milla. "You want to possess Hulda? You'd need your own demon for that."

"No. Not possess her. Just get inside her for a bit. Find out what she wants and if there might be a way to appease her. To end all this."

Hel scratched her chin thoughtfully. "Could be there's something could get you in there. Could be. But I'm going to need more maggots. Lots more."

Milla's stomach rolled and rose up to her mouth.

Hel took the cup from Milla and hummed happily while she worked. Milla forced herself not to look, not wanting to know. She heard Hel mashing something in the cup. Her stomach lurched and cramped, readying itself to refuse.

"Oh yes," Hel said. "That's nice. That's very nice." She brought the cup to Milla. Too late, Milla realized she should have held her nose. The steam that rose from the cup was as brilliant yellow as dandelions but the scent reminded her of dead mouse. The liquid itself was a sickly brown. And chunky. Milla thought she'd lose what was in her stomach before she even brought the cup to her lips.

"Now you drink all of that down," Hel said.

Milla looked up, her eyes stinging, fat tears rolling down her face. "All of it? There's so much."

"All of it. Hold the cup with two hands. You don't want to drop it when . . . well. You might want to drop it, but don't."

Milla pressed her lips to the cup and at first all she could think of was the unexpected thickness of Hel's potion. Or not thickness, sliminess. It was like drinking a slug. She took one sip and recoiled, sticking her tongue out like Kai spitting oatmeal.

"Drink it while it's fresh! You're wasting time, you silly girl."

"I'm not silly," Milla said. "I'm *disgusted*."

"You're not even a girl. You're a baby. A silly baby who wants to boo hoo about how hard her life is so someone else will fix it."

Milla narrowed her eyes at Hel, then she put the cup to her mouth and drank down every slimy, chunky sip and morsel. When she'd drunk it all, she continued to look at Hel while she ran her finger around the inside of the cup and licked it.

Hel laughed and slapped her knee. "That's my girly. My little demon girly. Now close your eyes and think of Hulda, not a thing else. The potion can't do all the work—you have to help it along."

Milla did as she was told, but other thoughts kept flooding in. Iris's confusion. Niklas's disappointment. Gitta's revulsion. Milla's own shame. The shame was dark and hard to see through and it made everything else ugly and untrustworthy. Milla's shame made her angry. She felt it consuming her, like fire. And this was how she found her way back to Hulda. The anger was where they both lived. The anger had transformed Hulda into a monster and it was transforming Milla even now. The anger burned up the air between them. The space. Then there was no air or space between them; there was nothing between them at all, because they were one and the same. They were Hulda.

Hulda remembered a time when she could be alone and not lonely. She remembered how she'd lay in the meadow, the grasses swaying and stroking her nose. She remembered having skin and hair and all the sensations of girlness. She remembered the salty taste of sweat that dotted her upper lip on a warm day. The delicious tickle of gooseflesh that bloomed in the night breeze. The vibration of her own laughter in her ears. She remembered all of this.

And then she remembered how it was taken from her. How aloneness became loneliness. And how loneliness became pain and then pain became terror and then terror became hate.

And hate became monstrosity.

Hulda didn't know why these memories were coming back to her now. Oh, but yes she did. She knew why. It was the girl's fault. Milla. The girl she'd cursed to be like her. The girl who wanted to apologize to Hulda for things that weren't her fault.

She remembered the cold. So cold. She remembered the midwife burying her. She remembered the snow in her face. How it froze the blood in her veins. The breath in her chest.

Hulda wrapped her snake arms around herself, listened to all the life that buzzed and crackled and squirmed in her tree. She was safe here. They couldn't hurt her anymore. She could talk to her snakes. She could talk to her demon girls. They would never leave her.

They couldn't.

Hulda writhed. They *would* leave her if they could. But they couldn't. They couldn't because she wouldn't let them.

So alone.

But. But. But. Hulda gestured with her snake hands, making her argument to the air around her. Their mothers and fathers didn't love those girls. Not the way Hulda did. Their mothers and fathers didn't *deserve* them. Hulda did, because Hulda understood them. And Hulda loved their ugliness. Their anger. These girls were lucky. Hulda had saved them. Now none of them would ever have to see the disappointment in a mother's eyes. Or a sister's.

Hulda was the mother now, and the sister. She was the one they loved, and who loved them back. She would never betray them.

Hulda remembered the mother, still. But those were sad memories. She remembered wanting something from her, something she could never have. It was like being hungry always. There was never enough for Hulda, because the sister got it all.

The sister. Gitta.

Why these memories now, Hulda asked herself. Told herself: *You don't need these memories. They only hurt you. Call to your demon girls. Make them come and tell you stories.*

But she didn't want the demon girls. They only loved her because she forced them to. Hulda knew that. She was a monster; she wasn't stupid.

Hulda wanted the sister. It had always been the sister she wanted.

Gitta.

31

MILLA DROPPED THE CUP. "SHE'S SO . . . SO LONELY."
Milla shivered in her dress, though the day was warm.

Hel rolled her eyes. "Boo hoo."

"Haven't you any feeling at all? She's *sad*. And I don't think she
has any idea how to lift the curse."

"Don't be a weak boo hoo baby," Hel said. Sverd and Selv
hissed at her. She laughed.

"How can I call up Vengeance?" Milla said.

Hel cackled. "Calling her up is the easy part. But what are
you thinking you'd say to her when you did? Girly, she's not
called Vengeance because she lifts curses. She punishes. That's
what she does. That's why she's a *demon*. I'm just an old witch,
not even the meanest, and even I wouldn't lift a curse. You hurt
someone, they hurt you back. You hurt a witch you get hurt back
worse. You go against a *demon* and you wish you were dead.

That's the way the world works and it makes good sense to me."

Milla looked at Hel, at the nightmarish mask her curse had made of her face. That was the price of so much hurt and hatred, and it did not make any sense at all to Milla. "You said it's easy to find her. So tell me how."

"You know, girly, you should be more respectful. Don't forget I'm a witch. You've got one curse on you already. You don't want another."

Milla's cheeks grew hot, half with anger and half with embarrassment. Half wanting to strike Hel, and half wanting to apologize for being rude.

Hel drew her white eyebrows together and lowered them over her small black eyes. She pinched her lips together so tightly her mouth seemed to disappear, sucked into her face. Black smoke poured from her nostrils and the stench of Vengeance rose around her.

Still, Milla refused to quake or step back. Instead she took a step forward, and Sverd and Selv rose up and hissed at Hel.

Hel laughed. "Good, girly. Never be nice, that's my advice to you. I spent years trying to be nice, though it wasn't in my nature. Then my dead husband's brother showed up on my doorstep and stole my farm. After that I didn't wish I'd been better at being nice. I resented every bit of time I'd wasted trying to be nice at all. Girls who run from what frightens them don't get what they want. Now let's call us a demon. It's a blood sacrifice we'll be needing. Demons like blood sacrifices."

Milla felt needles of suspicion at the nape of her neck and Sverd and Selv wrapped themselves around her throat, hissing. "What kind of blood sacrifice?"

"Something you can kill yourself. Maybe one of your pretty snakes?"

Milla backed away from Hel, and the witch closed the distance.

"I bet they'd make a powerful potion," Hel said.

Milla took another step backward.

Hel stomped her foot. "Girly! You're not going to find a demon by being a well-behaved child who runs away from scary things and hides behind your mother's legs."

"I don't do that," Milla said, feeling spite rising inside her.

Hel sighed. "I've lost patience." She walked over to a placid chicken pecking at the maggots that fell to the ground beneath the reeking hides. She grasped it by the neck in one hand, and pulled a knife from the pocket of her trousers with the other. She raked the knife across the chicken's neck, spraying blood across the earth between her and Milla.

Black smoke curled and rose from the blood, grew thick and alive and fierce with intent.

Hel smiled. "Girly, meet Vengeance."

Smoke poured into Milla's mouth, her ears, her eyes—choking her, deafening her, blinding her. She fell to her knees, unable to breathe. Sverd and Selv trembled and vibrated and she cried out—she thought she could hear their cries, too. It felt as if they were being ripped from her head.

Then it was over, and she could breathe, and she gasped and felt for her snakes. They moved against her hands and she was so grateful she thought she might cry.

When she opened her eyes, her tears dried. Her mouth did, too. The hissed refrain of Hulda's girls came back to her. *Terror . . . terror . . . terror . . .*

Vengeance filled Hel's yard. Black antennae branched from her head like horns, and what at first seemed like two black plate-sized eyes on either side of her head were made up of countless smaller eyes, all reflecting Milla back at herself. The demon's flattened nose was bright yellow, and two jaggedly sharp black mandibles wrapped round her chin, resting under her wide, black, ridged mouth. Her broad upper body was shiny-black and armored, her waist slender and flexible, and her lower body was all stinger, black slashed with yellow. Two sets of translucent, finely veined wings stretched out on either side of her from her shoulders, and her arms and legs were bright yellow and viciously serrated.

"Who calls me, and why?" Vengeance said.

Milla didn't know what she'd expected Vengeance's voice to sound like, but it wasn't this. Her voice was full, round, and motherly. If Milla had closed her eyes, she might have been deceived by it, but she kept her eyes open to remind herself what Vengeance was. A demon. The original demon.

No fear, she thought to herself. *Girls who run from what frightens them don't get what they want.*

"I called you. I want you to lift a curse," Milla said.

Hel muttered under her breath, "*Want,* she says. Like she's giving orders. Spoiled boo hoo baby."

"I see your curse," Vengeance said, "and I'm admiring of it, but it's not my curse."

"Hulda told me it was. That your words were in her mouth when she cursed all of us."

Vengeance hummed and Milla felt the vibration in her feet. "I am her demon. I cannot do what she doesn't ask me to do. Her curse is her own."

"Is there a way . . . a way to *make* her lift the curse?" Milla said. "Could you do that?"

"Nooooo," Vengeance said. "But you could."

"How?"

"You have three choices. The first is to ask for her forgiveness. And then she must grant it."

"I tried that. No. She's too"—Milla hesitated for a moment, then said—"vengeful."

"Hmmm," Vengeance hummed, shifting her wings. "Her demon suits her well." Vengeance took two steps forward. Milla felt each of the demon's eyes examining her. "That was a terrible thing her own family did to her. I remember how she cried out to me in the cold and dark because no one else would come to her. What kind of a mother and father would do that to a child?" The demon sawed the air with her mandibles, and Milla was all too aware of their sharpness and the wide mouth behind them. Then Vengeance grazed Milla's cheeks with her antennae, holding her still, and Milla was no longer in Hel's yard.

Milla was buried in snow, bound and shivering. Snow filled her mouth, her nose, and when she tried to breathe she breathed in snow. The cold was in her heart and in her lungs. The cold was in her bones. She tried to cry out, but she couldn't, so the scream was all in her own head and it wasn't a scream for Niklas or Iris, it was a scream for vengeance. She was dying, she was alone, and her only wish was for something to take this hurt away.

Milla cried out, and Vengeance released her.

"Settle yourself, girly." Hel patted Milla's shoulder, and it was almost soothing. "Don't be a boo hoo baby." Almost.

"What is my second choice?" Milla said.

"Kill Hulda," Vengeance said.

"*No,*" Milla said. "Never."

"Hmmmm. I thought you might say that. Your third choice

is the best, really. Simplest. Most . . . effective."

"What is it?" Milla said.

"Ask me to be your demon and let me kill her." Vengeance stood up on her serrated back legs and brought forward her long yellow and black abdomen. "Look at my children," she said, exposing her belly lined with translucent eggs, each containing a quivering larva. "There are so many. Vengeance is endless. I go on and on, and you may use me, all of me. My strength is the only strength you will ever need."

Milla felt Vengeance's strength and knew she was right. With Vengeance, she could destroy Hulda and save Niklas and Iris and Liss. With Vengeance she would never have to fear the revulsion she saw in Gitta's eyes—or anyone else's. She would never need to be pleasing again. She could live inside her anger and feast on it.

Milla might have said yes to that. But then she remembered lonely Hulda in her tree. That was where Vengeance would take her. And Milla wouldn't go.

"No," she said. "You're evil. And you're no choice at all."

"Oh, girly," Hel said. "You've done it now."

Vengeance spread and flapped her translucent wings and the wind that kicked up under them was furnace-hot. It knocked Milla back on her heels and singed her eyelashes. The air filled with buzzing, the sound familiar and horrible, the sound of swarming. The sky blackened as if the sun had gone out, a blanket thrown over them all, but the blanket was made of wasps. Milla thought she and Hel were surely dead, but the wasps closed around Vengeance, encircling her, lifting her from the ground and carrying her up and up.

Milla and Hel stood openmouthed, watching her go.

All was now silent in the surrounding forest. Not even a leaf shook. Hel's yard was strewn with feathers, the remains of her chickens. Sverd and Selv peeked from Milla's hair, while Milla struggled to think of something to say. "I'm . . . sorry . . . about your chickens."

Hel's long white caterpillar eyebrows were sizzled black at the ends. "Girly, I don't want your sorries. I'm no boo hoo baby. What did I tell you? Never be nice. We messed with a demon." She shrugged. "This is what we get."

32

Fulla stood chewing and waiting, unmoved by the appearance of a wasp-shaped demon. Milla rested her forehead on Fulla's and stayed there, wishing she could absorb some of the mare's calm. "All right, girl. Help me think this through. I can't kill Hulda. I wouldn't know how to, anyway." The very idea of it was ridiculous. Milla remembered her games with Niklas when they were little. Waving their imaginary swords through the air, hunting trolls. She had no sword and Hulda was no troll. "And I won't ask Vengeance to kill Hulda." That would be just as bad. No, it would be worse, because it would be cowardly. And then where would it end? With more vengeance. That's what the demon wanted. "So the only thing left is forgiveness. But I've already tried asking for that, and it made Hulda even angrier."

Milla wanted to scream, but instead she tried slowing her breath to match the mare's. How wondrous it would be to be an animal, Milla thought. How easy. Any kind of animal would be fine. No matter how short the life span. She'd live, sleep, and eat. Death would come quickly. As it was, Milla imagined her life if the curse continued to run its course. It rolled out in front of her, interminably. Her body fully covered in green scales, only snakes where she once had hair. She'd be a monster, forever alone. Punished for the sin of another.

Milla lifted her head from Fulla's, a thought blooming, tickling, making her ears itch. *The sin of another.*

It wasn't Milla's apology that Hulda wanted—needed. It was Gitta's.

It had always been Gitta.

Bless this horse's sense of direction, Milla thought to herself more than once. She said it aloud to Fulla more than twice.

It took the better part of a day for them to find their way back to Iris's cave, skirting as far around Hulda and the demon girls' territory as they could without losing their way. When they arrived, Iris was huddled in the dark, her face pressed to her knees.

Milla ran to Iris and crouched in front of her. Iris blinked as if to be sure that Milla was really there. "I came back to myself," Iris said. "I'm me. Your sister. You can see, can't you? I'm me."

Milla wrapped her arms around Iris. "Yes, dearest. I can see. You *are* my sister. And I'm yours."

Iris pulled away. She squeezed her eyes shut and buried her face. "I don't know why you still trust me. You shouldn't trust me."

"None of this is your fault. I trust *you.* I trust *my* Iris, *my* friend, *my* sister."

Iris let out a muffled sob.

"Come with me," Milla said. "I'm going home to get Mamma."

Iris lifted her head. "Gitta? Why?"

"I'd thought I needed to protect Niklas from Hulda, but now I know that it's not him she wants, or me. It's Mamma. Hulda loved Mamma more than anyone else, and Mamma betrayed her. And it's Mamma who has to make this right. So I'm going to ask Mamma to go to Hulda with me. Maybe if Mamma apologizes, Hulda will lift the curse."

"But you saw how Hulda is. She'll never lift the curse."

"I have to believe otherwise," Milla said. "I don't want to end up like Hulda. Even the thought is unbearable. And I must get her out of your head. And Liss's. And all the other girls. And . . . well. I want Hulda to have some peace."

"She doesn't give me any peace, Milla."

Milla sighed. "I know. But there's some part of her that isn't awful. I think there's a way to convince her to let us go." She picked up a coil of Iris's russet hair and held it in her hand. "At least I have to try. Will you come with me to talk to Mamma?"

"It's not safe. What if I lose myself? They'll tie me up and drag me away again."

"They wouldn't. I won't let them. Niklas won't let them."

"Neither of you could stop them before. And what if they drag you away, too? What if they see your snakes?"

"My snakes know how to hide."

Iris reached for Milla's hands and turned them over, showing her scales. "What about these?" Milla felt Iris's agitation growing, threatening to ignite. "Anyway, Gitta isn't safe with me," Iris said.

"What do you mean?"

"I hate her. We all do."

"But Mamma didn't do anything to you. Hulda did. And I

don't think Mamma really knew what she was doing to Hulda. She was frightened. And selfish. But how could she know what the midwife would do to Hulda? She couldn't possibly."

"I still hate her," Iris said.

Heat rose off Iris in waves. The cave felt airless. This was Vengeance, Milla knew. She could smell her, feel her. Sense her larva hatching in Iris, eating her from the inside out. "Well, I love you," Milla said, hoping to soothe the parts of Iris that didn't belong to Hulda or Vengeance.

Iris dropped her face to her knees again, and Milla stroked her hair, crinkly with hay and leaves.

"I'll come back for you, Iris."

Iris nodded into her knees but didn't speak.

It was midmorning a day and a half later when Milla arrived home—or the place she'd once called home. The farm looked faded, like a dress forgotten in the sun. The air buzzed with black flies that harassed Fulla and Milla both. Anthills leaned against fence posts, undisturbed, no one noticing or caring to sweep them away. The cottage itself seemed to sag in the center, as if exhausted with the effort of going on. All was quiet, and still, and sad, just like the village had been.

Milla led Fulla to the barn, unsaddled her, and gave her a big bucket of oats. The poor beast hadn't had a proper brushing in days. "I'll make it up to you," Milla said. Fulla was nose down in the bucket, unconcerned.

There was no sign of her father or Niklas when Milla walked back to the cottage. She didn't expect there would be—they'd be out in the fields, working, at this time of the day. But there was also no sound floating over from Stig and Trude's cottage. No scraping of chairs or stirring of pots or flapping of laundry. Milla walked inside and the kitchen was cold and empty, no bread rising or dinner preparations underway, even though her father and Niklas would be back in a few hours for their midday meal.

Milla found Gitta lying in bed, eyes open and staring, her blond hair loose about her shoulders. "Mamma? Mamma!" Panic rolled over Milla. Her mother looked ill. Or worse. Milla remembered the lie she'd told the midwife, that Gitta was dying. Had she made it so?

Gitta stirred, then raised her head from the pillow to look at Milla, her eyes struggling to focus.

"Milla?" She sat up.

"Mamma, what's wrong? Aren't you well?"

"I'm not dying, if that's what you think. I only wish I were." Gitta put her face in her hands. Milla felt a flash of disgust for her mother, like lightning. Gitta was so terribly selfish. Milla thought of what Hel would say about her. *Spoiled boo hoo baby.*

"Why do you wish you were dead, Mamma?"

Gitta's eyes trailed over Milla. "Look at you. You haven't had a bath in days, have you?"

Milla wanted to scream. A bath? Milla hadn't been home in months, and her mother could only remark on how dirty she was. "That's what you have to say to me, Mamma? That I need a bath?"

"Oh, Milla. Why must you be like that?"

Milla should have gone to her mother by now, embraced her. Isn't that what any other daughter would have done? She imagined what Liss would do if she hadn't seen Katrin in so long. She imagined what Katrin would do. Katrin would have held onto Liss and never wanted to let go. But Gitta went on lying there in bed, feeling sorry for herself. No wonder Hulda hated her.

"Do you want to know where I've been? Do you care? Or is it enough that you have Niklas home now?" Milla could see her mother's pain, how she suffered, but she didn't stop talking, remembering what Hel had said to her: *Never be nice.*

Gitta cringed, shrinking backward and inward.

And there, in her cringing and shrinking, was the face that Milla had grown up looking back at. The face that looked at Milla with fear. With dread instead of love. "Are you afraid of me?" Milla said. "Of these?" Sverd and Selv rose from her head, not hissing, only placid and staring. Milla's anger felt clean and right. It didn't belong to Vengeance or to Hulda, it was her own, and she could control it—and use it.

Gitta cried out and covered her face with her hands. "Don't make me look at you. Don't make me look at what I've done to my own child."

A space opened up in Milla at that moment. A space that allowed in a crack of pity, and of curiosity. She moved closer to Gitta. "What do you mean? What have you done to me?"

Gitta wept. "It's all my fault."

Milla remembered her mother's weeping when Niklas went to The Place with Iris. How was this any different? Gitta was more sad for herself than she was for Milla. "You mean you're disgusted by me."

Gitta dropped her hands to her lap and looked at Milla with anger. "You're so . . . *mean.* You always have been. Why are you so mean?"

"Mean? What have I ever done but what you've told me to?"

"Always begrudgingly, though. Always treating me like I'm simple-minded, such a bother to you. You and Niklas with your little jokes and secrets. Making me feel stupid. Niklas isn't the same with me now. I don't think he loves me anymore. He's so angry. And I can't make him understand that all I've done is to try to keep you safe."

"Safe? You mean from the curse you brought down on me? The curse that made me this way?" She turned her hands over and then rolled up one sleeve so that Gitta could see the scales, shimmering green.

Gitta reached out a tentative hand, and Milla didn't pull back, though she wanted to. Gitta stroked Milla's scales, and Milla trembled from her wrist to her shoulder. Her mother's hands were gentle, and Milla felt sudden relief that she could still feel the touch of fingers. She was overcome with longing to be a baby again, to start all over and be the kind of girl her mother could have loved. "Mamma," Milla said, "I'm a monster." And she sank to her knees and wept.

"Oh no, child. No, no, no." Milla felt her mother's arms around her, caught her mother's familiar scent of milky tea and parsley. Milla wanted to stay there, to put her head in Gitta's lap and pretend to be a girl again. A girl like she never was, with a mother like she never had.

Milla stood up, resisting all that temptation to soften. "But I am a monster. Or I will be. Even if you don't want me to be. And if you really want to help me, if you're truly sorry for what you've done, then you need to apologize."

Gitta reached up to grab Milla's hand. "But of course I'm sorry. I told you so."

"No, Mamma. I'm not the one you need to apologize to. It's Hulda. You must come with me to see her and tell her so."

Gitta scrambled backward on the floor and looked around as if for somewhere to hide. She shook her head wildly. "Oh no. No, no, no. I can't. I won't. You don't know what she's like. I didn't tell you that part, Milla. She's not like you. She really is a monster." Gitta wept and carried on so that it was all Milla could do not to roll her eyes.

"Don't be a boo hoo baby," Milla said.

Gitta looked at her strangely. "What?"

"A boo hoo baby, Mamma. That's what you're being. You lie up here crying because you haven't gotten your way. Hulda made messes for you, and then I made messes for you, and you can't wish your messes away. I'm here, Mamma. A big mess. And I'm taking you to your other big mess. And you will apologize, and you will make this right."

Gitta wiped her nose with the back of her hand and looked up at Milla with wet, pleading eyes. "Now?

"Right now," Milla said. "Get dressed and I'll saddle the horses. We're leaving before Pappa and Niklas can try to convince us otherwise."

As she walked to the barn, Milla imagined Hel off to one side cackling, slapping her knee.

33

M ILLA WAS SADDLING FULLA WHEN SHE HEARD HIS voice. "Milla! You're back!" Niklas ran to her and embraced her.

She held onto him for just a moment and then pulled away, fearing she'd break down if she didn't. "Not for long, though."

Niklas searched her face. "What do you mean? Why not?"

"Nothing has changed, Niklas. I'm still cursed and so is Iris."

"Milla, please don't go." Niklas looked so sad, so alone, and for a moment Milla felt a shameful sort of pleasure. For so many years she had been the one pining for him, pulling on his sleeve, wishing he'd stay. "It's awful here without you. Every day I wake up hoping you'll come home. Every night I go to sleep disappointed. Mamma clings to me so that I can't leave her alone for long. Pappa pretends nothing's changed. He won't even speak your name."

"He hardly ever spoke my name before, Niklas." Milla knew

it was unkind to be so cold in the face of his suffering, but she couldn't ease it right now. She had barely enough strength to cope with her own.

"Niklas," Mamma said, standing in the door to the barn.

Niklas looked Gitta up and down and confusion passed over his face. "You're wearing riding trousers." Then he turned to Milla and saw that she was saddling a second horse. "What's happening?"

"Mamma is going with me to Hulda, Niklas. She's going to apologize to her."

"What! No! Neither of you is going to Hulda. She'll kill both of you!"

Niklas was a full head taller than Gitta, and she reached up to place a gentling hand on his shoulder. "If she'd wanted to kill me she could have done so long before now. She wants me to suffer, not die."

"I'm going with you," Niklas said.

"*No,*" Gitta said. "There's no telling what Hulda would do to you, Niklas. And I can't bear to lose you again. That would truly kill me."

Milla bit her tongue and tasted blood. It wouldn't help to say what she was thinking—that, as ever, Niklas was everything to Gitta. That Milla could sink into the earth and it would mean less worry for her mother, not more.

"Milla, talk sense to her," Niklas said.

"I did talk sense to her, and that's why she's going with me. And she's right, Niklas. You should stay here. If you come along you'll only give Hulda something to use against us. She wants to hurt Mamma, and she'll know that the best way to do that is through you." She held his hand for a moment. "And I couldn't bear to lose you, either. You must let us go."

Gitta embraced him. "Stay safe, my sweet boy."

Niklas looked at Milla over his mother's head. "Come home to me. Both of you."

Milla nodded. She would make sure Mamma did, but could make no such promise for herself.

They rode for hours, until it was so dark Milla couldn't see more than a few feet in front of them. By then, she and Gitta were long past the village. They'd passed Ragna's empty cottage, falling in on itself, and then the wide, flower-dotted meadow that led to The Place.

"You know what that is, don't you," Milla said.

Gitta nodded, staring at the hulking fort off in the distance. "Niklas won't speak of it. Whenever I try to talk to him he tells me I don't want to know."

Milla cocked her head at Gitta. "*Do* you want to know?"

Gitta looked back at Milla. "No."

Mostly, the ride had been quiet. Gitta hadn't voiced a word of complaint since they'd left the farm. Gitta hadn't even delayed, though she'd had the chance. Milla thought her mother might make the excuse of stopping to speak to Hanna and Tomas, but she didn't. And she paid no attention to the stares of the villagers. Milla had grown so used to being an oddity that she'd forgotten what a strange thing it was to see a woman her mother's age in riding trousers, astride a horse. But Gitta seemed not to notice their gapes; she simply rode, her eyes forward.

After they'd eaten supper and rolled out blankets for sleeping, Milla said, "You don't seem afraid."

"I am."

"But you don't *seem* so," Milla said.

"I've had a lot of practice, not seeming afraid."

"Hm," Milla said. "I don't know if you were very good at it."

Gitta pulled a blanket around her and turned on her side to look at Milla. "What do you mean?"

"I mean, you've always seemed frightened. For the longest time I thought you were angry with me. There was this particular expression on your face when you looked at me, and it was so different from the way you looked at Niklas. I can't remember when it was that I first realized you were afraid. But once I did, it was all I could see."

"Well," Gitta said, "but did I seem terrified? Did I seem like I could barely get out of bed each morning because I lay awake every night wondering what might have happened in the night? Did I scream all the time, or look like I wanted to?"

"No."

"Then I'd say I was doing just fine at pretending. Because there wasn't a minute of any day since you were born that I didn't feel that I might die of dread."

Milla felt overcome by grief. The waste of all that time, neither of them having any idea how the other was tortured by the unsaid. "Why didn't you tell me? If you'd told me, then at least I'd have understood why you looked at me that way. I'd have understood why you couldn't love me."

Gitta shifted to her back and looked up into the branches overhead. "You're my daughter. Of course I love you."

"You can't even look at me when you say that."

"Oh, Milla. Why must you make everything so *hard?* Life is hard enough without your daughter making it more so."

"That's not the first time you've said that to me, you know."

"Well," Gitta said. "This must not be the first time you've needed to hear it then."

Milla closed her eyes, fighting back tears. Willing them not to come. "Goodnight, Mamma." She turned on her side, her back to Gitta. Sverd and Selv tried to soothe her, but Milla was ashamed to admit even to herself that it wasn't their comfort she craved.

When they arrived at the cave, Milla knew before they entered that Iris wouldn't be there. Even from the outside Milla sensed its blankness. Wherever Iris was, there was energy. Spark. But the cave was cold and empty. Gitta stood in one place, her eyes circling it. "This is where she's been living? That poor child."

"You said she was wicked, Mamma. You let them take her away."

Gitta turned on Milla. "You know, you resent me so much for how I've looked at you, and for what I did to Hulda. But you're looking at me right now like I'm a monster. Like I have no feeling. Like I should be the one with snakes growing from my head."

Milla sucked in air, stung.

Gitta's eyes widened. "I didn't mean you! That's not what I meant!" She buried her face in her hands. "Everything I say to you is wrong. You want something from me that I can't give you. But I've tried, Milla. I've tried."

"Mamma, listen to yourself. You act like everything's been *done* to you. I'm just me, Mamma. I've always been me. And all I've ever wanted is for you to love me. Even a bit."

"I told you I loved you."

"They're just words when you say them to me, Mamma."

Gitta reached for Milla, held her by the wrists. "I haven't

known a moment's peace since Hulda went . . . wrong. And everything I've done, I've done because I wanted to make things right. I was brought up to please. To please my mother and father, and then to please your father. Because that's what women do. That's how we live, how we survive. But Hulda couldn't be pleasing—she never could. I loved her when we were little, but when we got older I grew impatient with her. I wanted her not to be so . . . strange. And it made me angry that she was. I was afraid that Jakob wouldn't want to marry a girl with such a strange sister."

"Strange . . . like me?" Milla said.

Gitta's eyebrows knit together. She paused. "A bit, yes. And, Milla, just think. If you were like her, and you know how she turned out, then don't you think I was right to be frightened? And so every day I taught you how *not* to be like her. I taught you how to please. That's how I hoped to make your life easier."

"But you didn't," Milla said. "You made it harder."

"I know it, Milla. I know it. And I'm sorry for it."

Milla closed her eyes, felt her stony heart tremble and shake. She wanted to say something terrible to her mother. Wanted to make Gitta hurt, wanted her to feel the rejection that was as much a part of Milla as the snakes that grew from her head. But then she thought of Hulda and of what Milla asked her mother to do—to apologize to Hulda for all the pain. And if Milla held out any hope that Hulda could forgive Gitta, then Milla had to forgive her, too.

Milla looked into her mother's pale blue eyes, round and wet. "Thank you, Mamma." And as she said the words, she knew she meant them.

34

THEY SPENT THE NIGHT IN IRIS'S CAVE, HUDDLED CLOSE
for warmth. As Milla lay awake, she wondered what the future
might hold for her and Gitta if Hulda lifted the curse. Milla forgave Gitta for the past, but would Milla's heart ever fully open to
her? Could she bear to risk the terrible heartbreak of not being
loved well enough? Milla fell asleep not knowing.

The next morning they were both quiet and neither could eat.
"We should leave the horses here," Milla said. "I'm not worried
about Fulla, but your horse might get spooked."

Her mother nodded, then did something strange. Gitta had
neatly rebraided her own hair that morning, and now she reached
out to tuck a curl behind Milla's ear. When Sverd grazed her
hand, Gitta didn't gasp or lurch backward. "Oh," Gitta said.
"Oh." Her face remained gentle, and her hand as well. Milla's
heart opened to her mother just a tiny bit more.

Milla and Gitta hadn't walked far when the hissing started. Then the demon girls stepped from behind trees and crept over rocks and the hissing grew excited. Frantic.

She'sssssss here. The sssssssister. The sssssssister is here.

When Gitta reached for Milla's hand and squeezed it, Milla's heart opened still more.

They walked farther, the hissing building and blending and overlapping.

She'sssssss here. The sssssssister. The sssssssister is here.

When Milla and Gitta arrived at the clearing where Hulda's tree stood wide and tall, they were encircled by the demon girls. Among them was Iris. Milla searched her heart-shaped face for some sign of her friend, but there was none. The face that looked back at her belonged to Hulda.

"Sister," Gitta said, her voice hesitant at first, then growing stronger. "Sister, I'm here. And I have something I would say to you, if you'd let me."

Silence fell over the girls, and each of them cocked her head as if listening to a single sound.

A blast of heat rose from the ground, and Milla felt terror and a sense of wrongness so sudden and acute that she thought she would lose the contents of her bladder and her stomach at once. She wanted to take her mother by the hand and run. She wanted to tell her that this was a terrible mistake. Milla and Gitta had both been wrong: It wasn't safe for Gitta here. Because in that heat, Milla felt all the hatred and resentment that Hulda had nursed for her sister since Hulda had been abandoned in the snow. It was a well so deep it would never run dry.

But there was no time to speak, because from the tree slithered Hulda's snake legs, followed by the rest of her. And then so fast, too fast, and Milla should have known, should have *known* this would happen, Hulda had undulated forward and grasped Gitta around the throat, tearing her from Milla's side.

"Mamma!" Milla screamed.

Gitta's toes scraped the ground, and she struggled to stay on her feet.

Hulda pulled Gitta to her, her face just inches away. Her purple lips pulled back into a grimace. "After all thissss lonely time, Gitta, you've finally come to visit. You were always so frightened of me. Even when I was nothing but a strange girl who talked to snakes, you thought I was a monster. So what makes you sssso brave now?"

"I wasn't always frightened of you, Hulda. I loved you."

"Never."

"I did, Hulda. When we were little we slept so close our hair would tangle together in the night. Mamma would have to unknot us in the morning. Do you remember?"

"I remember you called me monster," Hulda said. "How the mother and father let them take me. Bury me in the snow. How the girl died that day and turned into thissss."

"I died that day, too," Gitta said.

Hulda howled, and her howling spread to the girls until the air was full of their agony. Milla felt their pain in her own heart, in her brain and lungs and blood. A sleek black snake with intricate golden diamonds down its back lifted from Hulda's head, and arched downward to graze Gitta's cheek with a long fang. "I could kill you right now, Gitta. And I should. For daring to compare your pain to mine. For *daring.*"

Milla stood helpless, watching Hulda tighten her grip around Gitta's throat, so tight her mother couldn't speak. Then Hulda dropped Gitta to the ground, and Gitta sank to her knees. Milla ran to her mother to help her to her feet, but then Milla felt herself lifted off her own.

Hulda dragged Milla backward toward her tree. Milla struggled to free herself, but it was like trying to bend iron. Iron that only coiled tighter the more she fought. "I could kill you, Gitta, but this is better. This way has always been better. I hurt you best by hurting what you love. Your child is mine now. She's a monster like me. And we're both monsters because of you."

Mine now.

Mine now.

You're mine now.

The voice was in Milla's head. Hulda's voice. Milla tried to resist. Tried to remember what her own voice sounded like. What her own heart felt and wanted. But where her heart had been there was only smoke. Hot and black and choking out all air, anything that wasn't hate. That wasn't vengeance.

Then there was another voice inside her, fighting through the smoke. A voice that Milla remembered but couldn't name.

The voice of a friend.

Come back, Milla.

Iris.

Iris was shaking Milla, then clawing at Hulda's iron-snake grip. Shaking and clawing, wild and frantic but herself, all herself. Milla was looking into the face of a friend, heart-shaped and russet-haired and syrup-eyed. "Iris," Milla said. And the friend smiled, but then the friend was flying through the air, hurled by Hulda. "Iris!" Milla screamed.

Hulda dropped Milla to the ground. Enraged, she rolled toward Iris, her black and diamond snake ahead of her, fangs spread and ready. Then a figure was between Iris and Hulda. A figure with long blond hair breaking free of its once-perfect braid.

"Mamma, no!" Milla cried out.

But Gitta had already thrown herself at Hulda, and the snake had already sunk its fangs into Gitta's exposed neck. Gitta's body jerked from the force, then went limp and sank to the earth at Hulda's feet.

Hulda screeched. "No, Gitta! No, sister! Not you!"

Milla ran to her mother, lifting her up, cradling her head in her lap. Touching her face as she never had. Stroking her hair as she'd always wanted to. Gitta's lips whitened and her skin chilled from pink-white to stony gray.

"Mamma," Milla said. She took one of Gitta's hands in hers. Milla remembered how she'd always loved the coolness of her mother's hands. But now Gitta's hands were cold. Too cold. Milla brought them to her cheek. "I'm sorry, Mamma. I'm so sorry."

Gitta looked up at Milla. "I love you, child. I always have."

Snake hands and snake arms wrapped around Gitta, taking her from Milla. "Wake up, Gitta. Wake up, Gitta. Wake up, Gitta." Hulda petted and petted her sister, hiss-whispering, "You are not to leave me, Gitta. Never to leave me. You stay. Sister. *My* sister. Most beloved. This was not my curse. Not my curse. You *stay*."

Gitta's lips moved, forming words. She looked up at her monstrous sister, eyes open and unflinching. "So much pain I caused you. Please forgive me." Then she closed her eyes, took one shallow breath, and no more.

For a long moment, Milla knelt by Gitta while Hulda held her, and the only sound in Milla's ears was Hulda's weeping.

Then her ears opened to the sounds of the forest. Wind shushing through needled branches. The call of birds.

So quiet otherwise.

Milla felt Iris beside her. Her friend, whom her mother had sacrificed her life for. Unafraid of Hulda, Iris kissed Gitta's forehead.

Milla set her mother's hand on her belly and she and Iris stood, backing away from the sisters, one cradling the other. Sverd and Selv settled their heads on Milla's shoulders.

Hulda's grief rose from her in waves, replacing the vengeance that had once radiated from her like heat. The girls gathered around Hulda and Gitta in a circle, each bringing their own sadness with them, like offerings. They laid hands on each other, on Gitta, on Hulda. And in the quiet of that clearing deep in the woods, where a monster had long lived while waiting for her vengeance, they wept together.

EPILOGUE

"Tell me a story," Liss said, her eyes bright with mischief. "The one about the girl and the witch."

Milla smiled, reaching out for a plump, red apple hanging from a low branch. She took a bite of the apple, warm from the sun, and juice ran down her chin. She caught the drip with a finger, then she wiped the stickiness on her skirt. The sound of a bell chimed in the air. "That's Mamma," Liss said. "Time for dinner. Come with us, Milla. Mamma and Pappa are always asking for you."

"Hm," Milla said. "Another time."

Liss sighed. "That means never."

"Doesn't." Milla tugged a chunk of Liss's hair. "It just means not now."

Liss took Kai's hand and picked up her basket of apples. "Mamma's making applesauce for the baby. I don't know why. None of it ever seems to make it into his mouth."

Liss's memories of the day when the curse found her had mostly faded. Just once, Liss had turned to Milla, a shadow passing over her face, and said, "Tell me about the wasps."

"It was a blight," Milla told her. "And it's over now."

Milla watched Liss and Kai walk away from her. When they were just two smudges off in the distance, Sverd and Selv untucked themselves from their hiding places in her hair.

Hulda's curse had lifted when Gitta died. Hulda had withdrawn to her tree, alone, and the girls no longer heard her voice in their heads. Many of the younger girls had returned to their homes, met by families who were happy to know that curses could lift. There were some who didn't feel they could go home again, though. Those women and girls made new homes for themselves where no one knew what had happened to them, where no one pointed or whispered or wondered if they really were themselves again. Iris was one of those. She'd visited her mother and father, thinking she'd stay. But she told Milla that they kept looking at her, like she might change back at any moment. And anyway, it was stifling living at home. And she was a curious girl.

Milla's pale green scales had faded away, leaving fresh skin behind, but her snakes remained—perhaps because she wanted them to. Life would have been easier without them, she supposed. But they were a part of her now. She could tuck them away in her hair when she needed to, but that never felt right. Sverd and Selv were restless creatures; they kept her honest. She couldn't pretend to be what she wasn't—or at least not for long.

When Milla had returned to the farm to tell her father and Niklas that Gitta had sacrificed herself to lift the curse, her father blamed Milla. He said she wasn't welcome in his house, that she'd as much as killed her mother and was just like her aunt: strange. Niklas had protested and said it was Milla's home just as much as Jakob's. Their father grew so angry he turned a shade of purple as dark as a bruise. His anger didn't frighten Milla the way it used to, though. She hugged her brother good-bye and told him not to worry: She would make her way. She hadn't wanted to stay there anyway, not really. The only hardship in leaving the farm was how much she'd miss Niklas. She'd been crying nonstop for a good two miles when Niklas came riding up behind her and said he was coming with her. "My home is with you and Iris," he said. Then she cried harder.

When Niklas, Milla, and Iris rode up to Otto and Katrin's farm, Liss spotted them first. Her squeal of delight split the air. Otto's and Katrin's smiles were wide and genuine. They didn't believe that Milla had caused the strange blight that descended upon them one day and lifted the next, and hadn't understood why Milla thought she had to leave. They never would have blamed Milla for such a thing, Katrin said. Milla thought of Hel and Hulda and Gitta, of vengeance and curses, and she smiled. People blamed other people for all sorts of things.

Katrin thought it odd that Milla hadn't mentioned having a brother, but was too polite to ask why. Otto's and Katrin's delight in having help with the farm and the children was so great that Otto offered to give Milla, Niklas, and Iris a plot of land and to help them build their own log cottage. Such a shame, Katrin said, that they were all orphans. She wanted them to know that they were always welcome at their dinner table. Niklas, Milla, and Iris responded gratefully, then chose a plot too far from Otto and Katrin's cottage to allow for casual visits.

"Are you sure you wouldn't like to live closer?" Katrin said.

Niklas shone his sunshine smile on her. "No, thank you." And in Niklas's usual way, he made it all right.

Milla was happy. She and Iris and Niklas made a companionable home together. When they weren't working on the farm, they took long walks in the woods telling stories about witches and lost children and demons. Well, Milla and Iris told the stories. Niklas mostly listened and laughed and criticized the endings.

Some nights, long after Iris and Niklas were asleep, Milla stepped out into the moonlight, alone. Sverd and Selv stretched themselves and tasted the night air.

Milla walked deep into the woods, ferns brushing her legs. She settled herself in the soft, pillowy moss at the base of a tree. Then she tapped her fingers on a tree root.

Tap. Tap tap tap.

On the fourth tap, the snakes emerged from their hiding places to gather around her. Green and brilliant yellow. Beetle-black and blood-red. Some wrapped themselves around her ankles and wrists; all raised their heads to look at her.

"Now," Milla always said to them, "from where we left off last time. Tell me your names."